# Hallum

## Casey Morales

AuthorCaseyMorales.com

## Chapter One

# Bauke

*"How wonderful it is that nobody need wait a
single moment before starting to improve the
world."*

Anne Frank, *Anne Frank's Tales
from the Secret Annex*

I hated early mornings in the autumn when the sun
didn't bother getting up before me.

My sister loved them. She was weird like that.

The third morning in October was no different from
any other. I crawled out from the warmth of my covers,
stretched, stopped by the bathroom to pee, then headed

toward the kitchen. My stomach gurgled as I whiffed the bacon frying down the hall.

*Is that Sarr?* I wondered.

Our *moeder* and *vader* told us never to name the animals, but we couldn't help it, and Lianne was worse than I was. She saw most of them before their own mother did, all gooey and gross. She practically wrestled them out of Papa's arms. Some of them wouldn't open their eyes for a while, but others, like Sarr, would blink up and make me want to squeeze them on the spot.

I hoped breakfast wasn't Sarr.

Sometimes, in war, we had to do things we hated, like eating the animals we'd named rather than selling them in the market or giving them to the Nazi collectors. I knew we had to do our part. The Hitler Youth at school taught us that. Still, it felt worse seeing them go to men with rifles than to other farmers or *Meener* Vermeer. He was the town's butcher—whatever that meant. He was always nice.

"Good morning, my *schat*," Mama sang as I stepped into the kitchen. She knew I hated when she called me "sweetie," but she did it anyway. "Hungry?"

I nodded and climbed into the wicker chair I always sat in when we ate. Lianne was already halfway through her breakfast. One of her long braids drooped in front of her chest and wiggled every time she used her fork. I giggled as it nearly fell into her plate when she reached for her juice.

She glanced up and stuck her tongue out, a grin tugging at the corners of her mouth.

A plate of two strips of bacon, a boiled egg, and toast with grape jam landed before me.

"Eat up. No school today. Papa needs your help," Mama said, before brushing my mop of fiery hair back and kissing my forehead. As soon as her hand left my head, the curls flopped back into place.

I couldn't decide whether to be more excited or frustrated. Papa needing help meant work. School meant work. The Hitler Youth made us work. It didn't matter where we were or what *we* wanted, we had to work.

I glanced at Lianne, hoping for some hint of the day to come. She shrugged and focused on her plate.

Barks rang out.

Mama peered out the window above the sink then laughed and shook her head. Our pack of Patrijshonden were as loyal as dogs came, but they were more goofy than helpful around the farm. Half the time, Papa had to scold them for terrorizing our poor chickens.

Their floppy ears were funny.

"Hurry up and finish," Mama said. "Papa should be in the barn with the cows."

At least we didn't have to work the fields. That was the one good thing about autumn and winter. The plants were asleep and the ground was solid, so the only things left to tend were the animals. Most of ours were cows.

Sometimes, it seemed like we had too many to count, but Papa always knew exactly how many there should be. He was smart like that.

We had a few sheep and a bunch of pigs too.

The pigs were my favorite.

I swallowed the last bite of bacon and downed my juice, then scooted the chair back and made for the door. Lianne reluctantly followed.

When we started before the sun, the days felt like they lasted forever.

By the time the sun reached her peak, we'd milked all the cows, fed the pigs, and shooed the sheep so they could eat whatever grass was still alive in the field. Papa had scattered hay along one fence row in case they were still hungry after the grass was gone.

As we stomped back toward the house, surrounded by our ever-present ring of pups who likely thought they were herding us home, Papa held his hand up to shield his eyes.

"Nazis are coming for their week's allotment," he said, more to himself than to us. "Go on, you two, get to the house. Tell Mama to get ready for Lieutenant Huber."

Lianne's eyes glazed over and her cheeks flushed. "What?" She shoved my shoulder. "He's handsome."

Papa rolled his eyes. "Go, run home. I want you inside before they get here."

The kitchen door swung shut behind us just as the German car ground to a halt, kicking up dust from our gravel drive in every direction. The truck that followed created an even larger cloud.

More than an hour later, the squeal of the kitchen door announced Papa's arrival.

"Isa," he called out to Mama. "Isa, they are gone. Where are you?"

"Coming." Mama's footfalls echoed against the wood of our hallway a second before her voice did the same. "Bauke is working his sums, and Lianne is reading another of her romance novels. I swear that girl will turn into a pool of syrup before she grows up."

Papa's rich laughter filled our home with warmth.

The moment they started whispering, Lianne and I tossed our books and headed closer. We hated when the grown-ups tried to keep secrets.

"... three pigs, two sheep, and they're coming back for a dozen cows," Papa said.

The groan of one of the kitchen chairs told me Mama had sat at the table. "So many?"

"Ever since the strikes ..."

Their voices were drowned out by the dogs braying at who-knew-what outside.

"The strikes?" I whispered to Lianne.

She cupped her hand to her mouth to hamper the sound. "Remember? In the spring, when miners and other workers walked off the job to protest how the Reichskommissar was forcing everybody to work for the Nazis."

Ah. *Those* strikes. The spring ones weren't the first, but they were the biggest. The papers—at least, the ones we could still get—said a lot of people had stopped working. So many farms in one region were set on fire that the sky turned red.

Reichskommissar Seyss-Inquart[1] had a lot of people shot after that.

Papa stopped letting us read the papers from then on. I never understood why reading a newspaper was dangerous, but that's what he said. Most of the big Dutch ones quit printing when the Germans came anyway.

We could listen to the radio some, but most of it was in German now. We studied German in school, but I still wasn't very good with it. For some reason, all the Dutch shows we used to listen to stopped airing a while back, too.

---

1. Reichskommissariat Arthur Seyss-Inquart served briefly as the Deputy Governor General in occupied Poland and, following the fall of the Low Countries in 1940, he was appointed reichskommissar of the occupied Netherlands.

We waited in silence for a long time before the sounds of Mama banging pots and pans told us their conversation had ended then scurried from our hiding spot as Papa rounded the corner, headed toward the living room and the comfort of his favorite chair. Most afternoons, after a long day outside, he would clean up, grab the same book he'd pretended to read for years, and fall asleep with it in his lap, only to wake when Mama poked him with the business end of a spatula or wooden spoon. The sudden hack of his interrupted snoring was our cue to get ready for dinner.

That night brought the smoky scent of sausage mixed with the tang of turnips, as Mama laid a steaming bowl of *stamppot*[2] on the center of the table. Since the Germans took over, a lot of people talked about how meat was rare, but I never noticed that. I guessed that was one of the lucky things about living on a farm. We had to contribute to the troops, but if the Nazis wanted milk, they couldn't take all our cows. I didn't know why they let us keep the others, but I was glad for it. *Stamppot* was one of my favorites and it wasn't nearly as good without the sausage.

---

2. Stamppot is a comfort food of the Netherlands made with mashed potatoes, smokey sausages, and a variety of vegetables such as carrot, onion, turnip, and spinach.

Lianna helped Mama clear the table and clean up, while Papa and I headed into the living room. We'd barely sat before his lids were closed and his breathing became low and steady. I sat on the couch opposite him, scanning the coffee table for anything to occupy myself. The corner of a newspaper peeked out from below a disheveled pile of old magazines. I reached down and pried it free.

I was surprised to find Dutch, rather than German, on the page. The title read *Trouw*[3] in bold block lettering. A hand-drawn image of Queen Wilhemina watching a rising sun underscored the forbidden nature of the page in Nazi-controlled Holland.

*DE KONINGIN SPRAK (The Queen Speaks)*
*Countrymen in the Netherlands ...*

"Son, what are you doing?" Papa snatched the paper out of my hands before I could sound out anything following the Queen's greeting. He folded it neatly, rose from his chair, and shoved it into a drawer in his rolltop desk. What he did next surprised me more than his snatch-and-grab had: he locked the drawer and pocketed the key.

---

3. *Trouw*, translated as "Faithful" or "Loyal" in English, was one of many underground papers printed and distributed in occupied Netherlands. *Trouw* began printing in 1943 and continues to this day.

When he returned to his chair, rather than lay back and drift off, he leaned forward and gripped my gaze with his own. "Listen to me, Bauke. I want you to forget you saw that, alright? It never existed. We are loyal to the Reich, and hold no love for the Queen. You hear me?"

My brows knitted together as I struggled with whatever bigger picture was at play here. All I could see was the Queen gazing at the sun. I knew Mama and Papa *loved* the Queen. None of this made any sense.

"Okay, Papa. But—"

"No buts. You do as I say. The only paper you've seen in this house for years is *Deutsche Zeitung*, and you don't read German well enough to know what it says."

"At least that part is the truth," I muttered.

His calloused hand gripped my shoulder. "Bauke, stop. This is important."

"Sorry, Papa. I promise."

He stared a moment, then released me and sat back. Still, he didn't relax. I could tell by how his forehead wrinkled and his eyes moved that he was thinking hard.

"Papa," I asked.

He looked toward me and grunted.

"Why don't we like the Queen anymore? You used to say she was like our *moeder* or something."

He stared, and his brow did that thing again. "The *moeder* of our nation, that's right." He nodded slowly. When he finally spoke again, it sounded like he was struggling to form his words. "Son, when you are older, you will find a wife of your own and leave our house. You will turn from your *moeder* to create your own family."

He gulped a time or two and looked down at his hands as he spoke. "Our nation has left our *moeder*. Now, we are married to the Germans."

His lips twisted like he had eaten something bitter, but he didn't go on.

I thought a moment. "Does that make Hitler our *vader* now?"

Something crossed his eyes and his whole body tensed, as if everything about him had seized up at the question.

"No, son, no. We have *no* parents now."

We didn't talk anymore that night. Papa stared into the bookcase until Mama and Lianne joined us some time later.

"Can we go outside now?" Lianne broke the interminable silence that had cloaked our living room in a feeling I didn't like.

"If you wrap up first," Mama answered. "And don't leave the farm. No further than the fence, alright?"

"Yes, Mama," Lianne said, hopping up and turning toward me. "Come on."

That's all it took.

I darted off the couch, determined to move faster than any protest our parents might issue. They'd given my older sister permission, but hadn't agreed to let me out of their sight. Fortunately, neither of them even watched me leave the room.

Moments later, Lianne and I were bundled in layers of sweaters and heavy coats. Winter had come early this year and the wind coming off the water was frigid.

We didn't care. Anything was better than the boredom of being cooped up in our house.

"You think they'll come again tonight?" I asked, smiling at the puffs that billowed from my mouth after each word.

She nodded. "I think so. They've come every night for almost a month."

As if hearing us from thousands of feet above, the distant hum of American bombers sang through the skies. I spun around and squinted up, seeing nothing but darkness and clouds. A second later, the distant wail of the air raid sirens in Emden sounded[4]. The bay was huge, and we were on the farthest point opposite the port, but sound carried over the water, sometimes making it feel like we were in the middle of the bombing runs rather than a country away.

"Here they come!" I hissed.

"Come on," she called, shifting from a steady walk into a jog.

---

4. The historical timing of the Allied bombing of Emden was altered to fit this story.

My pride wouldn't let a girl beat me in a race, so I kicked it up another notch and ran past her, nearly slamming nose-first into our picket fence. One of our cows, chewing lazily nearby, glanced up with mild interest.

The anti-aircraft guns fired first, then falling bombs screeched, followed by blasts that had us ducking like they were dropping on us. The night that had been black only moments ago was now lit with hues of scarlet and ginger. The city of Emden blazed even brighter.

"Two dozen," Lianne muttered as the bombs continued to fall. "Twenty-eight, twenty-nine ..."

"Why are you counting?"

She shushed me. "Thirty-one, thirty-two, thirty-three ..."

One of the bombers was hit and hurtled toward the ground, exploding into a million pieces somewhere on the other side of the town.

"Whoa! That was bigger than any of the bombs," I said.

Lianne was quiet a moment—still counting, I assumed—before she said, "They probably had bombs on board before they crashed."

She crossed herself and closed her eyes briefly.

I stared up at her. She didn't know anyone in those planes. She didn't even know anyone in Emden. Why would she pray over—

"Come on, let's get closer," she said. I watched, wide-eyed, as she climbed over the fence and hopped down onto the other side. "You need help?"

"Mama said—"

She cocked her head. "You coming or not? We'll be able to see better closer to the shore."

I started to argue, but the bombers were making their turn. They would likely go past us, then fly a wide arc until they were pointed back at Emden. They usually did two or three runs before the night stilled.

Fueled by a desire to better see the bombing, and aided by the thrill of doing something rebellious, I gripped the fence and climbed. Lianne had to grab my shoulder and help me over the top, but soon enough, I'd joined her on the other side and we were running toward the bay.

The bombers had made their circle and were nearly overhead. I could feel them as much as hear them.

I looked up to watch them pass and that's when I tripped, and the cold, hard ground reached up and smacked me in the nose.

Pain shot through my face and into my spine. When I reached up and touched my nose, my fingers came away wet and slick.

"Li!" I shouted, fruitlessly trying to raise my voice above the bombers. "Li!"

*I will not cry. I will not cry. I will not cry.*

It took a few seconds for her to realize I was no longer behind her, but then her hands were on my shoulders, lifting me into the light of Emden's embers as she examined my face. "Are you alright? Looks like you got your nose pretty good."

I nodded and bit my cheek, determined to be a man about my tumble, just like Papa taught me.

"I tripped over something big," I said.

We knew these fields like our own, and there were no boulders or logs, like there were near the forests further south.

Lianne's gaze moved from my nose to the ground behind me. She stared; her eyes narrowed, then they popped wide and her hand flew to her mouth.

She rocked back and rose to her feet, like someone had shoved her upward. "That's ... there's a body over there."

I leapt up and darted behind her, as though my sister could shield me from any danger the world had to offer. Sure enough, the long form of a prone body lay on its side a few meters away, the owner's face turned so we couldn't see it. The light of the bombs only offered a silhouette of whoever might lay there.

"What should we do?" I asked.

Slowly, she took a step forward, then another.

"Li, what are you doing?"

"Shh." She held a finger to her lips as she took several more steps toward the body.

I thought my heart might beat out of my chest. Plumes of heat exploded from my mouth as frightened breaths escaped.

When Lianne kneeled and reached toward the figure, I nearly bolted and ran for the safety of our house, but curiosity froze me in place.

"It's a man," she said, her hand pressing to his cheek. She carefully turned his shoulders so he lay on his back, then looked him up and down, hovering a hand over his mouth and nose.

"He's alive. But he's *freezing*," she said. "And his leg is bleeding."

"Is he a Nazi?" I asked, because I couldn't imagine who else would dare bleed on one of our farms in the middle of the night.

"No, I don't think so," she said. "It doesn't matter. He needs help. Go back to the house and fetch Papa."

"Li, I can't leave you—"

"Bauke, go. Run!"

# Chapter Two

# Bauke

*"The only thing we have to fear is fear itself—and possibly the bogeyman."*

Pat Paulson

Years of working a farm will make a man strong.

At least, that's what Papa says. Even so, the man we'd found was unconscious, soaking wet, and heavier than all of us combined could lift. Papa had to race back to fetch his tractor so we could move him.

The moment we stepped through the door, Mama was a blur. She had Papa lay the man on my bed, then shooed us out so they could strip him down and tend his wounds. She would emerge every so often, snatch up more towels or hot water, then disappear behind the closed door once more.

Lianne and I sat at the kitchen table, curiosity gnawing as we watched the commotion.

"Who do you think he is?" I whispered.

"How should I know?" she hissed.

I didn't think she was angry. She sounded more worried than anything.

"What was that rubber suit he was wearing?"

Her eyes darted from the door to me. "I think it was a diving suit, something to keep him warm in the water."

"That didn't work so well," I said. "His face was almost blue."

She turned and started to respond, but the bedroom door opened and our parents stepped out. It was still an hour before our usual bedtime, but they both looked exhausted. Papa joined us at the table, while Mama washed her hands.

"Lianne, what were you doing beyond the fence?" Papa asked in a calm, even tone.

Her eyes fell to the table. "I'm sorry, Papa. We just wanted a better view across the bay."

He leaned forward, eyeing each of us for an eternal moment. "It is dangerous these days. You know this. I expect better of you, Lianne, especially when you are with your brother."

He never addressed me or the fact I was beyond the fence too. I thought that was odd but let my good fortune be.

"Will that man be okay?" Lianne asked, breaking the uncomfortable silence that had settled over the kitchen. Mama sat beside me and took my hand in hers.

"I don't know," Papa said. "I think so, but his skin was colder than ... I've never felt anyone that cold. And his leg needs a doctor. There's metal in it that will need to come out."

"Did he wake up?" Lianne asked.

Papa shook his head. "No. He groaned as we moved him but he never woke."

"Who is he, Papa?" she persisted.

Our parents exchanged a glance, and Mama's lips tightened as she shook her head once.

Papa blew out a ragged breath, then leaned back in his chair. "I'm not sure, but I think we should keep his presence here a secret for now. Until we know more. Don't tell anyone, not even your friends, okay?"

Lianne cocked her head and scrunched her brow. "Why not?"

Papa sat forward again. "Lianne, listen to me. This is important. The Nazis don't like strangers. They like us helping strangers even less. We have no idea who this man is or what he might mean to them. Until we do, we can't risk catching their attention. Do you understand what I am saying?"

Lianne held his gaze a moment, then nodded. "Yes, Papa. I understand."

"Good. Bauke, you will sleep with us until the man is gone. I do not want you going in there without me."

"Yes, Papa," I said.

"Do you think he's dangerous?" Lianne asked, her eyes wide.

Papa started to speak, then stopped. Mama squeezed Lianne's hand and said, "We need to be careful, that's all, until we know more."

Lianne relaxed, slumping back in her chair. Mama always knew how to make us feel better.

"Now," Mama said, turning toward me, "you have had enough excitement for one evening. Go get ready for bed."

I wanted to stay up, to wait for the man to wake up or for the doctor to come, but sleep tugged at my mind the moment Mama mentioned it.

The next morning, Papa roused us before the sun again. My eyes fought to stay closed until I remembered the stranger in my bed.

"What are you going to do with that man, Papa?" I asked as we sat at the table and waited for Mama to finish readying breakfast.

His mouth was set in a thin line, almost exactly like Mama's had been the night before. "I need you and Lianne to start the chores. I'm going to get some help for our … guest."

"Aw, can I come with you?" I asked.

Papa shook his head firmly. "Absolutely not. You two start with the cows. I will help you as soon as I can. Remember, not a word to anyone about the man or what you saw last night."

I wasn't sure what else we had seen beyond an icicle in a rubber suit, but I nodded like I understood.

Papa was out of his chair and opening the door when a clatter sounded from my bedroom. Everyone froze.

"Stay here," Papa said. "I will check on him."

As he stepped from the kitchen, Mama reached out and touched his arm. They exchanged another of their looks, but he didn't stop walking. I watched as he turned the handle, opened the door, then closed it behind him.

Lianne started to rise, but Mama's glare locked her in place. "You two, eat," she said, dropping a plate of boiled eggs on the table. "Do not get up until I come back."

Without another word, she moved through the living room to stand outside my bedroom door, pressing her ear to the wood. A few minutes passed, then Papa called something and she vanished into the bedroom, leaving Lianne and me staring and unable to move.

That might've been the longest breakfast in the history of breakfasts.

When our parents finally emerged, their faces were unreadable.

Papa looked up, startled to see us still sitting at the table. "You two should go. Get started."

I could feel Lianne biting her lip. "Papa, what happened? Is he awake?"

Papa nodded. "He is in and out of consciousness."

"The poor man is in a lot of pain," Mama said. "He barely knew where he was."

"Did he tell you anything? Where he's from? Who he is?" Lianne asked, plucking the questions from my mind.

Mama gripped the back of one of the chairs. "He only said a few words. I am not even sure he knew what he was saying. I think he was himself for a moment ... before the pain took over. Barely long enough to give us his name. He called himself Wilhelm."

# Chapter Three
# Thomas

*"Touched bottom again. Decided to liberate myself... We are never trapped unless we choose to be."*

ANAÏS NIN, *THE DIARY OF ANAÏS NIN*

Everything hurt.

I tried to blink the bleariness from my eyes, but even that sent jolts of pain through my lids and into my head. My hip pulsed, as though someone had jabbed an ice pick into it and was wiggling it around in circles. A part of me wanted to cry out, but my throat was raw, and I had no idea where I was.

The mattress beneath me was soft, and the muted pastels of the walls offered some comfort, but I couldn't figure out why there were tiny cars on a shelf just beyond my feet.

The doorknob rattled and someone stepped in. I tried to turn, but moving my head felt like a herculean task. A moment later, the unresolved shape of a man loomed overhead. All I could think as I flinched beneath his gaze was *please don't beat me.*

Why would I think that? Where had I been?

"*Kun U me horen?*" he asked, sounding distant, like he was calling from a faraway room. The words bounced around my head, unfamiliar yet almost recognizable. The knitting of my brows as I concentrated sent another stab through my aching temples.

"*Begrijpt u mij?*"

I blinked a few times, allowing the man's face to sharpen in my vision.

"*Deutsch?*" he asked, finally in a language I understood.

My mouth opened, but only a guttural croak escaped. "*Ja, Deutsch.*"

"Here, drink some water. You must be parched," the man said, switching fully into German. His accent was ... strange, like he was singing his German rather than speaking it. I couldn't place ...

He held a glass to my lips. It smelled clean, and I was in no position to argue, so I took a tentative sip. Relief washed down my throat, and I craned my head upward to gulp more of the liquid.

"Easy, a little at a time or you'll choke," the man said, his voice firm but not unkind.

I slowed to sips, then let my head fall back onto the pillow. The effort to lean forward had sapped the last of my strength.

The man set the glass on a side table, then sat beside me on the bed.

"What is your name?"

My mind spun. What was my name? I couldn't remember. I could barely think. The name Will popped into my head, but something in me knew that wasn't right. Maybe I knew a Will. Did I have a brother? Flickers of a face flashed before me. I blinked them away.

An odd thought surfaced, more a memory than a thought: I was supposed to keep my name a secret. Maybe it was a good thing I couldn't remember it. Why was my name a secret? That seemed like an odd thing to hide.

Wilhelm. That was it. I mean, it wasn't my name, but it was what I was supposed to say. I didn't know why, but I was sure of that much.

"Wilhelm," I whispered, unwilling to test my voice further.

"I am Aart." The man blinked. "Where are you from, Wilhelm?"

"I ... I don't know. I can't ... remember."

A stab of pain nearly sent my stomach across the room and I moaned through gritted teeth. The man's hands pressed my shoulders down, holding me in place. The door opened and closed again, but I didn't dare open my eyes. Pain seared into me until ... everything went black.

Dreams replaced darkness, but they were even more jumbled than my waking thoughts, as if my subconscious couldn't order itself any better than the rest of me.

*A blond-haired man in a white uniform with gold stripes on black epaulets ...*

*A young woman in a crimson gown ... no, a black gown with a crimson sash about her neck. Her hair trailed fire in curls down the back, and her smile ...*

*A guy with thick spectacles ...*

*A familiar face ... so familiar ... a man no more than twenty, perhaps a year or two older ... his features sharp, his body lithe, the set of his jaw and eyes serious ... his gaze into mine so warm and ... I knew him ... I know him ...*

*Screams ... so many screams ... water everywhere ...*

*I call out, "ADAM! Over here!"*

*I can't breathe ... explosions and heat sucking oxygen and darkness from the night ... the wail of rending metal ... the stench of charred flesh ... then bitter cold ...*

*Then nothing.*

I woke again to find a different man bent over my hip. I would've bolted upright if Aart hadn't been holding my shoulders.

"Easy," Aart said. The other man barely looked up from whatever he was doing to my side. "He is a friend, here to patch you up."

I relaxed, and the pressure of his powerful hands eased.

"You have shards of metal in your hip that must be removed," the friend said, looking up from his work. "We do not have painkillers, so this will hurt … very much."

I peered down to find several metal trays and a couple of buckets. The second man wielded silver instruments that reminded me of a dentist's office. I closed my eyes and blew out a breath. "Do what you need to."

Aart held a glass to my lips. Water. I sipped greedily.

Then he held a second glass forward. The scent bit into my senses and I reeled back.

Aart grimaced. "It tastes terrible, but it will help with the pain."

He held the vile stuff to my lips, and I immediately recognized whiskey as it warmed my throat and chest.

"Put this in your mouth and keep it there," the would-be dentist said, handing a thick strip of leather to Aart, who held it to my mouth. "I hope you do not need it, but it is better to be sure."

The moment the leather was in place, a volcanic eruption of pain burst from my side, raging over the whole of my body. I cried out through the leather, more moan than scream, and Aart added pressure to his grip.

*Clink.* Metal landed in a bucket.

*Clink.*

*Clink.*

Seven more times.

Seven more eruptions.

By the last, there were no more cries. I'd lost consciousness again.

# Chapter Four

# Bauke



> *"Every man is surrounded by a neighborhood of voluntary spies."*

JANE AUSTEN

I t was strange, that first morning Wilhelm woke and joined us for breakfast.

He'd been in my room for more than a week. The doctor had said he shouldn't move for a few days, so Mama took meals to him, while Papa helped him to and from the bathroom. I wasn't sure why he was suddenly well enough to leave my bedroom, but Papa appeared with him draped over his shoulder then helped him into the chair opposite me—*Papa's* chair.

We ate in silence. I tried to keep my eyes on my food, but couldn't help looking up a few times to catch Wilhelm staring at me. His eyes were so empty, like whoever used to live behind them had moved away.

I'd only seen a few people with that look before. Their families had been sent away on trains.

"Do you feel better?"

I nearly shot up from my seat at the sound of Lianne's voice. What was she thinking, talking to him?

Wilhelm's hollow gaze shifted from me to her, and his head nodded, ever so slightly. "Yes, thanks to you. You saved my life." He looked back to me. "Both of you did."

I didn't know what to say to that. All I did was trip over him, then run for help.

"Where are you from?" Lianne asked, her voice strengthening with each question.

Wilhelm's brow furrowed and something sparked in his eyes. "I can't remember much, but I think somewhere with red banners and old brick, maybe a university. It's like the memory is right there, just out of reach."

"Why were you wearing a wetsuit?" Lianne persisted. I glanced over to find her stare intense and her jaw set.

"That's enough questions this morning. Wilhelm, would you like to lie down again?" Mama scooped up his empty plate and hovered. Her tone was the same as when she asked me about bedtime. It wasn't really a question.

Wilhelm looked up and smiled weakly. "Yes, that would be best, I think."

Papa rose from Mama's chair and helped him to his feet, then hobbled with him toward my bedroom.

"Why did you do that?" Lianne snapped.

Mama's head turned. "What?"

"Stop me from asking questions. He wants to remember. Besides, we need to know who he is. We could have a Nazi living in our house, for all we know."

Mama set Wilhelm's plate on the counter, then pressed her palms into the table as she leaned across, her eyes locked on Lianne's. "He is *no* Nazi. Don't you dare say that again."

Lianne pushed her chair back and rose. "You don't know that. You don't know anything. We are all in danger with him here. Now Dr. Kuiper knows he is here. It is only a matter of time before the black cloaks come looking for him—and questioning us."

Mama's face burned red. "Lianne, listen to me. Your *vader* and I will decide when we speak of this man to others, not you or your brother. You must trust us or we *will* all be in danger. This is no time to act on your own."

Lianne stared, her arms crossed, looking like she might explode. Then, as quickly as her anger rose, she blew out a breath and lowered her head. "Yes, Mama."

"Good. Now, both of you, go get ready for school."

School?

How was I supposed to think about math and literature when a mystery man with no memory had washed ashore and was sleeping in my bedroom? I'd gotten over the initial fear. Wilhelm seemed nice. But the curiosity was driving me crazy. Who was he really? How did he get hurt? Why was he wearing a wetsuit? Was he some kind of war hero or Nazi hunter? Was he secretly a Nazi and just covering it all up?

That thought chilled me.

I padded to my bedroom door and paused. I couldn't hear movement from within. I knocked, but no answer came. I slipped inside and crept to my chest of drawers. Wilhelm lay facing the wall, away from me. His shoulders rose and fell in a steady rhythm.

I grabbed my clothes and carefully slid the drawer shut. The dark woolen trousers I had to wear scratched my legs, but there wasn't much to do about that. We might live on a farm with food to spare, but we weren't immune to other things on the war ration list. Mama grumbled about our clothes, especially when Lianne stepped out of her room in the same faded blue dress she wore most days. I guess we were lucky. If I had to choose between clothes and food, there really wasn't a choice.

Wilhelm groaned behind me, and my trousers fell from my hand as I whipped around.

He was still facing away, but his breathing was now fast and his shoulders jerked with each moan. He muttered something I couldn't quite make out. I knew I should take my clothes and leave, but I wanted to know what haunted this man's dreams, so I took a step closer.

Then another.

"... not a good idea. We can't ... Will, please ..."

He wasn't speaking German.

It wasn't Dutch.

My mind tried to figure out the words. They weren't anything I recognized from any of my classes, but something about them was familiar. Then I remembered the radio broadcasts Papa listened to before the Nazis came. Most were in Dutch or German, but every so often they played updates from reporters in other parts of the world.

I froze, staring at the strange man's back as his dream continued to play in his mind and more words tumbled through his lips.

"Bauke." Mama's urgent whisper from the now-cracked door startled me almost as much as Wilhelm's words had. "Let's go."

I stepped toward the door, glancing back one last time, as if Wilhelm would rise and explain himself. Mama's hand gripped my shirt and yanked me out of the room.

"Get changed. We need to leave soon," she said, softly closing the door behind me.

I shuffled into the living room. My mind wouldn't stop spinning. Wilhelm's words rattled in my head.

"What's happening over there? You look like you've seen a ghost."

I hadn't even noticed Lianne enter the living room. She'd pressed her dress, but no iron could give it back its color.

I needed to figure this out, but Mama would only tell me to leave it to the grown-ups. I had to trust someone, and Lianne already knew about Wilhelm. Maybe she could help me understand.

"Wilhelm spoke," I whispered.

On any other day, I would be glad to sit in a class and hear stories about kings and queens of the past. School was a lot of work, but it was fun, my one respite from the endless work on the farm, and the only opportunity to see my friends throughout the week.

But on that day, I couldn't focus.

My teacher's voice buzzed in the background, as my conscious mind replayed the words Wilhelm had muttered in his dreams. The more I heard them, the more convinced I was they were spoken in English.

I didn't know anyone who spoke English. German and Dutch were the languages we learned. A select few might be chosen to join the French class, but I didn't care about that. I lived on a farm in the northeastern corner of the world. Why did I need to know how to speak to anyone in Paris?

But English?

"... you paying attention?" The teacher's voice was a whip-crack across my ears.

"Oh, sorry. Yes," I stammered, sitting upright and returning my gaze from the yard beyond the glass panes.

Dutch History was followed by Dutch Language, which led into two hours of Hitler Youth. Since the Nazis had replaced our Queen and flag, schools had also replaced physical education classes with Hitler Youth.

Most days, we were forced to play games or exercise or march in silly formations. I never understood why I needed to learn to march, but it felt good to get out of class and move around. The older boys were divided into teams and taught boxing or fencing, while the girls did ... whatever girls did in their own version of Hitler Youth.

Some days, the lieutenant who ran these classes just had us play games or run. I wasn't sure he cared what we did, just that we didn't bother him as he stood on the steps of the school and glared at us through his dark sunglasses. It was creepy how he always wore those dumb glasses, even inside.

That day, though, the lieutenant gathered our group of a baker's dozen and spoke of the virtues of the Reich. He praised Germany and its racial purity, then explained how the Führer believed those of us born in the Netherlands were also of the divine race and were, therefore, deserving of the full respect of people everywhere.

One of the boys asked if respect meant having German soldiers tell us what to do, and if we were so respected, why did they have to stay and make our dads work and send our friends away on trains?

The lieutenant demonstrated how quickly a hand could strike a cheek in reply.

The boy didn't rise from the ground throughout the rest of the lecture.

"Now, boys, we must talk of a very important topic: loyalty," the lieutenant continued, sneering at the fallen boy one last time before letting his gaze roam among the rest of us. "Our Führer is the father of us all. He works night and day to make this world a better place, to create a land where our people may take their rightful place at the head of the table. As children should respect and obey their parents, we must respect and obey our Führer. This means always remaining loyal to him and to the Reich."

He let his words sink in, his eyes like a brilliant spotlight in the night, shifting from each boy to the next, always searching, never settling.

"Unfortunately, as has been the case with every great movement, there are those who oppose our Führer's work. They would see him thrown down and our great Reich crumble. They do not understand the dangers those of inferior blood pose and wish to rebel against the will of our father.

"You have seen pamphlets and papers saying as much. They drop like petals from a tree throughout this country. Others wear flowers or coins in protest of our presence. Still some, those whose hearts are blind to the greatness of our cause, sow discontent and seek to destroy what we build.

"But you children have a vital role in stopping these saboteurs of civility."

"Us? We're just kids," one boy said, his face scrunched in confusion.

"That's right, but even the smallest among us may help win a war." The lieutenant nodded. "Let me ask something. Do you have eyes?"

The boy nodded slowly.

"Do you have ears?"

Another nod.

"Do you not see me every day?"

"Yes, Lieutenant," the boy said.

"What if you heard someone talking about printing one of those papers? Or if someone spoke ill of our Führer? What do you think the right thing would be for you to do?"

Several boys around me shifted uncomfortably as the one to whom the lieutenant spoke lifted his chin. "Tell you?"

The lieutenant smiled. He probably meant it to be friendly, but it might've been the scariest thing I'd ever seen. "That's right. I would never want a boy to put himself in danger. Oh no. Our Führer loves children. He protects boys like you. No, what he asks is that you share what you've heard and seen, especially if it might help save our soldiers or stop those who seek to harm our cause. That's all. Nothing more."

When none of us spoke, the lieutenant straightened both his spine and his face. "Now, is all of that clear?"

"Yes, Lieutenant," we barked in unison.

"Good." He glanced up to where the older boys were kicking a ball on the football pitch. "Go run three laps around the pitch, then move on to your next class."

"Yes, Lieutenant," we chorused.

I was turning to race toward the pitch when the lieutenant's hand fell to my shoulder, nearly scaring my heart into fits.

"Bauke, remain a moment." I turned back and stared into the darkness of his glasses.

"You would not look at me as I spoke, son. Is there anything you need to tell me?"

I tried to stare up, but my head fell as my eyes found my feet.

The man's fingers lifted my chin. "What is it, Bauke? Talk to me."

His voice was gentle, soothing, completely unlike the man I'd come to know. Conflict roiled in my chest, and my mouth suddenly felt like the inside of an oven.

His grip on my chin tightened. "What have you heard, Bauke?"

Tears welled in my eyes. I knew Papa would want me to be strong, but the lieutenant seemed like he already knew my secret. He always said it went worse for people who hid things. Would he hurt my family? Would he send my parents on a train if I refused to speak? I'd heard of others suffering that fate.

I blinked a few times, letting beads dribble down my cheeks.

Still, his grip was a vice.

"I found a man."

The lieutenant dropped into a squat before me. "Go on."

"He was hurt, so I got my Papa to help him. That's all."

He stared at me, waited, considered. "Where did you find this man?"

"In a field outside our fence. We ... my sister and I ... we were just ... we didn't mean to ..."

"It's okay, Bauke. You can tell me anything. I'm your friend." His voice was so comforting, like when Papa told me stories as I fell asleep. I wanted to believe him.

"The man's been in our house for a while now and ... he talks in his sleep sometimes."

"Really?" The lieutenant's brows rose above his glasses. "What does he say?"

"I don't know."

Now his head cocked. "You don't know? Why is that?"

"Because ... his words ... I think they were in English."

# Chapter Five

# Thomas

*"The only free cheese is in the mousetrap."*

Dutch proverb, origin unknown

Memories are funny things. They leave without warning and return with no rhyme or reason. At least, that's how mine began returning after a few days of barely conscious reckoning.

Faces would flash before me. Snippets of voices. Moments of frozen time appeared, then began to play, as though someone had flicked a switch on a movie reel. But just as I began to understand, to sense time and space, the reel halted, leaving me more confused and lost than before.

Deep within, I knew I was a confident man, but losing one's ability to recall even his own name was akin to the shifting of one's personal tectonic plates. Everything that had made me so sure before lay hidden beneath the surface of a pond of the blackest water. And, while the darkness of sleep beckoned me the moment my eyes would flutter open, its allure was as much in escaping a waking world I didn't recognize as it was about rest. My hosts were kind enough, tending my wounds, offering food and shelter, but I still wondered if they held me as a guest or a prisoner.

Worst of all, I had this sense that I hadn't arrived in this foreign land alone. There were people, friends perhaps, from whom I'd been separated. I could feel their absence, their loss. Sorrow lodged within my ribs like a boulder, weighing down my soul, though I couldn't even remember who I'd lost.

Emotions swarmed like hornets: anger, frustration, confusion, helplessness. Fear. If my head was swimming in a jigsaw of memories, my heart was drowning in a torrent of feelings.

I woke on the third—no, fourth—morning of my stay with the family. My head didn't swim when I sat up, a minor victory, but one for which I thanked anything holy that would listen. I'd barely gathered my bearings when the door creaked open and a man—Aart, I think—appeared.

He smiled. "Good morning."

It hurt to smile back. "Morning."

"How do you feel?"

I groaned. "Like someone dropped me off a tall building, then ran over me with a tank."

Aart chuckled. "You look worse, if that helps."

Was he ... *joking*?

"Thanks, I think."

His grin widened. "Would you like to try to stand? The children are at school. I kept some breakfast warm for you if you think you can eat."

My stomach growled. When was the last time I ate? I vaguely remembered sitting at a table with the children, but had I eaten? Everything was so muddled in my mind.

"Eating sounds great. Standing, not so much."

Aart stepped forward. "Here, put your arm around my shoulder. When you rise, keep your weight off that side." He pointed toward my heavily bandaged hip and leg.

I had no balance and nearly toppled on my first attempt. Pain radiated from my hip throughout every nerve in my body. I hadn't meant to dig my fingers into Aart's shoulder, but when he winced, I realized what I'd done.

"Sorry," I said, easing my grip. "That really hurt."

He nodded slowly. "Take your time."

The second attempt got me to my feet, but the pain refused to subside. Each step felt like someone striking my hip with a live jumper cable, sending spears of electricity into my wound. I'd never been so thankful for a simple wicker chair as I was when Aart set me down.

Then the salty tang of bacon wafted into my nose, and my stomach threatened to empty right there in the kitchen.

"Easy, Wilhelm," Aart's wife said. I couldn't remember her name. "Sip some water and let your head settle."

I took the glass she offered. "It's not my head I'm worried about."

"This will settle your stomach too." She smiled and watched me sip. "Perhaps you should start with something bland. Try a small bite of egg."

As I lifted the boiled egg to my mouth, I realized she had called me Wilhelm. Was that my name? I let it roll around in my head a moment, hoping it would find a comfortable home, but something about it was out of place, as if it belonged to someone else.

"You called me Wilhelm," I said, swallowing slowly. "Why?"

She sat in the chair across from me and cocked her head. "Is that not your name? It is what you told my husband a few nights ago."

Aart placed a hand on her shoulder, and her own hand lifted to cover his.

"I ... I don't know. Maybe, but ... I don't think so."

The couple watched me eat, my confidence growing with each bite, sure my stomach would remain in place and allow a proper meal.

"What do you remember?" the woman asked.

I ate the last of the egg and washed it down with more water, then wiped my mouth with a cloth napkin. "I remember a lot of things, but none of them make any sense. It's like my mind is a deck of cards, and someone came along and shuffled them in the most random order possible."

Aart freed his hand and took the seat next to me, leaning forward with his elbows on the table. "Tell us whatever you remember. Maybe saying it out loud will help some of the cards fall into place."

Aart's wife slid the plate of bacon toward me. My mouth watered, but my stomach clenched. "Maybe I should stick with eggs this morning."

She nodded once, removing the bacon from the table and setting it on the counter behind her. I took another egg from a bowl in the center of the table.

"I see these faces. Most are young, my age. They feel so familiar, like I know them well, like they're family or close friends. I dreamed about brick and stone buildings draped in red banners."

"Nazi banners?" the woman asked.

I shook my head. "I don't think so. There was a white letter in their center, not a swastika."

"You would remember that symbol well enough," Aart said, in a tone that I wasn't sure was still friendly.

"It's hard to forget," I admitted. "I know I'm not a Nazi. The thought of them makes me angry."

The couple shared a quick glance, and the slightest curl appeared at the corners of the woman's mouth.

"I was on a ship," I said suddenly, a memory returning unbidden to my mind's eye. "It was cold and loud. The sounds were … strange, like some animal wailing."

Aart's brows knitted. "Can you describe it? Can you see any writing on instruments or above doors?"

*Clever*, I thought, as I searched my mind.

A loud banging on the front door shattered my concentration, and Aart shot out of his chair.

*"Aart, het is Ignass van der Kleij. Ik moet je spreken."*

*Aart, it's Ignass van der Kleij. I need to speak with you.*

Aart and his wife gaped, then he whispered to me, "Ignass is the local police captain."

My heart leapt into my throat, though I couldn't quite understand why.

"Isa, help Wilhelm back into bed. I will try to delay Ignass."

Aart stepped out of the kitchen as Isa rounded the table and helped me stand. I struggled with her arm under my elbow until she said, "Put your arm around me. It is okay."

As her husband had done less than an hour before, Isa walked with me draped about her shoulders into Bauke's bedroom. We could hear the men's voices but couldn't make out their words.

Then the sound of heavy boots marching across wooden flooring sent my blood into a rage. A second set of boots added to the thunder of the first.

"Isa, where are you and your guest?"

Isa stared through me, her eyes even wider than before.

The door opened and a tall, iron-jawed man in the crisp military-style uniform of the Dutch police stepped in, a revolver gripped firmly in his right hand.

"You"—he pointed the gun like it was a school teacher's rod and barked in German—"come with us. Now."

Isa stood. "Ignass, he is injured."

The captain held up his palm. "Do not interfere, Isa. Not in this. I can only protect you and your family if you do not resist."

*Protect them?* My head reeled.

Isa leaned toward me and whispered, "I am sorry, Wilhelm. I must protect my children."

I nodded up at her. "It's alright. I will go."

A second officer, a young man with slicked-back black hair and crystal blue eyes, entered behind his chief.

"Bring him. He will need help walking," van der Kleij instructed.

The younger man looked from me to the captain. "Restraints?"

"They will not be necessary, will they?" van der Kleij asked me.

I shook my head.

The young officer helped me stand. I expected a rough grip and painful exit, but the man's support was gentle and sure. As we stepped onto the porch toward the waiting car, I heard Aart behind me ask van der Kleij, "Do *they* know about him?"

"Yes."

# Chapter Six

# Thomas



The cell floor was so clean it shone in the dim light breaking through the barred window. I laid atop the wafer-thin mattress with my head resting on the neatly folded sheet and blanket. The knotty pillow helped keep my hip elevated. I didn't fully understand why, but that seemed to keep the throbbing at bay. Based on the dip in the sun's position, I guessed I'd been there for a few hours, the sound of water dripping in a distant sink my only companion.

I tried to sleep, but every time I closed my eyes, explosions flared in my vision, and the overwhelming spike of fear that came from gulping in far too much saltwater jolted me awake. Each time, I found myself atop the cot, nowhere near the sea or balls of flame.

I still couldn't piece together any of the memories, though my gut was certain of their veracity.

"Stand up." A firm voice at the cell door jolted me out of my waking sleep.

I struggled to my feet and turned to find the younger of the two policemen who'd arrested me that morning turning the key in the lock. "Turn and press your hands into the wall above your head. Spread your legs wider than your shoulders and do not move."

I tried to comply but pain stabbed into my hip as I widened my stance.

"Easy," the officer whispered as he clamped a cuff on one wrist, then twisted my arm behind my back. "They will ask you questions, nothing more. The Nazis will come later, but I will try to help you before that. Do not trust the captain."

My mind spun. Why was this man helping me? Was this a test? A trick? Some game to gain my confidence so I would ... what? Tell him all the things I could not remember?

He gripped my other wrist and guided it down to lock into the other shackle. Then he turned me by my shoulders to look into my eyes.

"They know you mutter English in your sleep. Do not lie about that."

My mouth fell open. I had spoken English? I'd been speaking German because ... I didn't know why. It just felt right.

I nodded, not trusting words to form.

"Good. Breathe. These are only questions," he whispered, offering a weak smile before stepping beside me and gripping my arm. His voice rose to a command. "Move."

A moment later, I sat in a small windowless room, in a metal chair with my cuffs attached through a ring in a metal table. The younger officer had left as soon as I'd been locked in place. Thirty minutes, perhaps an hour, later, the door behind me opened and police captain Ignass van der Kleij rounded the table to sit across from me.

His face was a mask of emotionless disdain. "What is your name?" he asked, opening a folder then flipping a page in a small notebook, his pen at the ready.

"I do not remember."

He eyed me, then scribbled something. "How do you know the Vos family?"

"I don't know them. I mean, I didn't."

His eyes bore into me. "Until?"

"Until they found me in the field. That's what they told me."

"And you had never met them before that day?"

I shook my head. "I had never seen any of them before."

"And they simply took you in and treated your injuries? With no name or explanation? In the middle of a war?"

I'd wondered those things myself. "I guess ... yes."

He jotted more notes. "Where are you from?"

"I'm sorry, I do not remember anything before waking in the boy's bed."

He set his pen down. "The boy's name is Bauke."

I nodded. "Yes."

"He is a smart lad. A loyal boy." Each word felt more like a threat than a description of a child. "You slept in his bed?"

"Yes."

"It is something for parents to give their son's bed to a stranger, is it not?"

I started to dismiss the claim, but again found myself unable to argue with his logic. "Yes. They have been most kind."

"Why were you wearing a wetsuit?" he asked, switching to English.

"I don't know," I replied without hesitation in the same language.

One corner of his mouth twitched. "You speak English without thought."

It was another accusation.

"I ... I think so, yes."

He switched to Dutch. "*En je spreekt onze taal niet?*"

My brow furrowed. "I'm sorry. I don't understand—"

He switched to German. "You do not speak Dutch, yet you speak German and English?"

My eyes fell to my hands.

"Do not look away from me," he snapped.

My eyes darted up.

"Your accent, it is *American*."

"I do not know," I muttered.

But I did know.

As soon as he said the word, in my gut, I knew he was right. I was American. Why the hell was I in the Netherlands?

"Did you know the Americans began bombing the port across the bay from our border roughly five weeks ago?" He clicked his pen a few times, then looked up. "In truth, they have bombed Emden many times before, but their raid became quite intense recently. Why do you think that would be so?"

"I have no idea," I said.

Van der Kleij sat back, his chair screaming in protest. "Something interesting happened a few weeks ago, about the same time the Vos family found you."

When I didn't respond, he continued. "A team of men in boats slipped into the harbor and destroyed several vessels. The explosions were seen and heard across the water. They painted the sky red."

I remained silent.

"The Nazis are quite upset about this attack. Apparently, there was something dear to them on one of those ships."

"I don't understand—"

Van der Kleij rose and slammed his palm on the table. "We captured two of these men. They wore the same black suit you were found wearing. Do not lie to me anymore. Tell me who you are. Who is helping you? Is Vos your contact?"

"What? No. I'd never met—"

"I heard your lie. Tell me the truth. How do you know Aart Vos? What is your name?"

"I don't—"

"If you tell me you don't remember one more time, I will hand you over to the Nazis and they will peel the truth out of you, one layer of skin at a time."

Nazis. A wall of fear slammed into me, and my pulse pounded.

"Well?" Van der Kleij demanded.

"I'm telling you the truth. I don't remember anything. I want to remember, but I just can't. Everything is a jumble."

Van der Kleij considered me a moment, then sat and made a few notes. When he looked up, his voice was calm again. "What is a jumble? Tell me what you see when you close your eyes."

How did he know I spoke English in my sleep? Aart and Isa didn't mention it to me when we spoke about my dreams just this morning ... wait. Bauke. Maybe the boy came into his room and heard—

"What do you dream about?"

I decided honesty was best, considering I'd already told the Voses. "Buildings—brick and stone."

"Go on," he said, his pen scraping against paper.

"Red banners hanging down ... or ... on poles. I'm not sure. I can't see them clearly."

"What else?"

"Faces. I see faces of people I think I know, but I can't remember them now. They feel so ... familiar."

"Does anyone speak in your dreams?" he asked.

I shook my head. "Not so far, anyway."

"Anything else? What else have you seen?"

Explosions. So many explosions. The brightness of the night sky. The taste of salt and smoke and blood. The scent of death. I remembered those all too well.

"Nothing else."

The captain completed his observations, then closed his folder and notebook. "That is enough for now. A doctor will visit later to tend your wound. You are now a prisoner of war, but we Dutch do not aim to be cruel. We leave that to our suzerain."

He strode out of the room, leaving me alone to ponder my fate.

# Chapter Seven

# Will

*S*now drifts from above.

*Pinions fashioned to poles atop majestic buildings snap in the wintry breeze.*

*Brassy notes from a marching band play in a distant field.*

*As I tread the cobbled stones, fingers entwined in mine squeeze with familiar warmth, and my heart flutters at the touch.*

*I turn to see the one who has captured me so completely and*

*...*

I rubbed my eyes, frustrated that some distant noise had roused me from sleep's embrace. I turned, tussled my pillow, and let my mind drift free once more.

*Planes roar overhead.*

*The wail of falling bombs tear through the once-peaceful night.*

*One explosion, then another, then ten more.*

*The town blazes.*

*My arms ache from miles of paddling, but still we press forward. The other canoes are just ahead.*

*Thomas is just ahead.*

*As we drift away from our target, the mine successfully attached, I watch in horror as the water near Thomas's boat blooms with light. Men with rifles appear from the ship above and a smaller boat below. Angry voices call out and hands rise in surrender.*

*"We have to go back," I plead. "We have to help them."*

*Ward shakes his head.*

*"Ward! They're going to—"*

*"Shaw, stop. There's nothing we can do."*

*Those words stab into my heart.*

*There is nothing we can do for our comrades.*

*Nothing we can do ... for Thomas.*

*The ship that was our target bursts into flames; brilliance blinds our eyes. Seconds later, two more bursts ring out from ships moored nearby. The bay rocks as water churns. The twisting of metal sends eerie groans, the cry of vessels of war in the final throes of their deaths.*

*Of Thomas in the throes of death.*

Sweat poured down my face and soaked my shirt as I threw the covers off me. I'd long since ceased caring about the river of grief that lined my face. I no longer cared that my anguish was repulsive, my love an abomination. Others derided what Thomas and I were, what we had, but their castigation no longer held sway in my mind or heart.

The world be damned.

I hurled my pillow across the room, knocking several items off the deck in a clatter, then pounded my fists into the mattress, begging to punish anyone, anything, within reach.

"Emu?" The soft voice of Sarah Proctor, code name Sparrow, drifted through the door. "Are you alright?"

Despite knowing each other's true names now, we still followed protocol and used our OSS code names while living in the safe house. The agency had been kind enough to let me mourn in peace, but I knew that could change at any moment. The war waited for no man ... or woman.

"Emu, I'm coming in," she said just before the knob turned.

The moment she saw my reddened eyes and puffy cheeks, the door clicked behind her and she stepped forward. Her arms locked around me, pulling my head into her shoulder.

I wouldn't have stayed alive without her. I knew it. Her strength, her compassion, her unwavering friendship. She was the tether that moored me to life and the possibility of a future without unending pain.

"Will it ever stop?" I sobbed into her.

"Shh. It will get better. In time. The nightmares will fade. You just have to give it time."

I knew it was the best she had to offer, but still ...

Time was no salve. It was a sentence.

I don't know how long we sat like that. She never resisted or made to stand. She simply held me, occasionally stroking my hair or kissing the top of my head. I wasn't sure when we'd become family, but we had. The fires of war had forged us into something new, something stronger when combined, and I loved her for it. I needed her even more.

A knock sounded at the door, then again, more rapid and insistent.

"Master Emu," our host, George, called. "Master Emu, come quickly. A messenger has arrived from Downing S treet."Downing Street?

We were in Bedfordshire, only an hour's drive from London. Why on earth would the Prime Minister of England send a messenger to me?

"Come on," Sparrow whispered into my hair. "Let's go see."

Reluctantly, I let her release me, feeling safety and comfort flee with the loss of her warmth. She stood and extended her hand, then wiggled it to signal that she would not be put off.

I looked up and a pathetic smile tried to tease my lips.

"There he is," she said. "I knew he was still in there."

I blew out a breath, then rose. George was practically dancing outside the door when it opened.

"Downing Street!" he said, sounding more like an excited teen than the septuagenarian I knew him to be.

Sparrow patted his arm and strode past. I met his eyes but couldn't find the energy to return his smile.

We stepped into the foyer to find a tall man in a dark suit, a hat spinning in one hand.

"Oh, hello," he startled, nearly dropping his hat. His head bobbed quickly, as I suspected it might when a royal passed by, then he reached into his coat and retrieved a cream-colored envelope. "Are you the birds?"

The question sounded absurd rolling off his tongue. I nearly coughed a laugh, but Sparrow tensed.

"Who are you? And what do you know of birds?" she asked.

"Easy, miss," he said, holding up his hat like a white flag. "I am Jamison Hurt from the Office of the Prime Minister. Churchill sent me directly, said this was urgent."

I groaned. The last thing I wanted was to be thrown back into another mission.

Sparrow still didn't step forward to accept the envelope.

Hurt's lips pursed. "I assume you are Sparrow. This message is for Emu, but from the look on his face, he's not keen to receive it."

"Our last mission was . . . challenging," Sparrow said, winning an award for understatement of the century. "Forgive our caution. It's ingrained in our training."

Hurt's eyes twinkled. "Ah, yes. The vaunted Camp X. Our Canadian cousins are quite proud of the place."

Sparrow's jaw nearly hit the floor at this man's intimate knowledge of our journey.

Hurt winked.

The man actually winked.

"Despite what you Yanks think, there's little hidden from the Crown," he said, a sly grin parting his lips. "Be a champ and hand that to Emu. He will want to read it straight away. The PM requests his reply before I leave, and I should be on the road already."

Sparrow stepped forward, took the letter, then held it toward me. The simplicity of the return address embossed in the upper corner struck me as the most British thing I had ever seen.

My hand trembled as I took the note and tore it open. A single folded page contained the whole of Churchill's message.


*Emu,*


*We found them.*


*Lt. Cdr. Drake Raines*

Hurt was smiling when my eyes darted from the page to his.

"What the hell does this mean?" I said, my voice tinged with anger, sharp pain, and no small amount of hope.

Sparrow grabbed my wrist so she could read the note, despite my refusal to release the precious page. Her hand flew from mine to her mouth.

"It means exactly what it says," Hurt answered with a typical British non-answer. "Forgive me. I am only at liberty to deliver this message and receive your reply. What would you like to send back?"

"George!" I shouted, only to find the man standing right behind me. "Oh, sorry. Would you get our guest a tea or coffee, or scotch? Whatever the fuck he wants? Just keep him here for five minutes. I'll be right back."

I didn't wait for a reply or protest from Hurt. I grabbed Sparrow by the arm and dragged her down the hall back to my room. As I threw off my shirt and rummaged for another, she whispered, "What are you doing, Will? What's going on?"

"I'm not sitting here one minute longer if there's a chance Thomas is alive."

"Condor," she corrected.

"Fuck all that," I snapped, struggling to get my arm through the right hole in my shirt. Sparrow's slender hand guided the fabric until it settled into place.

"Look at me, Will." She held my arms so I couldn't continue dressing. "You *have* to care about things like that. Things like code names and missions, especially if you plan to go to London. Lives depend on us caring about them. *His* life might depend on them."

I wanted to argue, to shout, to scream, to do anything but stand there and admit she was right, but she was.

My head dipped. "You're right. Sorry, I'll be careful."

"*We'll* be careful," she corrected again.

My eyes widened. "What—?"

She released my arms, then crossed her own. "Do you honestly think I would let you leave me here while you run off to save your man—a man I care a great deal about too? Not to mention Egret and the others. We still don't know what happened to them, and the PM's note said they found *them*, not him."

"Shit, I missed that." The realization hit me like a hammer to the chest. "What if—?"

"Stop," she said, her palm pressing into the center of my chest. "We only know what we know. Think like Emu right now, okay? You need to be smarter than this. *We* need to be smarter."

I stared into her eyes. I knew that look. Her mind was set and there was nothing in the world that could change it.

God, I loved this woman.

I wrapped my arms around her and pulled her close. "Thank you, Sarah. Thank you," I whispered.

"Spa—"

"I know. *Sparrow*. It was a moment. You can let me have those, can't you?"

Her scowl softened as she reached up and smoothed my hair. "I love you too, idiot."

I laughed. I couldn't help it. It just tumbled out. Right there in the middle of my room, with no pants on and Sparrow smoothing my unruly hair, I actually laughed.

It was the first time I'd felt anything other than sorrow since we'd left the continent, and damn, it felt good.

By the time we returned to the foyer, Hurt was down to his last sip of whiskey.

"We're coming with you," I declared the moment we stepped into the entrance.

"Obviously," the Brit said through a smirk and dramatically raised brows.

Sparrow stepped forward, as if no one had spoken.

I gaped. "You knew I would want to come?"

Hurt spun his hat, plopped it onto his head, then turned toward the door and glanced back. "The Crown *always* knows."

# Chapter Eight

# Thomas

*"The prisoner, having reached the depth of his depression, gradually reawakens to the life around him. He licks himself and his wounded pride, opens his eyes, and finds that far away on the horizon there is still a ray of sunlight left."*

Philip Newman[1]

As I sat alone on the bunk in my cell, I realized how civil most of the process had been to that point. The Dutch police, a rural station with only a few officers and their chief, had been almost courteous in their handling of me. The one time the chief got angry during our questioning looked more like a performance designed to scare a prisoner than any genuine anger.

More curious was the absence of Nazi officers. I hadn't seen a single German in the station. No SS men visited my cell. The chief had barely spoken a word about them, except for the reference regarding how upset they were about the port attack in Emden.

I couldn't blame them for that. If the police chief told the truth, we'd destroyed an incredibly important and sensitive project.

The other thing that tickled my mind as I replayed the earlier interrogation was how brief it had been.

A distant memory of training crept in—in camp somewhere cold—instructors preparing us for endless hours of brutal questioning and torture. I vaguely remembered someone saying that all men broke, but our task was to delay that eventuality long enough for a possible rescue. They never spoke about how infrequently prisoners were saved from such a fate, and we never asked. There was something oddly comforting in hope, regardless of how rational it might—or might not—have been.

Wilhelm.

The name I'd given the Vos family. It was the first name that popped into my mind when they'd asked. It was the only name I could remember.

And yet, I knew it wasn't mine. I didn't understand why I knew that. I just felt it in my gut.

I leaned my head against the cold stone of the cell wall and closed my eyes. For a brief moment, my hip relaxed and the pulsing pain I'd come to expect ebbed to a low throb, uncomfortable but bearable.

A face appeared before me. It was the same face I'd seen in recent dreams.

The man was young, perhaps a year or two younger than me. Straight, sandy blond hair was cropped close to his head, except for a few tufts that refused to lie back and drooped across his forehead. Ocean blue eyes drilled into me, and I felt a warmth in that gaze. This man knew me, cared about me, and from the stirring in my chest, I knew him too.

Will.

*His name is Will.*

The recollection sent a shiver up my arms.

A sense of overwhelming affection and safety—two feelings I'd been without since my memory had vanished—wrapped me in a cloak and held all other emotions at bay. My cheek tingled as I imagined him reaching out and cupping it, his skin hot against mine, his smile—

"What are you grinning at?"

My eyes flew open and Will fled, replaced by the young policeman who'd claimed to be my ally.

"I think I remembered someone ... someone special," I admitted.

"It may all come back in time." He unlocked the cell door and stepped inside. The clank of the metal lock resetting behind him echoed off the barren walls.

He stepped forward to stand only a stride away, then whispered, "I only have a moment. The captain has notified Berlin of your capture. The Nazis are quite keen to get their hands on you, both for what you know and to administer retribution for your actions."

"My actions?"

He cocked his head like I was a child whose mouth was covered in powdered sugar but still denied eating a forbidden dessert.

"Wilhelm, you are *American*. I hear it in your accent when you speak English. Hell, I hear it in your German at times. You wore a wetsuit, and we found boats, canoes, hidden on the beach. Some of the equipment on those boats matched what you were wearing. You were part of the mission that blew up ships in Emden. Of this, there is no doubt. I believe you lost your memory, but this is who you were—who you are."

"I ... I don't know ..." Flashes of moments played like a broken reel in my mind: visions of other men in wetsuits, paddling in a strange canoe, explosions. I could feel the heat, the water pulling me down, the helpless surrender as darkness—

"Wilhelm, look at me," he said.

My vision resolved to the present and I met his gaze.

"The Nazis are sending two high-ranking SD officers to take over your interrogation. Once you are in their custody, you will be lost. You will live as long as they can keep you breathing, but every moment will be agony. You will beg to die, but they will refuse you. This *cannot* be your fate."

I sat forward and rubbed my eyes with my palms. "What am I supposed to do from in here?"

"We have one thing on our side. The SD men are either too important or too proud—or too lazy—to drive all the way here. We are in the middle of nowhere to them. We are nothing but slaves for food."

I gaped at hearing him speak so openly of his disdain for the Nazis. His words would earn him the same fate he ascribed to me if he was overheard.

"They will arrive by plane in Amsterdam in one week. They are to meet with Reichskommissar Arthur Seyss-Inquart[2] and then turn their full attention to you the next

---

2. https://en.wikipedia.org/wiki/Arthur_Seyss-Inqua rt  was appointed reichskommissar of the occupied Netherlands in 1940.

day. We have been instructed to transport you to Amsterdam in six days. That is the time we have to plan your escape."

I found myself holding my breath as he spoke.

Six days stood between my freedom and a miserable end to life in the hands of the Nazis.

Then something struck me.

This man, this police officer who had arrested me, said *we* had six days.

"Why are you helping me?" I asked without thinking.

He hesitated only a moment. "My name is Fons Boswel. My father was head of the resistance who led the farmers' strike in the spring, while our countrymen, miners, doctors, and others also refused to work. Our protests were met with rifles and ropes about necks.[3] My father was hanged from a tree that grows a few paces from our porch. There is a swing on that tree. His body swung beside it."

"Fons . . . I'm sorry," I breathed, desperate to wash the image from my mind.

---

3. https://en.wikipedia.org/wiki/April%E2%80%93May_strikes (also known as the milk strike or mine strike) were labor strikes in 1943 in the Netherlands against forced labor and was the largest strike in Dutch history.

His head remained bowed for only an instant before snapping up. "We do not have time for this. Continue having no memories, if only when questioned. I will return when I know more."

When he turned to leave, I reached out and gripped his wrist. His head whipped around.

"Thank you, Fons."

He stared for a long moment, then nodded crisply once and strode out of the cell, slamming it shut behind him.

The silence that followed that iron echo rang louder than any bell that ever tolled.

"Six days," I muttered to myself.

I tried to close my eyes and recall the image of Will, the man who'd radiated fondness and regard, but the only image I could conjure was that of Nazi officers with rifles pointed at my head as they barked orders above the din of the water beneath. I could feel the waves rocking the boat, feel the shift of my legs as I struggled for balance.

The German soldiers' eyes were filled with anger. No, it was more than that. We were enemies striking at their fatherland, inferior people rebelling against their betters. The hatred in their eyes was malice, contempt, and disdain, and it was all consuming.

I rubbed my eyes again, this time harder, desperate to erase one of the few memories that remained so clear. The irony in that brought a rare turn to my lips, and something in my chest eased.

The soldiers and ships vanished. The rocking of the boat stilled. Even the man at my side, the one I'd paddled with only to be captured, whose name I still couldn't recall, faded away.

*He* returned.

Will.

*His name is Will.*

I repeated that phrase again and again, at first in my head, then whispered aloud.

I *loved* this man.

I could feel it. I knew it.

And he loved me.

We were together before ... before all this, whatever *this* was.

We were one, and my very soul cried out to return to him. Whatever it took, I had to be with him again, by his side, in his arms. I was meant to walk this life with this man, and not even a great war could stand between us.

I swore it over and over, willing myself to believe it was possible, steeling my resolve for the days to come, for the challenges that surely would test everything I had ever known, possibly the very spirit of who I was.

But I *would* endure.

Overwhelming love surged through me, a wildfire loose on an endless wood.

I squeezed my eyes shut and watched us strolling down city streets, laughing and jostling. Then we lay beneath a twisted tree on a sea of grass in a park I instinctively knew held meaning beyond measure.

His lips pressed against mine. I felt the graze of his tongue, the thrill of his fingers as they worked the buttons of my shirt.

His skin felt so smooth, so perfect and right.

Our bodies entwined. Our hearts beat as one.

Then we were one.

My eyes flew open, and I gulped in air.

Six days.

I had six days.

# Chapter Nine
# **Will**

*"Bureaucracy gives birth to itself and then ex-
pects maternity benefits."*

Dale Dauten

Midway through the drive into London, Sparrow reached across and gripped my hand. I'd tried to settle, to calm my nerves and stop my leg from bouncing, but my heart hadn't stopped racing from the moment I'd learned Thomas might be alive. I could barely contain myself.

It didn't help that the Brit the PM had sent to retrieve us refused to talk about anything more substantive than the cloud cover that shrouded London's skies like some celestial blanket. I tried asking him questions; first about the note, then about who the "them" was in the note, then about Lieutenant-Commander Raines, our mission commander from the Emden raid and the note's author. When none of those queries worked, I asked where we were headed.

"Broadway." Hurt chuckled. "Isn't that where every American wishes to go when they visit?"

"Broadway?" I repeated, glancing sideways at Sparrow. She shrugged and shook her head.

"Broadway is where you want to be, take my word for it."

"Is that where the Prime Minister is?"

Hurt's laugh swelled beyond a chuckle. "Of course not. You didn't think—"

"You said you were from the PM's office," I persisted.

He glanced back through the rearview mirror. "I am. I am also a servant of the Crown. In that sense, I was sent by the King as well. Did you know, the PM and the King now meet often? I am told the PM consults with His Majesty on matters of war. Isn't that remarkable?"

I wanted to rap him upside the head to show just how remarkable I thought it was. "Mr. Hurt—"

"You may call me Jamison."

"Jamison"—Sparrow squeezed my hand, and I took a breath to level my tone—"Jamison, please understand that these men are important to me ... to us. Until you arrived, I

. . . we . . . believed they were all lost. Now, you give us hope that they are alive but refuse to offer any explanation." "I was only authorized to deliver the note and bring you to Broadway. I am confident you will receive answers once we arrive." His eyes softened in the mirror. "Christopher Ward, your canoe mate in *Catfish*, received the same note. Unfortunately, he was already pending transit to the continent on other matters and could not join us."

"You talked with Ward?" I hadn't even thought about him, but of course he'd want to know. He and I were the only ones to make it home, besides MacLeod and O'Connor, whose canoes capsized before they ever left the sub. They had missed the most dangerous part of our mission altogether.

"I did, just yesterday. He sends his regards." He was silent a moment, then added, "I believe his exact words were, 'Tell Emu to bring Condor home.'"

I fell back against the seat, letting my head bang against the rest, and stared up at the ceiling. I had put all the possible things that could be happening to Thomas as we drove to London out of my mind—until that moment. The mere mention of his code name brought them thundering back to life. My heart seized, and I struggled to suck in air.

Sparrow's other hand sandwiched mine. "Try to breathe. We'll be there soon."

Another twenty eternal minutes passed before we entered London proper and pulled out front of a ten-story building whose brick and stone facade appeared more retail than governmental. A brass plate beside glass double doors read *MINIMAX Fire Extinguisher Company*.[1]

"A fire extinguisher company?" I asked, enunciating each word as if they tasted of bitter herbs.

Hurt opened his door and stepped out. When we didn't move, his head reappeared, and that infuriating smile returned. "Come along."

Sparrow released my hand so I could open the door. As soon as I'd stepped out, she scooted across the seat and exited from the same side. Hurt stood by the doors, one hand resting on a handle.

We stepped inside to find sales clerks behind counters that lined each wall. Glass cases beneath the counters displayed a variety of extinguishers, axes, and other firefighting and escape-related equipment.

---

1. 54 Broadway served as the headquarters for the British Intelligence Services beginning in 1924. The brass plate and the cover for the headquarters were real, but the hidden entrance was fictionalized for this novel.

A stunning young woman whose blonde hair had been pulled into a tight bun smiled broadly. "Welcome," she said. "Can I help you find anything specific?"

I nearly laughed at her absurdly accurate question.

Hurt ignored the woman and led us to the far side of the sales floor where the side of an antique firetruck decorated the back wall. He reached up and squeezed the black bellows that would normally sound the truck's golden horn, then pulled outward. The entire front of the truck opened to reveal an unmarked door. He stood aside and gestured for us to enter. The moment we did, he followed and closed the faux truck behind us.

A pair of British soldiers sat at desks just inside the door.

"Sign in, please," one said to us, spinning a book around and holding out a pen.

Hurt stepped forward and completed a few lines, then turned back. "Follow me closely. The Secret Service does not take kindly to wandering strangers."

One of the soldiers held up a hand. "Wait here, sir. All guests require an escort."

Hurt's brows rose at this. I thought he was going to protest, but the soldier vanished faster than our guide's mouth could move, leaving us standing before the desk with the other guard watching dutifully.

"The Secret Service?" I asked, since we had some unexpected time.

Sparrow looked as baffled as I felt.

"This is the headquarters of His Majesty's intelligence services. We prefer to be more ... what's the word ... *subtle* than you Americans. Bombs dropping on your heads will do that for a people."

Sparrow chuckled and whispered "subtle" in a sarcastic echo.

Moments later, the guard returned with a young woman who couldn't have been a year older than me. The top of her hair barely reached my chest, but her thin frame stood in contrast to the obvious strength that flowed from her eyes. Something about her reminded me of a sharp-tongued grandmother chasing a pack of unruly children with a wooden spoon.

"Arms out, please," one guard said as the other stepped forward.

"Is this absolutely necessary? I am from the PM's office." Hurt clearly couldn't hold back any longer.

"Only if you want to continue past this desk," one guard said.

The woman cocked a brow at Hurt. "The PM understands our need for security better than anyone, does he not?"

Hurt huffed out a breath. "Right, then."

"Arms and turn," the guard said, resuming his patting routine.

Once satisfied, the guard turned to the woman and nodded, then took his seat and made notes in his log, no longer interested in us. The woman eyed each of us, then spun and led us through a series of hallways, each lined with more unmarked doors, before stopping before a simple stairwell.

"Please forgive me for this climb," she said cryptically, before leading us up ten flights of stairs. "The view up here is brilliant, but the climb is a leg killer."

My thighs agreed.

"You will be meeting with Major General Stewart Menzies, the head of the service," the woman said, as if a visit to a major nation's intelligence head was a common occurrence. Then again, in this building, it was. We were the outliers.

We stepped onto a floor whose carpet and walls were as utilitarian as any military office building, yet the air somehow thinned at our approach. Unlike the other floors we'd seen as we climbed the stairs, where everyone was hidden behind unmarked doors, on this highest of floors, men and women sat in desks along the main walkway, as if guarding the offices that stood at their backs. A few looked up as we passed, but most kept their eyes on their work and showed little interest in the newcomers. The double doors to the last office were guarded by two secretaries and flanked by a pair of armed soldiers.

Hurt stepped forward before our escort spoke. "The PM sends his regards to Sir Stewart, along with two guests."

Both secretaries looked up, then one scanned a page and spoke, "You are?"

"Major Hurt. This is Sparrow and Emu," he said, motioning toward each of us. Neither secretary showed the slightest surprise or interest in his use of code names for our introduction. The one who'd spoken simply slid her finger down the page until it settled by a series of entries.

"Stay right there a moment," she said before vanishing through the doors. Barely a heartbeat later, she returned. "You may go in."

When Hurt stepped forward, the woman's hand shot out, blocking his path. "Just your guests—Sir Stewart's orders."

Hurt's eyes widened, then he turned toward us. "I will wait for you here."

"Downstairs," the woman's voice cracked. I suddenly got the impression Hurt was a frequent guest in this building and not a favorite of the staff.

"I will wait for you downstairs," Hurt said, a grin playing at his lips. "I hope you find what you seek."

As he strode back down the hall, one of the soldiers opened a door and motioned for us to enter.

The office was enormous, but nowhere as grand as I would have expected for the head of a major power's intelligence service. A fifty-something man with thinning hair and a neatly trimmed mustache rose from behind a long mahogany desk.

"Come in. Sit," he ordered, though not unkindly. "Would either of you like a drink?"

I followed his hand to the bar and wished desperately for an entire bottle of whatever he had.

"No, sir. Thank you," I said.

"Let's not bother with introductions. You will not give me your names, in any case." Menzies's clipped words were refreshing, like an ice bath in the middle of winter. "What you did in Emden was nothing short of a miracle, the stuff of novels. I know what you destroyed and what our enemy intended to do with it. This nation, the whole world, really, is in your debt, though it will never admit such a thing. Our work lies in shadows, not platitudes."

We stared, unsure how to respond.

"Enough of that. We believe we found one of your men. That is the good news." He sat in a heavy leather chair across from us. "Here is the other news: he was detained by Dutch police in a rural town in the northeastern farmlands of the country. The Dutch are technically still neutral, but with the Nazis running the place, they may as well be an enemy state."

"Who is it? Which man? Do you know his name?" spilled out before I could think better of it.

Menzies shook his head. "The report did not say. We only know he was found wearing a wetsuit, was injured, and received treatment—though by whom we do not know—and has lost his memory."

"Lost his memory?" I repeated.

Menzies nodded. "Your man is scheduled to be delivered to the SD in Amsterdam in five days."

"The SD?" Sparrow muttered.

"Yes," Menzies said. "Two senior SD officers are flying from Berlin to retrieve him. It appears your mission garnered the attention of the Reich's inner circle. Right pissed them off."

I thought a hint of amusement crept into his granite tone, though his face showed no sign of it.

"What can we do? We've got to go in, to try to—"

Menzies held up a palm. "The PM has authorized air missions to intercept the plane carrying the SD men. They will never lay hands on your man."

"What about getting him back?" I asked.

"We have other operations that make any direct intervention impossible at the moment," Menzies said. "As soon as we can—"

"Sir," I said, suddenly realizing I'd interrupted one of the most powerful men in Europe. "Forgive me, sir. It's just ... these men are important to us. We thought they were lost."

"Son, *every* soldier is important, but we cannot risk vital operations for one man, especially a man held on Germany's doorstep. A rescue mission would be foolish."

"That's the exact word they used to describe our last mission," I said defiantly. "We didn't listen then either."

Menzies sat back and fiddled with his tie, finally smoothing it into place. "I will talk with the PM. That is the best I can offer."

"Thank you, General," I said, pressing myself up by the armrests.

"We want to join," Sparrow said, as I was half out of the chair. "When the PM gives you the green light, we want on the team."

"That's quite a request. This would be a British team."

Sparrow actually laughed at the head of British intelligence. From the look on Menzies's face, it was something akin to a slap across his cheek.

"What is so funny, young lady?" Condescension dripped from each word.

"We are Americans, trained at a Canadian base by British instructors, assigned to an impossible mission on a submarine manned by Scottish sailors. We've been passed from the hands of French resistance fighters, through Swiss agents, to German priests who were actually spies. I believe we have proven our ability to navigate in international waters, *Mr.* Menzies." Her emphasis on the honorific was another slap to the proud man, and his pursed lips showed he felt it fully. He stared at her as if examining a bug pinned to a board, then stood and paced around his desk. Once settled back into his leather chair, Menzies donned spectacles, looked over their rims at us, and said softly, "I will try. You have my word."

# Chapter Ten

# Will

*"Bureaucrats are the only people in the world
who can say absolutely nothing and mean it."*

HUGH SIDNEY

"It's been two days," I said, as I paced the few yards of my bedroom in the Bedfordshire safe house. "Two days without a word from Hurt, Menzies, the PM, the SOE[1], or anybody who might give a shit about helping."

Sparrow sat in a chair upholstered in patterns of garish flowers who'd long ago lost their color. She watched me pace, but remained silent.

"What are we going to do if they say we can't go? Or worse, if they say *they're* not going? What if they don't even try to get him back?"

"Them," she corrected.

I froze and turned toward her.

"Them. You said *him*. We need to get Egret and Adam Roth back too."

"We don't know they're alive."

She crossed her arms. "We don't know they're not."

I fell onto the bed, hands pressed to my face. "You're right, but what difference does it make if they don't—"

A loud banging on the door startled me out of whatever I was about to say.

---

1. Special Operations Executive, the umbrella organization for the British intelligence community responsible for espionage, sabotage, and reconnaissance in occupied Europe (and later, also in occupied Southeast Asia). One of SOE's primary missions was to aid local resistance movements.

"Anny, Tobias, come quickly. There are men here to see you."

I wasn't sure which sent my pulse racing more, the fact George used our cover names instead of our code names, or the urgency in his voice as he spoke of whoever was here. Sparrow and I bolted for the door.

Lieutenant-Commander Raines and another man whose uniform bore the patches of the RAF[2] stood in the living room. Raines stepped forward and embraced each of us as we entered.

"You look disappointed. Were you expecting someone else?" Raines said through a smirk.

I smiled weakly. "Sorry, I was just hoping—"

"That someone from the government would tell you it's time to go get Wilhelm?" Raines yanked the words from my lips. When my eyes widened, he laughed. "We *are* the men from the government, you idiot. We're here to help you get our boy back."

I could barely believe it. Sparrow shot forward and wrapped her arms around the commander again. I was only a heartbeat behind. The RAF man must've thought we'd lost our marbles.

---

2. Royal Air Force, the British military air force.

"Whoa, okay. Good to see you too. What's with all the hugging?" The teasing lilt I'd come to respect wove through Raines's words. "You Americans are so excitable."

"When do we leave?" I asked.

Raines held up a palm. "Take a breath, soldier. We need to talk this through first, then you have some training to do."

"Training?" Sparrow gaped. "We only have a few days. There's no time for—"

"There is time, and this is necessary. What we're about to do is beyond fucking insane. I'm not about to let you jump out of a perfectly good airplane unless I'm confident you won't break your neck when you hit the ground."

The room was silent.

Sparrow stepped back slowly.

Raines looked from me to Sparrow, then a smile curled his mouth. "What? You want him back or not?"

"Yes, but ..." Sparrow struggled to find her words.

"But what?" Raines asked, now toying with us. Bastard.

"Jump out of a plane?" Sparrow asked, her voice barely a whisper.

"Sure. Jumping is actually the easy part. Landing is where things get tricky. The Crown's throwing in a parachute to increase your odds. Isn't that nice of the King?"

The RAF man barked out a laugh.

Sparrow sat and stared up, her mouth still open, though covered by her slender fingers.

"Alright, it sounds like there may be things we need to talk through," I admitted. "Come on. Let's sit at the dining table. We can lay out maps in there."

"I'll make tea," George said.

"Fuck tea. We need whiskey," I said, earning a laugh and a clap on the back from Raines as we strode into the dining room.

Reluctantly, Sparrow rose and followed. I'd never seen her face quite that shade of yellowish green. She might've actually *needed* tea.

Once everyone was seated with a glass of whiskey before them, Raines unfolded a map and spread it across the table.

"This is a detailed map of the Netherlands from 1941. The red indicates roads or bridges that have been destroyed."

"There aren't many of those," Sparrow said, leaning over to get a better look.

"No, France and, more recently, Germany have taken most of the bombs. Still, they're worth noting." He pointed, then dragged his finger up and to the right. "Here's Amsterdam. Up in this corner, almost as far to the northeast as you can get, is the village of Loppersum."

"Loppersum? Never heard of it," I said.

"Unless you're a Dutch farmer, you wouldn't have. The population was in the hundreds a few years ago, and has probably declined since the arrival of the Nazis."

Everyone reached for their glass as that sobering thought sank in.

"The village is small, but it serves as a central market for many of the farms in the surrounding areas. The town center only has a few shops, a couple of houses converted into restaurants, and a police station that doubles as the civic center for the northeastern tip of the province of Groningen. Wilhelm is in that police station."

We stared at the dot on the map representing a village of a few hundred souls, as if Thomas might leap from the page and appear before us.

"We were within a few miles of that place after the mission," I thought aloud.

"You may have even passed by it without realizing it was there. It would've been on the way to your rally point." Raines nodded. "The asset's information was brief, but we know Wilhelm was found by locals who treated his wounds.""He's hurt?" I nearly leapt out of my chair.

Raines motioned me back down. "He *was* hurt. Whoever found him treated him. Somewhere along the line, the police learned of his presence and took him into custody. Word from our asset traveled the same day he was arrested."

"That's pretty remarkable," Sparrow said.

"Yeah, it is," Raines agreed. "If he'd been captured in France—or pretty much anywhere else—I doubt we would've heard about it for days or weeks. When it comes to propaganda, printing, communications, and the like, the Dutch are in a league of their own."

"Sounds like it," she said.

Raines continued. "The Dutch resistance is less aggressive than their French counterparts, but they are very effective at gathering information. One of the four policemen who work in that station is an informant. He notified Amsterdam, who called their government in exile here in Britain, who notified the SOE. And here we are."

I stared at the map without really seeing anything. The lines and dots had all run together. I wanted so desperately to see a plan, to look at the paper and know we could save him, but my mind was a jumble of fears, hopes, and dreads.

"The bombings of Emden have eased since your raid, with fewer planes hitting that route. Most have been diverted to the new German missions. Still, the Allies have maintained nightly runs of at least a half-dozen." Raines paused long enough to force me to look up. "You with me?"

"Yeah, sorry. Go on."

"In two days, more than two dozen bombers will hit targets in and around Emden. Besides the port you're familiar with, there are other areas on the northern coast where the Germans resupply ships. To date, we have not hit those mini ports. That changes now." He marked three places on the northern coast above Emden. "On the second turn of those runs, our plane will join the formation with the bombers. We will drop from it and land here"—he marked a spot a few miles from Loppersum—"it will be the best cover we could hope for."

"Can you stop there a moment?" Sparrow said. "You're serious? How the hell are we going to drop out of an airplane?"

"That's where this guy comes in." Raines nodded and pointed to the RAF man. "Sorry, we would have made introductions sooner, but Tobias looked like he was about to pee his breeches."

"I can't help—"

"Relax," Raines said with a grin. "This is Edward Ingles of His Majesty's Royal Air Force. Eddie will be your instructor tomorrow."

"Instructor?" Sparrow said with more than a hint of apprehension.

"Ya didn't think we'd drop ya out of a bird without a wee trainin', did ya?" The Scottish practically oozed out of Ingles's mouth as he spoke. "We'll spend the mornin' jumpin' off wooden rigs, then move t' the real thing in the evenin'."

"Is it normal to only spend one day training to do this?" Sparrow's hands hugged her tumbler of whiskey like it was a precious jewel.

"Nope," Ingles said. "I normally git twelve days wit' a lad before he's headed to battle."

"I'm no lad," Sparrow said, sipping from her glass.

"Right ya are. Ye should take t' it quicker. Say, in a day."

Raines couldn't hold back any longer, and a deep rumbling laugh filled the dining room. Sparrow and I glared daggers at him, while Ingles joined in with a chuckle.

"Sorry," Raines said. "I don't mean to laugh. What the hell, yes I do. You should see your faces."

Neither of us cracked a smile, which only encouraged the men's mirth.

"You'll be fine," Raines said. "Remember to pull the cord, and don't land on your head. Simple as that."

Sparrow's eyes widened.

Ingles rolled his eyes. "T'isn't *that* simple, but it's close. We'll get ya ready on the morrow."

"Great," Sparrow and I said in unison.

"There really is nothing to worry about," Raines said with more amusement than reassurance. "If you get nervous, Eddie will just shove you out."

The next morning, we rose before the sun and were driven to a military base nearby. Young men who looked like they should've been in school rather than uniform strode to and from buildings, mostly in formations with a sergeant barking the entire time.

It was a strange thing, to step onto a base and realize I was technically a soldier but had never experienced a single day of training like these boys were enjoying—though I doubted "enjoying" was a word they would have used to describe it.

Ingles, whose insignia bore three stripes like a sergeant but with a crown atop them, stood on one of the barracks' steps smoking a cigarette.

"Welcome, bairns. Ready t' play?" The glimmer in his eyes made me shiver.

Raines and Ingles shook hands like old mates, then Raines excused himself to attend to his usual duties. "I will return later tonight to retrieve you. We should have a full brief prepared by then. Try not to break anything, please."

He and Ingles shared a grin as Sparrow and I tried not to throw up.

As promised, we spent the morning learning the parts of a parachute, then practicing jumping off short beams, landing, and rolling. Ingles insisted our body position be in perfect order before each jump, correcting even the slightest stiffness of the knees or back. Once that was perfected, he took us to taller and taller devices, and we repeated the jumping, landing, and rolling technique until it was as natural as one day's practice would allow.

The final tower, a metal scaffold with a wide platform on top, served as our ultimate challenge. A small training chute was attached to a cable high above, so when we dropped, the whole thing dropped with us and allowed for a controlled descent. We dangled freely, learning how to pull the cords and guide our chutes, then plunged to the ground.

The sun had begun to drop over the horizon by the time Ingles led us to a small air strip at the edge of the base.

"Time for the real thing," he said, leading us to a waiting plane. "Tomorrow, we'll spend an hour on the rig, then ya climb aboard that bird and jump."

"Are we ready for this?" Sparrow asked.

"Nope. Not even close," he said. "But that cannae be helped, can it?"

"You okay?" Sparrow whispered, resting her hand on my forearm.

I nodded, but didn't trust my voice. How could she be so calm?

She smiled weakly and leaned in. "I'm scared to death too. But Wilhelm needs us."

That was all it took to stiffen my resolve. No fear in the world could outweigh my need to bring Thomas home.

# Chapter Eleven

# Thomas

*"If you lose hope, somehow you lose the vitality
that keeps moving, you lose that courage to be,
that quality that helps you go on in spite of it
all. And so today I still have a dream."*

Martin Luther King, Jr.

Three days passed without word from London. I could tell by the tension at the corners of Fons's eyes that he was beginning to question if help would come in time. Captain van der Kleij, also keenly aware of the ticking of the clock, chose to make the most of the time we had together. We spent hours in the interrogation room each day, me handcuffed to the same table and the chief asking the same questions.

Remembering events wasn't an issue. Making sense of what I remembered felt like piecing together a thousand-piece puzzle with only a few hundred fragments. Nothing made sense.

"Let's start again," van der Kleij said, as we began our afternoon session on the third day. "What is your name?"

I tried to keep sarcasm out of my voice. It was beginning to be as challenging as ordering my mind. "Wilhelm."

Van der Kleij clucked his tongue, then gently laid his pen on his notebook, fidgeting with it until it lined up precisely at the center of the page, perpendicular to the table's edge.

"We Dutch dislike to brag," he said, leaning back and painting a pleasant smile on his lips. "We are diligent, for sure. We are intelligent and inventive. Our people have pride in these things, but we are not proud. To be so would not be very Dutch of us. You understand?"

I didn't. This man was odd.

He continued as though I had agreed. "It would do no good for me to take pride in breaking you. The Nazis would simply claim credit for themselves. They are a proud people. They are not shy in saying so either. They would bellow from the rooftops about capturing an American spy, helping him reclaim his memory, then forcing him to recount everything he knows. They would take great pride in your shame."

He picked up his pen again.

"And then they would kill you in front of cameras, perhaps at one of their parades with thousands lined up and marching like little metal ducks, all while you dangled from the end of a rope."

He waited for me to speak. I didn't.

"Would you give them so much? Wilhelm, what good would that do?"

I leaned forward as far as the restraints would allow, as though I wished to whisper something intimate across the table. Van der Kleij leaned in.

"I can't tell you what I don't remember," I said quietly.

He pushed back from the chair, hurling his pen against the wall, shattering it into several pieces.

"Now look what you have done. That was my favorite pen. Now it is as broken as you will be soon," he said, before storming out of the room, leaving me alone with his forgotten journal of useless notes.

More than an hour passed before the door opened again and Fons entered. He closed the door behind him, stepped to the table, and unhooked my handcuffs from the metal loop.

"The captain is frustrated," he whispered. "You may want to feed him something, just so he feels like he is winning."

"That isn't how this works," I said. "Any word from our friends?"

He walked around the table and gathered the broken pieces of van der Kleij's pen, then closed the notebook and stuffed it under his arm. "The Americans and British have stepped up their bombing runs. They have begun striking Frankfurt and other key cities inside Germany. It would not be unusual for word to travel slowly through the network, especially if some larger game is afoot."

"We have two days, right? I lose track of time in this place."

He sat across from me, returning the notebook to the table. "Two days until the SD men arrive. On the third day, van der Kleij and I will take you to meet them. I have asked for aid from resistance leadership in Amsterdam, but they too remain silent. It is as if someone threw a blanket over the Netherlands when we most need to see the sun."

I watched him in that moment, as his eyes closed and fingers pinched the bridge of his nose. He genuinely anguished over my situation, this man I barely knew.

"Thank you, Fons." He looked up, his brow furrowed. "I know you are trying, and you don't even know me. Whatever happens, I sincerely appreciate everything."

He held my gaze for a long moment, then rose. When his hand landed on my shoulder, it wasn't the grip of an officer returning his prisoner to a cell. It was that of a friend offering unspoken strength to another.

"Come. I have work to do," he said, urging me up.

# Chapter Twelve

# Will

*"Those who don't jump will never fly."*

Leena Ahmad Almashat, *Harmony Letters*

The original plan was for Raines to collect us at the end of the day and return us to the safe house in Bedfordshire, but at seven o'clock, an hour after his anticipated arrival, Ingles stepped from an office building, a scowl across his face, with a young airman struggling to keep up a few strides behind.

"Ya be our guests tonight. This lad'll show ya to the officers' barracks." Ingles nodded toward the uniformed man

who'd finally stopped behind him. "Be ready for trainin'
at oh-seven-hundred."

Sparrow rose and dusted off her pants. "What happened
to Raines?"

"Detained with Crown business," he said, as if those
sparse words fully explained everything, then spun on his
heel and marched away.

"Have you eaten?" the young man asked after Ingles was
halfway toward another building.

"No," I said, standing and shaking my head.

"Alright. I'll take you to the mess hall first, then we can
get you settled for the night."

At precisely oh-seven-hundred, Ingles opened the door to
the barracks. "Wee birds, time t' fly."

Sparrow laughed nervously.

I groaned.

"Come now, that was funny. Give a lad some credit," he
chirped.

"You really aren't funny. You know that, right?" I said as
we exited the barracks.

"Ya sound like that arse Raines," he said through a
chuckle.

"You two known each other long?" I asked.

Ingles nodded. "A few years. He sends all o' his people to me fer trainin' o' one sort or the other."

"You train more than just parachuting?" Sparrow asked.

Ingles grinned. "When ya've been in the King's service as long as I have, ya do a bit of everythin'."

That really didn't clear anything up, but the metal structure towering before us as we rounded the corner ended the inquiry.

"This mornin', ya do live drops. Another instructor will be on the loudspeaker coachin', so listen up and do what he tells ya. Questions?"

Our heads shook, and he gestured toward the bottom stair. "Up ya go."

We climbed to the top, where a pair of airmen buckled me into a practice chute attached to a thick cable that ran from a crane-like extension protruding from the tower's peak. The wind billowed stronger than it had the day before, and the tug of the chute was almost impossible to resist. One of the men had to brace himself to keep me from being sucked over too soon.

Seconds later, the mechanism within the structure hauled me off the platform to dangle with nothing below my feet for hundreds of yards. Gusts buffeted the chute, swinging me like a pendulum and sending my pulse on a sprint. I recited the instructions for landing we'd learned the previous day to give my mind something to focus on beyond the terror that threatened to freeze me in place.

"Straighten your legs and feet together, number one," a voice boomed over speakers attached to the structure. I shifted my weight, desperate to gain some sense of control, and stiffened my posture, snapping my boots together in the process.

"Number one, drop your paper," the voice commanded.

I let the slip fly free, my marker to judge the wind's direction and strength. It flew away so quickly I barely had time to register its path.

"Ready, number one."

I sucked in a breath.

"Drop, number one."

Like the eye of a hurricane, there was a moment of dead calm, then a mechanical click snapped far above me and my body lurched downward.

"Let up on your risers," the voice boomed.

I spread my arms high above my head, releasing the tension on the guides. The chute billowed, and the sideways swinging eased.

"You're okay, number one," the voice called.

*Easy for him to say. He's standing on the fucking ground,* I thought.

"Keep your feet together," he barked.

I snapped my boots again.

"Check your landing altitude!"

Oh, shit. Landing.

I'd barely had time to register the ground below before my feet touched down, my knees bent, and I rolled forward several times, just like we'd been taught. The chute jerked me forward as the wind continued carrying it away from the landing point. Several airmen positioned nearby raced to assist, lifting me to my feet while disconnecting the chute.

"Nice landing, sir," one of the guys said, a toothy grin parting his lips. "Fun, isn't it?"

Fun? My heart still felt like it might burst at any moment.

"Yeah, just great," I said. His grin widened, somehow revealing even more crooked teeth.

"Sarge said to send you back once you had your feet under you again."

*Great. Just what I was hoping for.*

"Thanks," I said, wobbling away on shaky legs.

I'd made it halfway off the field when the speakers vibrated. "Ready, number two."

I looked up to find Sparrow's diminutive frame dangling, her feet perfectly together, her body relaxed.

*How the hell is she so good at this ... and so comfortable?*

She dropped a second later, never received a word of instruction, then landed perfectly, popping up after her third roll. She unclipped her chute and threw her arms in the air, shouting excitedly. By the time the men arrived to take her chute, she'd bolted across the field and was bouncing beside me.

"That was the most incredible thing I've ever done! Wasn't it amazing? We were flying, Tobias. *Flying*!"

"Actually, we were falling. There was no flying involved," I said drolly.

She shoved my arm. "Lighten up and have a little fun."

"I'm too terrified I'll shit my pants to have fun."

She howled at that, shoving me playfully again.

"Again!" Ingles barked as we approached the tower. "Get back up there. This time, use yer knees on landin' or ye'll break 'em both."

Sparrow elbowed me. "He's talking to you."

I rolled my eyes. "Thanks, I wasn't sure."

"Move," Ingles barked and pointed.

By the fourth drop, the abject terror I'd felt on the first attempt had dulled to sharp-toothed butterflies in my stomach, and my landings no longer jarred my senses on impact. Sparrow clapped and cheered with each drop—hers *and* mine. Her cheeks were bright from the chill in the air, but excitement thrummed through her every step as we strode from the landing zone that last time.

"Go eat somethin'," Ingles ordered. "After lunch, we take the bird up for live drops."

Sparrow squealed and gripped my arm, like some child who'd just learned Santa was stuck halfway down the chimney. The way my stomach lurched at the thought of a live jump, I wondered if eating was such a good plan.

A few hours later, two airmen led the way, flinging themselves out of the plane like it was the most natural thing in the world. Sparrow was in line next. She glanced back, winked, then screamed her way into the endless sky.

"Move!" Ingles barked.

I stepped up to the opening. Wind blasted my face, billowing my flight suit. The acrid smell of fuel threatened to finish the job the fear of jumping had begun, spilling my guts in all directions. Somehow, I managed to gulp down my dread.

"Yer not makin' love t' the door. Just jump," Ingles shouted above the combined roar of the plane and wind.

My knuckles whitened as I gripped tighter, the opposite of every instruction.

"Tobias!" Ingles shouted. "Yer last in line. Dinnae be a fribble."

*A fribble? What the hell—*

"Fucking arsehole!" I screamed as Ingles's hand shoved all conscious thought—and my body—out of the plane. I shouted every curse I could think of as the din of the engines faded, replaced by the whistling of the wind.

*Pull the cord. Pull the cord. Pull the cord.*

*Yank!*

The chute whipped out of its pack, quickly caught the wind, and jerked me upward so hard I thought my shoulder might've come out of its socket.

Then nothing.

Absolutely no sound, save a gentle breeze between gusts.

I had time to scan the horizon, taking in towns and villages scattered miles around. England's ever-present clouds had parted for the blessed moment, warming my skin and filling my chest with hope.

*Dear God, this is beautiful.*

My fear had fled, replaced by an awe I never knew possible. The weightlessness was invigorating, but the perspective of soaring above the world nearly brought tears to my eyes.

"Land!"

A faint voice screaming through speakers jolted me out of my reverie. I looked down to find terra firma racing toward me.

"Shiiiiiiiiiiit!" I screamed, remembering to relax my knees at the last moment.

My feet hit the ground and I pitched forward, tucking into a ball and rolling several times before settling. Unlike Sparrow's near-perfect landing, I finished my bowling ball roll flat on my face.

"Way to use your pretty side, sir!" a smart-ass airman I hadn't seen running forward teased, as he hauled me to my feet.

"At least you think I'm pretty," I said, proud of having any wits left, much less quick ones.

The airman barked a laugh and slapped me on the back, then pointed me toward a car at the edge of the field. A tall man in a white cap and navy uniform leaning against the sedan lifted a hand and waved, then gave me a thumbs-up. Sparrow was already headed in that direction, so I shrugged off my empty pack and followed.

# Chapter Thirteen

# Will

*"Spontaneity is a meticulously prepared art."*

Oscar Wilde

"Are you ready?" Raines asked the moment the car doors shut.

"Two days of what is usually a twelve-day training? Sure. We're champs now," I said, trying to get my heart to slow to a normal pace. I'd given up on calming my breathing.

Raines's tight smile through the rearview mirror only added to the jitters raging through me.

"Our window shifted," Raines said. "We leave in two hours."

Sparrow gasped. "Two hours?"

Raines nodded. "The weather report for tomorrow is terrible. Experienced jumpers would struggle in what's coming. If your plane made it to the jump zone, the fall would likely kill you both. We go tonight or not at all."

Sparrow gripped my hand, the first time she'd shown any nerves in days.

"Fine," I said. "What do we do now?"

"Briefing in fifteen at the base HQ. Your team is already assembled and waiting on you."

"Team?" I asked.

Raines chuckled. "You didn't think we would send you into enemy-held territory on a rescue mission alone, did you?"

"I ... no, I guess not."

Sparrow squeezed my hand. An amused smirk twisted her lips.

"The briefing should only last ten or fifteen minutes. You can grab something to eat afterward and get to know the team. Your gear will be packed and waiting on the plane, so we won't be going back to the house."

The rush of excitement and terror that slammed into me when he first told us we were leaving that night crashed in wave after wave. Sparrow's comforting hand was the only thing keeping me from prying the window open and jumping out of the moving car. I wanted to save Thomas more than anyone, but the whole rushed mission concept chilled my bones.

"Listen," Raines said. "I know this was unexpected, but you'll be fine. The guys we're sending with you are the best. You'll be landing in a rural part of the country where cows are more of a threat than Nazis. Just don't kill your-self landing and you should be fine."

"Was that a pep talk?" I asked. "I don't feel very pepped."

Raines's grin widened. "Get your shit together before we walk into the briefing room. The guys won't respond well to their new spook teammate shaking like a leaf before you even take off."

*So much for gentle reassurance*, I thought.

"You were a lot nicer on the sub," I said, trying to find my misplaced sense of humor.

Raines grunted. "I'm at home under the water. Up here, it's one shitshow after another."

A shift from gravel to smooth pavement heralded our return to the living and office areas of the base. Raines pulled the car into a parking space beside a long two-sto-ry building whose face fluttered with a row of flags. Old Glory snapped beside the British banner near the front entrance.

It was odd how seeing that tiny piece of home eased my breathing.

We followed Raines inside, down a short hallway and into a conference room. Three men sat at the far end of a table for twenty: one RAF officer, a Royal Marine, and, to my surprise, an American soldier. They rose as we entered.

"Gentlemen," Raines said as we stepped closer. "This is Tobias Richter and Anny Bedeau of the US Army."

Raines gestured toward the gray-templed man at the head of the table. "This is Group Captain Acheson. He handles most missions originating from this base."

Acheson gave us a curt nod, then took over the introductions by resting a hand on the shoulder of the Royal Marine. His voice was like the grind of angry sandpaper. "This is Lieutenant James of His Majesty's Royal Marines. Don't let his pinup looks fool you, he's the best sharpshooter in Britain."

James stood only a couple of paces away, but even those few strides swaggered as he stepped forward and extended a hand. Dimples formed as he smiled, and a curl of hair bobbed on his forehead. I tried not to stare into his rich hazel eyes, but there was something magical in his gaze. I nearly laughed when a flush crawled up Sparrow's neck and into her cheeks, as James flashed his perfect teeth and bobbed his head in her direction.

Acheson pointed his open palm toward the American. "This is Major Sikes, Airborne Ranger. Sikes kicks ass in pretty much every direction. I am told he has more rescue experience than any man in the army and is a certified jump instructor. He'll be your team lead."

Sikes nodded but didn't move to shake our hands. Raines leaned between us and whispered loud enough for everyone to hear, "There's no one alive I'd rather have on my six. Sikes is a legend."

Sikes's hardened expression didn't so much as budge at the praise.

"Right. Seats," Acheson ordered, then unfurled a map of Europe and grabbed a pointer leaning against the wall behind him.

"The main air wing briefed this afternoon, so I will spare you the details. Check your flimsies for the following plot points. Your bird, under the command of Air Captain Mercer, will depart at twenty-hundred hours, which is zero hour for this mission. You join the main air group at splasher zero seven at approximately zero minus thirty minutes. The group will fly north, maintaining a distance of fifty miles from the coast, until reaching Schiermonnikoog here." He pointed at a large island off the northern coast of the Netherlands, almost at the border with Germany. "At this point, your bird and one escort will break off from the main formation to head to the drop zone. We have no reports of Nazi air defenses in that region, so you will approach for a low altitude drop of approximately one thousand feet. Adjust your pull timing accordingly."

"You getting all this?" Sparrow whispered.

Acheson cleared his throat and willed her back into her seat with a vicious glare.

"The port town is eighteen-point-five miles from the LZ, well within a normal patrol's range. There is the chance the Nazis will have moved fighters into position for patrols, but our intelligence indicates that risk is low, especially given the weeks of bombing runs that have reduced most of the city's AA capability to rubble and the beating the Germans have been taking on their Russian front. Still, you should be aware of the possibility." He eyed each of us, as if gauging how that tidbit might've shaken our confidence. "Your LZ is here. You will scuttle your chutes, then hike two miles to the target, retrieve the package, and proceed to the exfil site here." He pointed to a small section of coast that appeared barren on the map. "There is a motor boat hidden in the brush, which you will take to the island of Rottumerplaak, directly across the Groninger Wad. For those not up on their Dutch, that is the bay between this island and the mainland."

James chuckled, but Sikes remained stone-faced, never breaking eye contact with Acheson.

"A small reconnaissance plane will extract you from the island at zero minus six hours. Be at the extraction zone on time or you will have to swim home."

Sikes almost cracked a smile at that.

"Questions?"

No one spoke.

Acheson glanced at the map one last time, then nodded toward Sparrow and me. "Sikes is in command. Do what he says and you will come home alive. Dismissed."

# Chapter Fourteen
# Thomas



Maya Angelou

I had to give the police captain credit, Ignass van der Kleij was a determined man. For the fourth consecutive day, he dragged me into his interrogation room, attached me to the table, and asked the same questions again and again. Exactly the same questions. Word for word.

He was determined, but not very creative.

The lack of spontaneity in our routine made sticking to my memory loss story easier than it might have been with a nimbler inquisitor. In truth, I had begun to recall things, and most of those were childhood memories, which I was fairly certain would be useless to the Nazis.

I had, however, become reacquainted with Will and our time together. His face now shone brightly in my eyes, as I traced every curve and line with imaginary fingers. The day we spent traipsing around Boston was crystal clear, and our first real moment alone beneath the Old Timer sent shivers of pleasure up my spine. More than anything, I recalled how his gaze softened when his eyes found mine, and how my chest thumped each time he smiled. I loved this man, and each memory that returned offered longing and resolve. I would find a way back to him or die in the effort.

*What if he thinks I died?*

My heart lurched into my throat. I tried to imagine what it would feel like to believe him lost, and the shroud of sadness that fell over me threatened to drag me into a place of such darkness—

"Wilhelm." Fons's familiar whisper saved me from the depths. I turned to find the officer fiddling with his keys.

"Anything?" I asked.

The lock to my cell clicked, then he entered and closed the door behind him.

"No," he said, leaning against the wall beside my bed. "Not a word."

The depths beckoned me once more.

"This is it, isn't it?" I asked. "You have to take me to Amsterdam tomorrow, right?"

He shook his head. "It's the day after tomorrow. You've got your days scrambled."

I blew out a breath. "Thank God."

"We should have heard something by now. Even if the answer is 'you are on your own,' we should have received a reply. The government in exile is never this out of touch."

"The Nazis might've found your transmitters. They've gotten pretty good at hunting."

Fons lowered his head. "Perhaps."

"What time is it?" I asked, looking over his shoulder out the barred window. "It gets dark so early here, I can barely keep time."

"Almost eleven o'clock," he said. "Lights will go out any minute."

"Are you headed home?"

He shook his head again. "No, I work all night tonight. The other man who normally works nights has a sick child."

"And you need to, what, babysit your only prisoner?"

He grunted, almost a laugh. "Yes, actually. You are an important prisoner. The captain would not let you go unguarded."

"Fons, there are more cows than people in this part of the Netherlands." This time he did laugh. "And the cows are very attractive, no?"

"You might make me want the bars between us again."

He grinned. "Humor. That is good. Keep that. There is still hope."

I sucked in a breath and rested my head against the wall. "Yeah, that's what I keep telling myself."

"Would you like company tonight? There might be a bottle of something in the break room. We could share a drink?"

I nodded. "A drink would be great. Company with a cow lover? If that's the best you can do ..."

He snorted as he walked to the door. "Give me a moment to lock the outside doors."

"I'm not going anywhere," I said.

Moments later, the cell door opened. Fons set two coffee mugs and a bottle of golden liquor on the floor by my cot. He then stepped out, returning with a baguette and a large chunk of cheese.

"I thought you might be hungry," he said, raising the cheese.

I nodded. "The food in this restaurant is almost as poor as the service."

Fons chuckled, then squatted onto the floor so his back leaned against the cot. He filled the mugs halfway, then handed me one.

I raised the mug to my mouth, but stilled as a sharp, unfamiliar scent found my nose.

Fons grinned. "Never had genever before? It is a Dutch specialty, something like gin but with herbs or other flavors to hide the bitterness."

As if to ease my trepidation, Fons lifted his mug and downed a gulp.

"Here's to Dutch prisons," I said, raising my mug, then pressing it to my lips. "Dear God," I spat once the liquor hit my tongue. "You said this was bitter, you didn't say it was vile."

Fons chuckled and took another sip. "After one or two mugs, you will not taste the bitterness. Trust me."

"I won't have any taste buds," I grumbled, downing another mouthful and shivering at the acrid flow as it oozed down my throat.

"Here, have some cheese. It will help." Fons ripped off a piece of the bread and handed me the cheese and a small knife. When my brow rose and I hesitated, his eyes drifted toward the utensil. He quickly spun the knife so the handle extended toward me. "Go on. The cheese is good."

We ate and drank in silence for a few long moments. Fons seemed lost in thought, and I barely knew what to say. He said he was a resistance man, that his father had been killed for leading the strikes, but we really didn't know each other. And yet, everything in his bearing, the kindness in his eyes when he spoke, told me he was a good man who could be trusted. There was no rational explanation for it. I just knew.

"Did you always want to be a policeman?" I asked, startling him out of whatever daydream had captured him.

"Oh, yes. Very much so. Since I was a little boy. My brothers and I would pretend to be police and criminals, hunting and chasing each other all over the farm. It drove our father mad."

The distant stare of one traveling into the past came into his eyes, and a thin curl punctuated one corner of his lips.

"You have brothers?"

All humor drained from his features as he nodded. "Had. Three."

"Fons, I'm sorry—"

"One died when he was young. It was a silly accident on the farm. We lost the other two after the strikes. They were with Papa when … The Nazis made them watch our father hang, then shot them as our mother and I stood helpless on the porch."

Fons lowered his head. He had lost so much.

"Forgive me. We have all lost much," he said, shaking his head free of the images I was sure still haunted him. "What do you think of the cheese?"

I had already finished the pieces he'd given me. "It's great—almost makes that drink bearable."

Fons hefted the bottle and refilled our mugs. "I tell you, by the third mug, you will dream of genever."

I took my mug and grinned. "By the third mug, I might never be able to taste anything again."

He passed the baguette and cheese. "What about you?"

"What about me?"

"Your parents? Brothers and sisters? What was life like, growing up in America?"

I downed another bite, then washed it back, surprised that I no longer shivered with each sip.

"One brother," I said, trying to find a way to answer his questions without lying about who my family really was. Will was among the only people in the world who knew that my family line was practically American royalty. It was a secret I'd learned to keep many years before, and practiced answers, now suddenly fresh in my mind, rolled off my tongue. "My parents live outside of Boston. Dad is a businessman, mostly in textiles. My mom stayed at home with us, though I suspected she was always the real brains behind my dad's success. She's the sharpest person I know."

"So, you are an American after all." It was a statement, not a question.

Shit. I couldn't believe what I'd just done. Maintaining cover was one of the core missions of any OSS agent, and I was damn good at it. How had I just—

My throat worked as I tried to speak, but nothing came out.

"Wilhelm, it's alright. I already knew. You talk in your sleep, remember?"

Right. "Yes, I'm American," I admitted.

"The Americans will save us. That is what is said among the resistance. Your bombers already attack German soil, and rumors say that will only increase."

He said that with an almost dreamlike quality, like America was a whiff of smoke he wanted to grasp, some ideal rather than a place filled with flawed people trying to make something of themselves.

"Do you know how long it will be?" he asked quietly.

My brow furrowed. "How long what will be?"

"Before American soldiers come."

I didn't mean to laugh, but it just flew out. Fons looked like I'd slapped him.

"I'm sorry, Fons. I meant no offense," I said. "It's just … I'm stuck in here, and I'm not exactly a general or anything. I have no idea what they're planning."

He nodded slowly. "I had to ask. That day cannot come soon enough."

There was such sadness in his voice. It seeped into my chest, and my heart squeezed. I'd seen the horrors of the Third Reich when we landed in France, and knew how much worse the Nazis were willing to do if it meant flying their wretched banner above every building in Europe, but to hear another man long for salvation, for his people's freedom …

"If you weren't a policeman, what would you do?"

I had no idea why I asked that, and, from the way Fons's face scrunched up, he couldn't figure it out either. Oddly, we found ourselves smiling at each other as he spoke.

"My father was a farmer. I hate farming. God, if I have to milk one more cow ... and the pigs. Wilhelm, they are vile little creatures, always squirming and squealing."

My grin widened. "I always thought pigs were cute."

"Cute?" He nearly spat the word. "They eat slop and live in filth."

"But when they're little—"

He raised a palm with one hand and slammed back the last of his drink with the other. "Yes, baby pigs are adorable. Fine. But, like people, they grow up."

"Are you saying big people live in filth and eat slop?" I raised the cheese and wiggled it.

His answer was to refill our mugs.

"Perhaps I dislike them because my earliest memories were of cleaning out their pens. That will scar anyone." He drank from his refilled mug. A glassy sheen had taken hold in his eyes. "I wanted to be king of the Netherlands."

My brows shot up.

"What? We have a wonderful Queen. She lives in Britain for now, but she will return. She is the picture of grace and everything beautiful about this land. I would follow in her shoes. I could be a good king. King Fons the First, just think of it. My people would love me."

He was babbling now. I tried to hold back a laugh, but he hefted his chin and pretended to wave at a crowd. That's when liquor sprayed from my mouth all over him. In a flash, we were both doubled over with tears threatening our eyes.

# Chapter Fifteen
# Will

*"With a heavy heart, I pulled out my own pocket knife and carved three little words beneath Archer's. A plea and a wish, in a form I could never take back: return to me."*

ASHLEIGH ZAVARELLI, *UNDER THE CYPRESS TREE*

There is something about flying in the middle of a wing of dozens of bombers that is impossible to describe—like a flock of enormous metal birds migrating for the winter. It felt like being part of something so much larger than myself that I could easily be swallowed up and forgotten in its midst. And none of that accounted for the immense power contained in the belly of each of our beasts, payloads that would kill untold numbers and litter the landscape with rubble. I'd never really thought about bombing campaigns as anything beyond the degradation of an enemy, but our brief stint in post-blitzkrieg London had wrested that innocent delusion from my head.

War was indeed inglorious.

"Five minutes to splash," Sikes shouted over the roar of the engines, indicating the waypoint when our plane would break from the main formation.

Sparrow reached over and gripped my leg.

"Easy," I said as her nails dug deeper. "I might need that leg to land."

She jerked her hand away. "Sorry. Guess I'm a little nervous."

I nudged her with my shoulder and smiled as warmly as I could muster, then leaned toward her ear. "I'm scared shitless too."

"Why do they have to call it 'splash?' We're flying over water, for heaven's sake."

Despite everything, I grinned. Sparrow was one of a kind.

The plane angled so we would've slid into each other had we not been strapped in, announcing our turn toward the Dutch mainland. The rapid descent that followed nearly sent my stomach into my brain.

"Drop zone in three minutes. Harnesses," Sikes ordered.

Without standing, each of us turned and unhooked the parachute hanging above our heads, then began strapping it on. Once everything was in place, we performed the routine check on each other to ensure buckles were firm and rip cords weren't tangled.

The door opened and frigid air whooshed in. My skin pimpled at the cold, and the thunderous roar of the wind and whine of the engines made hearing each other nearly impossible.

"Stand!" Sikes barked. "Hook in!" He held up one finger to each of us, and we echoed the gesture. "One minute. Get ready!"

Lieutenant James was first in line. At Sikes's motion, he stepped to the door and gripped the sides.

Sikes held up three fingers.

Then two.

Then one.

"GO!" he bellowed.

And James leapt from the plane.

With no time to think, Sparrow stepped up. Sikes didn't give her a countdown.

"GO!"

Then it was my turn. The world somehow slowed and sped up at the same time. All I could do was react, follow orders, and try not to think.

"GO!"

And suddenly the world lost all sound.

The wind whistled by, but given the deafening roar we'd just endured, this was more like a gentle kiss than true sound.

I glanced around to find two chutes already deployed with Sparrow and James floating beneath, their legs perfectly straight, feet together.

Pull! The chute ripped out of its pack. The wind caught it and yanked me upward.

Then ... nothing; even quieter than before. The wind no longer whistled. The planes grew more distant. There were no lights below, no cities or towns illuminated against the darkness of night. Even the moon and her stars lay tucked beneath a pillowy blanket. It was at once peaceful and utterly disorienting.

I hoped our intelligence was correct and the fields were indeed sprawling and barren. The thought of landing in a forest or somewhere inhabited terrified me. Either way, we wouldn't be able to see it until we were a lot closer—far too close to alter course.

James and Sparrow dropped and rolled, their chutes flattening as they landed. I bent my knees, readying for impact, but misjudged the distance and struck before I was fully ready. A jolt of pain fired up my legs and into my spine, and my ankle bent at an unnatural angle. I rolled as best I could, throwing off the momentum, but every movement sent another shock through me.

"Fuck!" I muttered to myself.

Heartbeats later, I watched Sikes hit, roll, and pop up like the pro he was.

"Bastard," I grumbled. I hadn't actually wanted him to injure himself, but he didn't have to make it look so easy right after I'd practically face-planted in the dirt.

By the time I gathered my chute, which took far longer than it should have as I limped around biting my cheek, Sparrow and James stepped up.

"Are you alright?" Sparrow asked.

I waved her off. "Fine. I'll be fine."

I reached down to gather more chute and lost my balance, tumbling to the hard-packed ground.

"You're not alright. Where are you hurt?" she said, kneeling beside me.

"My ankle. I don't think anything's broken, but it hurts really bad."

James peered down and whispered, "Happens. We can wrap it up, but you'll have to push through the pain."

Wasn't he a ray of fucking sunshine?

Several minutes later, Sikes arrived. "Let's get these chutes stowed and move. Only thing I see are cows, but we're exposed out here. I'd guess the target is a little over a mile in that direction." He pointed south.

A mile of hiking. The thought made my ankle throb, but this was Thomas. I would walk through hell to bring him home.

"James, wrap his ankle while Anny and I scout ahead. We'll approach in pairs until the target's in sight. Understood?"

We all nodded, and Sparrow gave my shoulder one last squeeze before rising to follow Sikes.

The farms were eternal, spreading in every direction, with only the occasional house or barn in sight. While there were no trees or crops to avoid, the rows of tilled soil were tricky to navigate. The hike toward the village was brutal. Each step sent new spasms up my leg, especially the missteps when I dropped into an unexpected divot in the soil. Had it not been for the tight wrap and James propping me up, I might not have made it.

"When we get there, you'll be our lookout. We'll position you across the street, somewhere you can have overwatch. The real trick will be extracting you after we have the package. If you are positioned atop a nearby building, one of us will need to help you down."

I nodded. "Just bring him out safe. We can worry about me afterward."

James eyed me sideways as we hobbled after the others. I hadn't meant for a pleading to enter my tone, but I was sure it rang clearly in his ears, as it had mine.

A paved road, far wider than the graveled paths we'd crossed between the farms, marked the ending of the agricultural sprawl and the beginning of the village proper. A smattering of humble homes lined the far side of the road, while two- and three-story buildings popped up behind them. For a village of only a few hundred residents, the center appeared more like a small American town than the ramshackle huts I'd envisaged.

Sikes motioned for us to join him and Sparrow at the road's edge.

Once we were together again, he whispered, "You alright? Leg okay?"

"Fine," I said. "I'm good."

He and James exchanged a glance, then he nodded once. "The police station should be two blocks west, on the northwestern corner of the village. Our maps show its drive connecting to this main road and the other one that crosses going north–south. We'll follow the road on this side until we can see the building, then cross. Got it?"

Each of us nodded, and Sikes turned to walk parallel with the artery, motioning for us to follow close behind.

Most of the buildings we saw as we crept along the road were shrouded behind trees and lush foliage. For a chilly land standing on the edge of winter, it was surprising to find such dense greenery.

The station emerged exactly where Sikes had predicted, wedged into a triangle of primary roads, allowing officials to move quickly in any direction. The small wooden sign out front looked like any rural police station one might see in a thousand tiny towns across America. Faded lettering was etched deeply into the crackled wood alongside a pristine painting of a police shield; the entire plaque swayed in the stiff Dutch breeze. The station itself was little more than a house converted for official use. Thick shingles overlapped a slanted roof above a one-story brick building that resembled a ranch-style home in southern Florida.

Sikes scanned the area, then motioned for us to duck down and huddle. "James, position Tobias atop the apothecary there—" He pointed to a two-story building directly across a side street from the station. "Heads on a swivel. Someone may live on the upper floor."

He glanced back to the station. "Anny, you and I will circle to the back—" He pointed to the end of the station's L-shape. "The cells are likely in the back. We'll search for an entrance while we wait for James."

Sparrow nodded.

"Remember, if the place is secure, we may need to blast our way in, which will be loud. If things get loud, we work fast. Let's move."

Sparrow and Sikes shot across the road, while James and I hobbled toward our target.

## Chapter Sixteen

# Thomas

*"Amidst the chaos, we clung to hope like a fragile flower in a storm, refusing to let it wither away."*

Anonymous Dutch resistance

fighter

"God, it feels good to laugh," I said to Fons through wheezes. "I can't remember the last time—"

Everything lurched as a blast tore through the back of the building, sending shards of metal and brick flying past the cell. Dust and debris billowed up the short hallway.

Fons shot to his feet and stumbled toward the cell door. His eyes widened, then he stepped out, moving to grab the sidearm I hadn't realized he was still carrying on his hip.

A shot echoed. Fons cried out, gripping his side, then collapsed to the ground.

Before I had time to react, a man in dark, dust-covered fatigues, rifle raised, burst into the cell. "Wilhelm?" His voice was hushed, urgent.

I nodded.

He grabbed my arm and hauled me to my feet.

"Wait. He's on our side." I pointed to where Fons lay bleeding.

"There's no time. We have to go," the man insisted, dragging me out of the cell, where we ran headlong into

...

"Sparrow?"

I could barely believe what I was seeing. Why was Sparrow here, in the Netherlands, with a rifle?

A quick flash of a smile shone on her lips, then her face returned to stone.

"Reunion later. Go, now!" the man gripping my arm hissed.

"Wait," a weak voice called from behind.

I looked back to find a frighteningly pale Fons reaching up with one hand.

The man pulled me toward the blown-out door. I tugged against him, but he was ridiculously strong.

I glanced back toward Fons, desperate to help my friend.
"Your other men ... they are alive," he called out, his
voice failing. "The Nazis have them."

# Chapter Seventeen

# Thomas

*"In the crucible of captivity, the human spirit's flame can burn even brighter, defying the darkness of war."*

UNKNOWN ALLIED PRISONER OF WAR
SURVIVOR

Everything froze.

The massive man was still barking in the background, but Fons lay in a swelling pool of crimson, as I stared openmouthed, unable to think or move.

"They're alive?" was all I could say as I jerked against the iron grip of my savior. "Stop, wait!" I shouted, no longer thinking of our own safety.

"Quiet," the man hissed.

"We can't leave him. He'll die," I pleaded. We were nearly at the door and I still hadn't turned away from my friend's prone body.

"We have to go. The extraction window is tight. Move!" The man heaved, and I stumbled through the blown-out door and into Sparrow, who wrapped her arms tightly around me. But this wasn't another attempt to tow me free; it was an embrace.

She released me and I gazed into her face. When she smiled, I swear the sun lit up the onyx night. "I've got you. You're safe," she whispered. "And remember, aliases only."

"Move," the big man, who was clearly in charge, growled.

Sparrow turned, but I gripped her shoulder. "We have to go back. Adam's alive. Heinz is alive."

Sparrow looked like I'd punched her in the gut at the mention of Egret's alias. She nearly toppled over. "What are you talking about? Heinz's—"

"Alive," I finished. "Fons—the guard who was helping me—he just said—"

"Anny, we've got to go. Now," another man hissed in a decidedly British accent. "Sikes is off to collect Tobias. We've got to move."

"Tobias?" My head spun, and now my legs nearly gave out. "Tobias ... is here?"

"He's overwatch." Sparrow gathered herself and nodded. "Who said Heinz is alive?"

The world tilted. Will was here. He'd come to rescue me.

"Wilhelm!" Sparrow snapped. "Look at me. Where is this man?"

"Inside. He's shot."

The Brit grabbed Sparrow's arm like the big man had done to me, but she jerked free. "We go back inside. We're not leaving an ally to die."

Without waiting for a response, she darted inside. I looked to the stunned Brit, then raced after her.

Fons was unconscious and deathly pale when we reached him. It took both of us, with one of his arms over each of our shoulders, to drag him out. Blood streamed behind.

When we re-emerged, a light rain was falling, and the large American had returned.

"Wilhelm?"

It was a voice I would know anywhere.

I looked up and my eyes locked with Will's.

"Go," Sparrow whispered. "I've got him."

I bolted from under Fons and nearly bowled Will over. We hugged tighter than any hug in history, and I had to fight back tears as his scent flowed into me.

"They're brothers," I heard Sparrow explain, and the lie rang as true as any fact in my ears.

Thunder clapped in the distance. At first I thought it must've been bombs, but a streak of lightning brightened the sky a second before another boom. Light rain grew into a pelting, driving downpour.

"We'll never make it to the boat in this. We need shelter," the Brit said to the large man.

He cursed, then nodded. "Fine. Back to the second farm from the road, the one with the barn a hundred yards from the house. We'll hide there. Now move!"

This time we didn't resist. Sparrow and the Brit helped Fons, as I struggled to keep Will moving. It killed me to see him hurt, but no force in the world could've separated us in that moment.

In the midst of a war, when the world was ablaze, we'd found each other again.

<hr>

We crossed a road that separated the town from sprawling fields. The barn stood nearly a half-mile away, well out of view in the darkness and ever-increasing rain. Thunder bellowed almost with every step and lightning struck so close we all ducked a few times, for whatever good that would've done against Mother Nature's wrath. Beyond the misery of being soaked, the temperature had dropped a solid twenty degrees since we'd first stepped out of the police station. I found myself shivering despite the warmth of Will pressed against me.

"At least no one can see or hear us," I had to strain to hear the Brit tell Sparrow, though they were only a few strides ahead of us.

Will's fingers dug into my shoulder again and again, sending his unspoken love. At one point, he nuzzled his head against my neck and I felt chapped lips on my skin. It might've been the sweetest kiss ever given. I wanted to return it so badly, but ours was not a love shared in front of anyone, even those who'd just risked their lives to rescue me.

Nearly an hour had passed before the large American slid the barn door open and we stepped out of the storm. While the American checked to ensure we were alone, Sparrow and the Brit laid Fons out on a wooden table.

"I need light," the Brit said.

"No!" the American barked.

"Listen, this man might die if we don't do this right now. The storm will cover us. Get me a light." The Brit sounded like he might go toe-to-toe with the burly American if he argued.

"Fine," the American growled. "There's a lantern. You have something to light it with?"

"In my pack," the Brit said, shrugging the straps off his shoulders and tossing it to Sparrow.

With the efficiency of a trained professional, the Brit stripped the shirt and trousers off Fons. As soon as the lantern blazed to life, he began assessing the wound in Fons's hip.

"I can help. I've got field training," I said, handing Will to Sparrow.

"Wilhelm, right?"

I nodded.

"James," he said without looking up. "And the big fucker over there is Sikes. Bullet's still in. We'll need to remove it, clean the wound, and stitch him up. He'll need antibiotics and really should get some blood. He's lost a good amount."

"Give me your watch," I said, holding a hand out to Sparrow. I then pressed fingers to Fons's wrist and counted. "Pulse is weak but steady."

"Anny, there's a field kit in my pack," James said. "Get it out. We'll have to use the alcohol to sterilize. Wilhelm, hand me the iodine swabs."

What felt like half the night later, James and I stepped away from Fons, whose pallor still resembled cow's milk.

"That's the best we can do here," James announced. The others were seated or stretched out on piles of hay nearby, covered in dusty blankets. Their clothes hung over rails, still dripping water onto the dirt floor. "The bullet was intact, no fragments, and we got it out without opening anything else up, and the bleeding stopped a while ago.

He's healthy and athletic, but it could still take hours or days for him to regain consciousness, given his blood loss. It looked like a lot back at the station, but in the darkness, who knows?"

Fons moaned quietly.

"Did you give him anything for pain?" Sparrow asked.

James nodded. "I just gave him a shot of morphine. It should kick in quickly. And I have eight sulfadiazine tabs. That will keep any infection at bay for four days once he's awake enough to swallow them."

"You have all that in your pack?" I asked.

"Yeah, I was a nurse before the war. I became a sharpshooter, but they still make me carry a full med kit everywhere I go."

"Good thing too," Will said.

James looked back to Fons. "We need something to keep him warm through the night."

Sparrow rose, pulling the blanket tight around her, then grabbed another couple from a stack and laid them across Fons. Once he was settled, she grabbed another blanket and tossed it at me.

"You and James need to strip out of those clothes," Sparrow said to me. "You're still soaked. You'll freeze to death in here."

James didn't flinch, stripping off his shirt, pants, and even his underwear right there in front of everyone. Sparrow looked away, though I caught her sneaking a peek once. The flush that filled her cheeks when our eyes met nearly had me doubled over.

I turned from the group and peeled off everything but my underwear. Once the blanket was securely tight around my shoulders, I stepped to sit on the hay beside Will, but not so close as to raise the brows of James or Sikes.

"How did you get hurt?" I whispered.

"Jumping out of a perfectly good airplane like an idiot," Will said, a half-smile playing on his lips.

A thrill ran through me. God, I loved that smile.

"Your brother's a tough little fucker," Sikes said. By the way Sparrow and James gaped, I gathered compliments from the team's leader were rare. "Though I'd prefer it if he'd landed using his knees rather than his head."

"You hit your head?" I asked, suddenly alarmed.

"No. I just landed on my ankle wrong." Will rolled his eyes. "You'll learn to ignore half of what that meathead over there says."

"I work hard to be a meathead, thank you very much," Sikes said, raising his arm and flexing his grapefruit-sized bicep.

"Bloody hell, why are you encouraging him?" James asked.

"Boys," Sparrow said in the scolding tone of a sleep-deprived mother. "Can we keep our voices down? We need to be figuring out what to do next, not trading schoolyard jabs."

"Aw, Mom. You're such a drag," Sikes said with an accentuated drawl.

Sparrow glared, then raised her middle finger.

"That's the first time you've saluted me proper, little miss. Thanks so much." Sikes's teeth beamed in the near darkness.

"Switch that lantern off," Sparrow said. "Please tell me you had a contingency plan in case things went south with the boat."

James and Sikes glanced at each other.

"There was no back-up," Sikes said.

"Seriously?" Sparrow looked like she wanted to strangle them for their shortsightedness.

"This mission was thrown together, then pushed up a day because of the storms. Good thing too, given they came even sooner than the weather geeks predicted," Sikes said.

"He is right," James agreed. "We were only given notice of this operation a few hours before you arrived for the briefing."

"Fine," Sparrow said. "We need a plan now though. Do any of you know anything about the Netherlands?"

"Amsterdam is supposed to be a lot of fun," Sikes said.

"I swear I'm going to throw something at you," Sparrow snapped. I found myself turning to Will and sharing a grin. Despite everything, it was good to hear Sparrow's spunky voice again.

"You two, not a word," she commanded. "Unless it's about how we can get this man medical attention without raising the ire of the Nazis. Oh, and then how we can get back home in one piece."

I cleared my throat.

"What?" Sparrow asked, her very annoyed brow raised.

"Heinz? Adam?"

Sparrow's other brow shot up. "Oh, shit. Right."

"We don't even know where they are, only that they are alive," I said. "If Fons doesn't make it, we'll lose three men, not one."

When I looked back at Will, his eyes were closed and his breathing had slowed to a steady, calm rhythm. I wanted to talk more, to come up with a plan, to know there was something we could do, but we were hidden in a barn in the middle of nowhere with no way to contact anyone who might offer guidance. Frustration warred with anger until exhaustion interceded and I drifted off to fitful dreams.

# Chapter Eighteen

# Will

*"In the darkest hours ... the human spirit has the remarkable ability to find light and strength."*

ADMIRAL JAMES STOCKDALE

The rain continued pounding the barn's metal roof throughout the night and into the morning. If it hadn't been for the stack of horse blankets, cold would've found its way into every part of my body. When my eyes fluttered open, the first thing I saw was James standing over the Dutch man, his fingers pressed into his neck and his eyes pinned to his watch.

"Is he awake?" I asked, rubbing my eyes.

James ignored me, his concentration fixed. A moment later, he removed his fingers and looked up. "Not yet, but his pulse is stable and color is returning to his face. I cleaned his wound and changed his bandages. It looks as good as I could hope, given where we are, but he needs a doctor."

"Will he make it?" I asked.

James started to answer, then closed his mouth and shrugged.

Thomas groaned, like a young boy struggling to wake on a school day.

"Morning," I said, watching his eyes pry open and adjust to the dim light in the barn.

"Is it?" he groused then looked around. "How can you tell? It's still dark."

"That's the storm. The weather guys said it would be like this all day. It's why we came a day early."

"Early?" He stared. "They were about to take me to Amsterdam—"

"To hand you over to a Nazi interrogator," I finished.

Bafflement bloomed in his eyes. "You knew?"

I nodded. "The Brits got a tip from someone in the resistance."

Thomas glanced to where Fons lay. "That would be him. He's been promising to get help, but no one was responding. We were starting to think none of his messages made it through."

I shifted into a sitting position and tried to cross my legs, but pain shot through my ankle.

"Hey, you okay?" Thomas asked.

"Yeah, my ankle hurts. That's all."

"Let me look." He started forward.

My gaze darted to where James was watching us from across the stall. "I'm okay. James wrapped it."

"Tobias, give me your damn ankle."

Reluctantly, I tossed back the blanket enough to free the leg with the busted ankle, keeping the rest of me comfortably warm beneath the cloth. Thomas unwrapped the tangle that had once been a neat wrapping, the one piece I hadn't removed to dry the night before.

"No wonder," Thomas said, annoyed. "You walked across the soggy field last night in this thing. It got soaked and loosened to the point of being useless. It probably did more harm than good."

I glanced up. James remained silent.

When the last of the wrap fell away, Thomas whistled. "You're swollen pretty badly."

"I have acetylsalicylic tabs in my pack that should help with swelling," James offered.

Thomas nodded. "Yeah, good idea. I wish we had some ice."

"Just call room service," I quipped, earning stern gazes from both my caretakers.

"Do you have another wrap in there?" Thomas asked James as he was rooting around for the tablets.

"Yes, here." James tossed a sealed pack over Fons. Thomas snatched it out of the air and quickly began rewrapping my ankle. The pressure made me wince, but offered almost immediate relief from the worst of the pain. James stepped up and handed Thomas two white pills, which he promptly shoved in front of me.

"Take two of these and call me in the morning," Thomas said without a hint of a smile.

James actually snickered behind him.

"Very funny. You have such a bedside manner," I said, popping the pills into my mouth and wishing I had a glass of water.

"Is that a good or bad manner?" James asked.

I cocked a brow. "It's *a* manner. Let's leave it at that."

Sparrow finally woke and scooted over next to us. "It's still raining?"

The three of us nodded in unison.

"Where's Sikes?" she asked.

I glanced around, realizing for the first time since I'd woken that our leader was nowhere in sight.

"No idea," James said. "I have been up for an hour and he was gone when I woke."

"What time is it?" Sparrow's voice carried all the weariness I felt in my bones.

"A touch past eight," James said. "You slept in."

Sparrow snorted. "If that's your idea of sleeping in—"

"You are US Army. Are you not used to rising before the sun?"

Sparrow eyed him. "I'm in the branch that likes to sleep late."

James chuckled. "Well played."

Sparrow stood and stretched, then peered through a crack between the wall boards. "The sky is black. This must be some storm."

"It is a good thing. This barn is a half-mile from the nearest house, and I doubt anyone will come here in this weather," James said.

Thomas, his nursing duties complete, sat leaning against a bale of hay. "Yeah, it's definitely a good thing. We'd either have to move Fons, which he might not survive, or kill whoever came in here—and I'd rather not kill any innocent Dutch farmers if we can help it."

That thought sobered the conversation.

The rain drumming against the barn lulled us into a comfortable silence and nearly put me back to sleep, but the creak of the barn door jolted me wide awake. James had his rifle up and pointed before Sparrow or Thomas could stand.

"Easy," Sikes said as he secured the door behind him. Water flowed from his olive poncho, turning it more black than green. He shed his rain gear, draping it over a stall to dry, then strode toward us. "The whole countryside is quiet. Looks like nobody wants to move in this mess. Visibility is almost zero."

"You were gone a long time. Find anything?" Thomas asked.

Sikes removed a small sack from beneath his coat. "Breakfast."

He handed the sack to James, who quickly removed two baguettes and a half-eaten hunk of cheese.

"Where—?" Thomas started.

"A house, about a mile west. It was dark, so I checked it out. Nobody was home."

"You stole bread from a house?" Sparrow gaped.

"Call me Jean Valjean."

When no one laughed, he reached under his coat and retrieved two canteens. "Fresh water and wine—at least, I think that's wine. It was in a wine bottle, but tastes a little like alcoholic shit."

Sparrow rose and took the canteen filled with water. "When you say it like that, I can't wait."

Sikes grinned, a toothy, gruff gesture that would likely frighten anyone who didn't know the man.

We passed the crusty bread around, ripping off chunks, then sliced a bit of cheese with a knife Sikes proffered, one of several he kept sheathed in various places, a few of which I didn't care to know.

"Who knows anything about the Netherlands?" Sikes asked. "We need to think through our next steps."

"I read some intelligence prior to our last mission, but it wasn't very detailed. The Dutch government fled as soon as the Nazis came. The Queen and her ministers rule in exile from England."

"We know that much," Sikes said. "Anything about resistance organizations? People? Connections that might help?"

James swallowed down bread. "The Dutch resistance has primarily been through their underground press, printing newspapers and leaflets. Farmers, miners, and doctors staged a series of strikes, but each was met with brutal reprisals."

"Fons's father was hanged after the spring strikes," Thomas said quietly.

All eyes turned toward the resting man on the table. The sound of the rain thundered through the barn.

"What about the priesthood?" I asked. "They have a network inside Germany. What about here?"

Sikes thought a moment. "That's a possibility. What else?"

"Doctors," James said. "He needs one anyway, and they protested through strikes. There is likely still a fair amount of backbone among that lot."

Sikes nodded. "Okay, that kills two birds. Other ideas?"

"This is pointless until Fons wakes," Thomas said. "We wouldn't even know who to approach. He's our only contact in the whole damn country."

"We could try to find a transmitter," Sparrow said. "I'm a pianist. Get me a piano."

"Like we'll find one of those lying around," Sikes grumbled. When Sparrow's face darkened, he added, "But it's a good idea if we can find one. Add it to the list."

Our conversation meandered. One moment we brainstormed how to find and approach suspected resistance members, the next James was sharing stories about his childhood in Staffordshire. By a quarter past noon, we'd run out of things to talk about.

And that's when Fons woke.

James leapt to his feet. Thomas wasn't far behind.

Fons's eyes opened but didn't focus.

"Anny, fetch the thermometer from my pack. Wilhelm, get the water." James turned Fons to face him, watching his pupils closely. "Does he speak English?" "I don't think so," Thomas said, returning with the canteen. "We always spoke German."

"You'll have to translate," James said, then looked down at Fons and spoke in a soothing tone, placing his palm at the center of Fons's chest. "You're alright. Just relax and breathe."

Thomas translated, but Fons simply groaned.

As quickly as he'd woken, Fons drifted off again.

"Given his blood loss, it could have been days before he woke. This is a good thing," James said to the rest of us while testing Fons's forehead.

"Fever?" Thomas asked.

James shook his head. "I do not believe so. That is the best sign yet."

"He should wake in a few hours," Thomas said.

"I agree." James stepped back from Fons. "He made it through the night. If we can get antibiotics into him quickly, he should be out of trouble.""He won't be able to put weight on that side for a while though," Thomas said, as much to himself as to the rest of us.

"How are we supposed to carry him around a country full of Nazis?" Sikes growled.

Thomas looked up. "We need a vehicle. Two would be better."

"We're going to have to split up anyway," Sparrow said, turning heads in her direction. "Think about it. A group of five with a wounded man? We're far too easy to spot. James and Wilhelm have medical training. They need to take the policeman."

"That leaves the three of you to find your own way to wherever we're headed?" Thomas asked.

Sparrow made to respond, but Sikes cut her off. "No. Anny and Tobias go together. Play a couple. That'll be the most believable act."

"That leaves you alone," Sparrow challenged.

Sikes nodded. "It's easier for me to hide in the shadows by myself."

I couldn't believe what I was hearing. Thomas had been lost—dead for all we knew—only days before. We'd just found and recovered him, and now that we were together again, the team wanted us to split up? The logic was solid, but my heart didn't care one whit about logic. It only wanted to fall into Thomas's arms and live there forever.

"Your brother will be fine. James is a sharpshooter and Fons is a native," Sparrow whispered, reading my thoughts. Her comfort didn't help, but I nodded anyway.

"Sikes, do you speak German or Dutch?" Thomas asked.

"No."

"Shit. How are you supposed to go anywhere without language skills? You can't make it without someone to translate and cover you."

Sikes looked like he wanted to object, but thought better of it. "You're right." "Wilhelm, I know you just got out of jail, but you need to be the solo man here. You'll do better on your own than any of us," James said.

Thomas looked back to where Sparrow and I were sitting. If eyes could plead or scream—or cry—his did in that single glance.

"Fine," he said, resigned. "Now we just need a plan to get into Germany."

"Germany?" Sikes nearly spat the word.

Thomas turned and squared with Sikes. "I'm not leaving without our men. Fons said they're alive. We have to go after them."

"Are you fucking crazy? There's no way—"

"He's right," Sparrow said, rising to her feet. "If Heinz and Adam are alive, we have to go after them."

"You don't even know—" Sikes was nearly shouting. If it hadn't been for the raging storm and the distance to the nearest house, we would've been at serious risk. As it was, a raised voice was still irresponsible.

"This isn't a debate," Thomas said, using his commanding naval officer voice I'd only heard a few times. He hadn't been in the pre-mission briefing where Sikes was named the leader. Then again, Thomas never was one to take second place when principles were at stake. "The question is how, not if. Start thinking. When Fons wakes, we'll need to plan quickly and move even more so."

Consciousness did not agree with Thomas's desire to move quickly. Five hours later, as the sun made her final descent, Fons moaned and his eyes opened again.

"*Aletta? Ben je daar, mijn liefste?*"

"Any idea what he said?" James asked.

Thomas hopped up to join him by the table where Fons lay. "Dutch isn't German, but they're related. I think he's calling for his wife."

"*Aletta, waar bent je? Ik heb je nodig.*" Fons reached up as if to grab Thomas's face. "Aletta?"

"Fons, it's Wilhelm," he said in German.

"*Waarom klink je zo vreemd?*"

"No idea what that meant," Thomas said.

James shook his head. "Try to get him to drink. He's likely dehydrated, and we'll need to get those antibiotics into him as soon as possible. His head will clear in time."

Thomas uncapped the canteen and held it to Fons's lips. "Drink this."

Fons tried to pull back from the canteen, but Thomas held his head steady. "Easy. Take a sip, my friend."

Fons allowed the liquid past his lips. A heartbeat later, he drank greedily.

"Whoa, slowly," Thomas said, tipping the canteen up to allow him to swallow.

"*Dokter? Wat is er gebeurd? Mijn hoofd bonkt, en mijn heup...*"

"I don't understand. Can you remember German?" Thomas asked softly.

"*Duits?*" Then something resolved in his eyes, and he switched languages. "*Ja, ich glaube schon.*" *Yes, I think so.*

I watched Thomas's shoulders visibly relax as they transitioned to a common tongue.

"Fons, try to relax. You were injured and have been asleep for some time. Your mind will clear, but you need to remain calm. Here, take a few more sips of water."

"Water, yes. I am so parched. Why is my mouth so dry?" Fons said, allowing his head to be raised to drink again. "Doctor, where am I?" He glanced around. His eyes were so glazed, I doubted he was seeing anything clearly. "This is a strange hospital. It smells like horses."

Thomas translated, and he and James shared a look. Then Thomas smiled at Fons. "You are safe. We will take care of you, Fons. Can you swallow a pill? You need antibiotics.""A pill? Yes, I think so."

James handed Thomas the tablet. It took a couple of tries, but Fons finally swallowed the medicine, then let his head fall back like he'd done a day's work lifting it.

Thomas and James stood in silence as Fons lay there, staring at the ceiling.

"How long do you think it will be before his brain works?" I whispered to Sparrow.

She shrugged. "Who knows? Hopefully soon. The storm sounds like it's losing strength. We need to be out of this barn before things clear up and someone comes back."

It was in that moment that Fons returned to himself. "Wilhelm?"

Thomas clasped Fons's hand and leaned over him. "I'm here, Fons."

"I thought you were a doctor. Everything is so strange ... my side feels like it is on fire."

"You were shot in the hip," Thomas said. "We got the bullet out, but you lost a lot of blood."

James leaned in. "Tell him he needs rest and that we only have a few days of antibiotics. He will need to see a doctor soon."

When Thomas translated, Fons turned toward James and tried to focus. "I do not know him, Wilhelm. Why does he speak English? Who is this man?"

"It's okay," Thomas said, his use of German soothing Fons. "He is a friend, one of a team who answered your call."

A hint of a smile reached Fons's lips. "They did receive my message? This is good."

"Yes, they did. You saved me, Fons. You saved my life."

Thomas translated for James and Sikes without looking from Fons, as the policeman drifted back to sleep.

"He's a brave man, standing up for a random American caught in the net," Sikes said.

"That he is," Thomas agreed, finally releasing the man's hand and stepping back.

"He should wake again soon. I expect he will need more water than what's left." James shook the nearly empty canteen. "He will need food too. We all will."

"Tobias, your ankle is shit. You stay and help with the policeman. Anny, come with me. The pair of us can use the doting couple cover while we look for vehicles and supplies," Sikes ordered. "If anyone comes into this barn while we're gone, try to kill them silently. Guns attract soldiers."

With that uplifting admonition, he turned and vanished into the rain-soaked night.

# Chapter Nineteen

# Sparrow

*"In the midst of winter, I found there was, within me, an invincible summer."*

ALBERT CAMUS [1]

The rain had eased to a steady drizzle, just thick enough to obscure our vision and be utterly annoying. Sikes led us across the barren field to the house where he'd liberated the bread and cheese. Dark smoke billowed from the chimney, and lights flickering inside told us the home was no longer vacant.

---

1. French philosopher, author, dramatist, journalist, and political activist.

"Well, shit. I was hoping they were away on holiday or something," Sikes said.

"In the middle of a war?" I asked.

Sikes's mouth twisted. "Maybe they need a holiday from the war."

"You're an idiot," I replied, amusement in my voice. "Where to now?"

"If we go toward the town, we risk running into more people. This place is so small, they'll know strangers on sight." Sikes thought a moment. "Let's go north, stay the same distance from the barn, see if we can find another house without the owner."

"That won't help us find a car," I said.

Sikes considered a moment. "Maybe, but I'd rather try a low-risk house before going that route. There could be Nazis holed up in town."

That thought ended the discussion and we headed northeast, careful to stay low and out of sight of the windows that now glowed with life.

The second house we approached was identical to the first, smoke streaming skyward and lights glowing behind curtained windows. There was no debate this time. We simply continued east. This took us across the largest farm yet. When the main house came into view, we were surprised to also find two barns and a small second house behind the primary one.

There was no smoke or lights in sight.

"Let's start with the house in back," Sikes said.

We crept along the fence line, careful to avoid several small gatherings of cows, who looked more irritated by the rain than our presence.

"What time do you think it is?" I asked.

"Has to be after eight by now," Sikes said.

"When would curfew be? The Nazis impose one everywhere, don't they?"

"That's a good point. These are farmers too. They could be in bed." He stopped walking and turned back to face me. It only took him a moment to make up his mind. "It's worth looking out for but can't be helped. We move on."

Order issued, he turned and trudged forward.

We snuck up to the back of the smaller house, well hidden from the view of anyone who might peer out a window of the larger one. Three glass panes stared out at the farm beyond. Each was cloaked in thick curtains.

Sikes placed a palm over his eyes, indicating he couldn't see through. We crept to the second, then the third window, each resulting in the same blinded signal. Sikes paused, then turned back and signaled for me to stay in place while he moved toward the side of the house.

The rain had picked up again, now more sheets of biting drops than the irritating mist we'd experienced for most of the night. My socks squished with each step, and I briefly wondered how pruny my feet must be. It took all my strength not to shiver under the chill.

Sikes's head poked around the corner, and he motioned for me to join him. A heartbeat later, we stepped into the dryness of the farm's secondary home. The relief from stepping out of the rain was balanced by a sinking stomach, as I peered around the abandoned house. Furniture was upturned, several torn with stuffing strewn about. Glasses lay shattered by tables whose legs had been broken, and lamps lay like lifeless bodies beneath their crumpled shades.

We moved slowly, quietly, from the living area into the only bedroom. The scene was more of the same. Clothing covered the floor from open drawers in a tall dresser. More broken lamps from toppled side tables lay in pieces. Black stains marred walls painted some light color I couldn't discern, while pools of the same liquid had dried on the floor and in the center of the bed.

But it was the Star of David crudely drawn in the same blackish substance above the headboard that caused my heart to still. Dribbles ran connecting the interlocking triangles in ways never intended, as though the ancient symbol wept.

Sikes broke protocol and whispered, "We won't find anyone alive here. They've either been killed or sent on trains. Let's look for supplies and get back to the barn. You take this building, then join me in the main house. We can check for cars last."

I nodded, not trusting my voice, then watched through the curtained window as his silhouette crossed to the larger home.

Somehow, I managed to turn back to my task, and that's when I saw the toys.

The glassy eyes of a rough-sewn doll, her ropy hair stained dark crimson, stared up from her bed of discarded socks, each no larger than my palm. A stuffed bear lay atop a lion whose fur had long since worn away.

My eyes traveled from the floor to the bed, where deep depressions beneath the dried pools offered insight into the parent and child who must've once slept there. Tears began to fall like the rain outside, and I had to brace myself with a hand on the dresser. I covered my mouth and fled that room, only to return to the horror of the den, a different yet equally clear representation of vibrant lives snuffed out by the darkest evil.

After a cursory search, I turned toward the kitchen, where the stench of spoiled meat was nearly overpowering. I grabbed a few pieces of fruit, potatoes, and a loaf of bread whose mold was mild enough to be cut away, stuffing them in a burlap sack I found in a cabinet, then headed across to join Sikes.

I stepped from the yard into a mudroom just off the kitchen, where Sikes was rummaging through cabinets. He looked up as the door creaked, announcing my entry.

"Don't go upstairs."

I cocked a brow.

"Just trust me." His voice was almost as devoid of life as the home. "This must've been a well-off family. Check out that refrigerator."

Only about half the homes in the US boasted a fridge. For someone in the rural northeastern corner of occupied Netherlands to possess such a luxury was surprising.

"Bottles of water," I called. "Spoiled milk, old meat, a few pieces of fruit that look okay, an uncut wheel of cheese, a couple jars of jam. That's about it. Everything else has turned."

"There's bread on that counter." He pointed across the long, galley-style kitchen counter. "Grab those cookies too. They're not much, but they'll keep the stomach from rumbling."

I added what I could to my sack, then began opening cabinets. "Looks like someone was a canner. Here's some kind of fruit preserve in jars."

"I gathered some clothes from the bedrooms. We'll be lucky if anything fits, but we need to blend in." Sikes straightened. "We need to look for cars and head back. It's past ten o'clock. We don't want to be out much later, no matter how well the storm hides us."

His mention of the bedrooms piqued my curiosity, but I decided better of seeking answers. If the burly American said it was a scene worth avoiding, I knew better than to resist, so I shoved another jar into the overstuffed sack and heaved it over my shoulder. "After you."

Sikes led us out the kitchen, through a large sitting area whose couches and chairs once nestled around a large stone hearth—that is, before someone turned them over and tossed them about. The scene we'd witnessed in the outer house was repeated here on a grander scale. I had to step over shattered wooden frames and broken legs as we moved toward the front door. As Sikes stepped out, I noticed a shiny bowl on one of the few tables whose legs hadn't been knocked from under it. In the bowl was a pair of keys on a silver ring. I snatched them up and stepped outside, closing the door behind me.

The gravel drive that led to the house was empty of vehicles. I looked across to find Sikes, his hand covering his eyes from the rain, following a gravel off-shoot from the main drive, striding toward a small barn a few hundred paces away.

I followed him inside the small structure to find him opening the door to a black Opel Olympia, a popular German compact sedan.

"Look what I found," he said. "A couple of crossed wires and we're on our way."

"Before you go tearing the thing apart, try these." I tossed him the keys.

His brows shot up. "Where'd you—"

"Where anyone might leave keys. In a bowl by the front door."

"Nice," he said, climbing inside and turning the key. It took a couple of tries for the cold engine to fire up, but she was soon purring to life. "Hop in. Let's get back to the others."

I tossed the sack with our supplies in the back seat and settled in, while Sikes opened the massive sliding door that took up much of the barn's front face, then returned to pull out into the rainy night.

"Wish we could've found another—"

"Stop!" I shouted, not intending to sound an alarm.

"What is it?" His head wheeled about as his hand gripped the handle of a gun holstered at his side.

"Look." I pointed to the side of the barn we couldn't see from the house, where a dented maroon truck was parked so close to the barn I wondered how anyone in the passenger seat could get out. "A wooden bed. That's—"

"An Opel Blitz; 1939, I think," he said. "You didn't happen to see another set of keys in that bowl?"

I shook my head. "No, just those."

"Alright. You take the car. I'll go work on the truck. No headlights. We'll have to go slow."

Faster than I thought possible, the truck roared to life and the headlights flashed.

When we got back to the group, we parked the vehicles on the far side of the barn, well hidden from the view of the long drive that led to the building. Anyone working the fields would see the vehicles, though it was well past the harvest and the storm would keep most folks indoors at least until the morning.

"Easy, boys," Sikes said as we entered to pointed rifles and pistols. "I know you missed us, but this is a bit much for a welcome, don't you think?"

"We couldn't see who you were, just heard the engines." Thomas lowered his rifle. "A car *and* a truck? You did well."

I stepped forward and set the sack on a bale of hay. "We found a home the Nazis had ransacked. Pretty rough scene. I can't understand why they would leave the cars though."

"They were after Jews, not cars," Sikes explained. "The soldiers looted jewelry and anything else they could stuff in their pockets, but will probably go back for larger items later. That's pretty typical, especially in a rural area like this."

I looked past Thomas and was surprised to find Fons awake and partially propped up. More color had returned to his face, though his eyes looked a bit glassier than I remembered from hours earlier.

"He just got another shot of morphine," James said. "Went from wincing to giggling in a matter of minutes."

"Funny guy when he's knockered," Will said with a grin. "He was singing in Dutch a minute ago, sounded like a bawdy drinking song."

Thomas helped me pull items out of the sack and lay them out on the hay. "We learned a bit from Fons before he got his happy shot."

Sikes grabbed a loaf of bread and tore off a piece. "Let's hear it."

"He said one of the key resistance groups in the country is the doctors. Apparently, a couple years ago, they held a strike, refusing to treat wounded Nazis to protest the occupation. Some were killed as public examples, but the Germans were cautious about eliminating the Dutch medical core. Fons said the doctors still form a significant backbone of the resistance movement."

"Okay, what else?" Sikes asked.

"There are four major resistance groups—"

Fons cut Thomas off with a drunken, "*Landelijke Organisatie!*"

"What the hell does that mean?" Sikes asked.

"The primary group is called ... that," Thomas answered, clearly unwilling to attempt the Dutch pronunciation. "The LO for short."

"Thank God," Sikes said.

"They are the core of the resistance, focused on things like document forgeries and hiding targeted families. Fons said they aren't especially close to the government in exile and might not even be able to make contact."

"That's not encouraging," Will mumbled.

"The second group, called the OD—"

"*Orde Dienst*!" Fons shouted.

"Shh," Thomas hissed in German. "Quiet, Fons. Remember, we are hiding."

Fons ducked his head like a schoolboy who'd just been scolded, then mumbled in German, "*Tut mir leid.*" *I'm sorry.*

Thomas grinned at the policeman, then returned his attention to Sikes. "The OD is mostly former army officers planning for when the Germans retreat."

"There's dreaming," Sikes said.

"The OD has a radio network and might be our best shot at contacting London." Thomas glanced around, then continued. "The NC—National Committee in English—is the third group, the one with the best spy network. They gather intel and share it locally and with the Allies. Then there's the RVV, loosely translated as Council of Resistance. They run the widest radio network across the country."

"*Raad van Verzet*!" Fons shouted, then giggled, covering his mouth like he'd told a racy joke.

"Fons! Shh!" Will and I said in unison.

"Great history lesson, but none of this helps us if we don't have a contact." Sikes tossed himself onto a pile of hay.

"I was getting to that," Thomas said. "Back to doctors. Fons's father was a leader in the spring strikes. He was close with several local doctors Fons believes are quiet resistors, which fits with how most of the Dutch resistance movement has worked."

"What does that mean?" I asked.

"The Dutch haven't thrown themselves into sabotage and large-scale armed resistance like some of the other occupied countries. Most of their rebellion has occurred through leaflets or shows of defiance. One of the first was the birthday of the Crown Prince, where many across the Netherlands wore a carnation to express support for the royals in exile."

"Carnations? That's how they're fighting back?" Sikes shook his head.

"The Germans have them at the business end of a rifle. What do you expect them to do?" Thomas replied. "As benign as that protest was, the Nazis still carried out public executions and passed laws banning newspapers from talking about the Queen and her family. When her birthday rolled around, there wasn't a flower to be seen."

"You said Fons thinks these local doctors are resistance. Does he think or does he know?" I sat beside Will and crossed my arms.

Fons lifted his head and his eyes brightened, *"Hij weet het*!" *He knows!*

His head swam after the effort, and James had to brace him as he lay back again.

"There you have it," Thomas said. "This is the same doctor the family contacted when they found me. He came to their house in secret and treated my injuries. I might not have made it if it hadn't been for him, and I don't think he was who turned me in to the police."

"What about going back to that farm? See if that family can help connect us with someone?" Will asked.

Thomas shook his head. "Someone turned me in. I don't think it was the farmer or his wife, but someone did."

"How can you be sure? What about the doctor?" I asked.

Thomas thought a moment. "I'm not sure of anything, but I don't think it was either of them or the doctor."

"The kids?" I asked.

Thomas shrugged. "Maybe. Regardless, we can't go back there. We might not know who the leak is, but we know one exists."

"So, where does that leave us?" Will asked.

"Fons should be lucid again in a few hours. We all need to eat a bite and get some rest." Thomas glanced toward Sikes. "We should probably leave here before dawn."

"That's what I was thinking. Be gone before a farmer or his worker wanders into this barn again." Sikes nodded.

"Did Fons say where the doctor lived, the one he thinks is a good contact?"

Thomas nodded. "A town called Winsum, little more than nine miles west of here."

## Chapter Twenty

# Thomas



*"We were all in it together; we were all in it for the duration."*

Norman Rockwell

We loaded the truck with several bales of hay, figuring we would look less suspicious if we were carrying some sort of load through farm country. Sikes stepped back after tossing the last bale and adjusting it to ensure it didn't fly out.

"Nothing we can do to disguise the car," he said, as much to himself as to us.

I had taken to translating English into German so Fons could participate in our planning. Fons, who was awake and refusing another morphine shot until we made this next leg of our journey, spoke through the sedan's rolled-down window.

I relayed, "He says this is a common car in the Netherlands, even more so with the German occupation."

Sikes grunted as though mollified, but the scowl on his face remained. "Tobias, you, James, and Wilhelm go with Fons in the car. Anny and I will continue playing the couple in the truck. We need to stay far enough apart so it doesn't look like the vehicles are traveling together, but I don't want us to lose sight of each other either."

"This is fairly flat land. That shouldn't be a problem, even from a distance, especially once this rain lifts," I said.

"I'd rather it rained for the next week," Sikes said. "It's the best cover we could've hoped for. Plus, it would keep lazy eyes from looking too closely."

"How should we play this when we get to the doctor's house? Does he have family? Will we be waking him?" Sparrow asked.

All eyes turned to Fons. I translated, then listened to the injured man's answer.

"Fons says Dr. Kuiper has a wife, Fresia. His idea is for one of us to knock on the door and tell the doctor that Fons was injured in an incident at the jail. He knows Fons, and it wouldn't be unusual for an officer to come to him for aid."

"At his house?" Sparrow asked incredulously.

"Fons says that's the weak link, but it can't be helped. Once we're inside, we can explain what's going on and ask for help to contact one of the resistance groups."

"Where is this house? Is it in the middle of a neighborhood? How exposed will we be?" Will asked.

"He says it's a typical upper-class neighborhood in a small town, with large homes on lots that back up to either a forested area or neighboring farms. A river runs down the center of town, and small branches snake their way throughout like streets. Many of the clusters are basically islands connected to one another by a single road. The doctor lives on the northwestern corner near his clinic."

"Who knocks on the door?" Sparrow asked.

"It can't be you or Sikes. You're in the truck," Will said.

Fons and I went back and forth a moment before I turned back toward the group.

"He says it should be either Tobias or me because we speak the most fluent German. Dr. Kuiper is used to German officers demanding all sorts of things, so that language will not immediately raise an alarm."

"What if his wife answers the door?" Sparrow asked.

"Fons says she will react much the same as the doctor. We stick to the story," I said.

Sikes pushed off from where he'd been leaning against the truck. "Alright, let's go. Anny and I will lead. You follow as far behind as possible without losing visual."

The ancient wooden sign welcoming us into the town of Winsum boasted some two thousand residents. The collection of homes and shops, though more numerous than any we'd seen so far, looked strikingly similar to those we'd seen in Loppersum.

As we crossed from farmland into the town proper, we switched on our headlights.

"Everyone's still asleep," James said absently.

Shops were shuttered. Houses remained still and dark.

I glanced up at the clock tower above the town square to learn it was just past five o'clock.

"I bet more people would be stirring during the planting season," Will said.

I almost asked how he would know that but quickly remembered our new cover as brothers and clamped my mouth shut.

"Unless they have animals on their farm, there's no point to waking at this hour," Fons said. I glanced at the policeman to find his eyes unfocused and glassy again.

"Are you alright?" I asked.

"Is it that obvious?" He grimaced. "I did not realize how much the morphine helped until it started to wear off."

"Sitting upright in a car can't help either," Will said.

Fons nodded and gritted his teeth in reply.

"We are almost there," James said, turning the car from the small commercial center of town onto a cobbled road lined with trees. "Sikes will continue driving when we stop at the doctor's home. They will return each hour until we can reconnect safely."

Trees bowed over the narrow lane, and homes on either side grew larger. When we reached the last house before the dead end, Fons pointed. "That is the house."

The house, though modest, exuded authority and warmth. Its brick facade, kissed by weather and time and adorned with creeping ivy, was decidedly Dutch in design. Deep green, ornately carved shutters framed large windows, and two towers crowned with stepped gables bracketed the home like majestic bookends.

"It's beautiful," Will said, his breath fogging the window.

"Show time," James said. "Wilhelm, good luck."

I sucked in a breath, unfolded myself from the car, and climbed four stone steps. Wrought-iron lanterns bracketed the front door, like a pair of guards standing sentry. A gilded knocker shaped like an anchor rested against a brass plaque. A metallic clank echoed throughout the neighborhood each time I struck it.

A moment passed before lights on the upper floor began to glow through the windows, then one on the main floor flared to life. When the door opened, a fifty-something man gaped up at me.

"Wilhelm?" His eyes widened, then darted from me to the street beyond, searching for what, I couldn't tell. "What are you doing? You were captured—"

"Doctor, there was an incident at the police station. Fons Boswel was shot. He needs your help."

The doctor startled as if I'd punched him. "Fons?"

"May we bring him inside? He is in the car." I turned and pointed. "As you say, we must stay out of sight."

"Yes, yes. Of course. Bring him inside."

I turned and gave a thumbs-up signal. The others were moving before I turned back.

A woman's voice called from deeper inside the house. Dr. Kuiper replied in Dutch, then turned back to me. He lowered his voice and switched back to German. "We should go to my clinic. I have more equipment there and no one will intrude. My wife is loyal, but the fewer who know of your presence, the better."

I nodded once. As I turned to tell the others to get back in the car, Dr. Kuiper said, "Give me a moment to put on some clothes."

"We know where the clinic is. We will meet you there. It is best no one sees us together."

The doctor considered, then nodded. "Very well. Park behind the clinic. There is a small alley. No one goes back there."

"Thank you, doctor. This is the second time you have saved me."

Kuiper gave me a tight smile, then shut the door.

# Chapter Twenty-One
# Will



*"Nothing is accidental in history. Every current, every phenomenon, every person, appears at a certain time, through certain events, in a way that shapes the future …"*

"The Fall of Mussolini," *Het Parool*, underground Dutch newspaper, 1943

Dr. Kuiper proved as competent as he was swift, cleaning the wound on Fons's side, stitching it back up, then administering a more comprehensive round of antibiotics and painkillers.

"I wish your father were still with us," the doctor said as he inserted a needle in Fons's arm. They spoke in German for our benefit, but I still had to translate for James. "He had far more contacts than I do. After our strike failed[1], most of us were too afraid to resist openly and returned to simply caring for the ill and injured. Your father, bless his soul, refused to let fear grip his soul."

"You knew him well?" Fons asked, a small boy yearning for the closeness of one lost.

Kuiper glanced up, as if examining Fons for the first time, then nodded slowly. "Quite well. He came to me when there were ... how do I say it ... special requirements. On occasion, when someone was injured, I would receive visitors at my home. Sound familiar?"

The doctor's easy smile belied the deathly serious events of which he spoke.

"He was a good man, Fons," he said, patting the officer on the shoulder. "As are you. I was never sure where you stood, being a policeman, but I know your father would be proud to see you helping those who would win back our freedom."

Fons lowered his head, lost in his own memories.

"Now," Kuiper said, turning toward me. "Let me have a look at that foot of yours."

By the time the rest of the town was rising to start their day, we were packed into a truck and two cars and headed

---

1. Reference to the general strikes of 1941.

west. The only delay came when we had to double back to our pre-planned rally point east of town to meet up with Sikes and Sparrow. They'd driven through some of the outer farm roads to avoid spending time in the more densely populated town where the risk of exposure was greater.

James, Thomas, and Fons rode in the sedan, Sikes and Sparrow continued playing the farming couple, while I rode in Dr. Kuiper's car. Spreading out made for a less conspicuous, more comfortable ride, but I missed feeling Thomas pressed against me in the back seat. It had been too long since I'd held him, felt the caress of his skin, enjoyed the simple thrill of his lips brushing against mine. In the rush of our escape, there had been no time for such things. In fact, we hadn't had a single moment alone, a single moment when we weren't pretending to be brothers.

We were a million miles from home, fighting on foreign soil, and still we had to hide.

Staring out the doctor's car window, watching the sprawling fields of Holland drift by, I wondered if it would ever be so.

"You know your mission is a death wish, yes?" Kuiper's voice startled me out of my thoughts. He chuckled. "Forgive me. Did you go somewhere?"

I turned. "Just remembering home."

"We do a lot of that here."

My brow furrowed. "But ... you *are* home."

"No, we are not. As long as the swastika flies overhead, this is not ..." His voice trailed away as he stared blankly at the road ahead.

"Doctor?"

Now it was his turn to startle. "Yes?"

"It's all true, isn't it?"

He glanced sideways across the seat. "What is true?"

"The Jews being sent from here by train. We read about it in the papers and see reports on the reels, but it's sometimes hard to tell what is true and what we are being told to ramp up support for the troops."

"Whatever you have been told, the truth is far worse." His face darkened. "If *Trouw*[2] is correct, nearly all the Jews who once lived here have been relocated."

"Relocated?" I nearly spat the word. "We heard—"

"Yes, they were killed in Hitler's camps. We do not speak such words to give hope to those who choose to believe their loved ones still live, but ..." He swallowed hard. "I have given many years to the saving of life. To watch so many be extinguished, so many friends ..."

---

2. While many small pamphlets and publications flourished as non-violent resistance to the Nazi occupation, the four most prominent Dutch underground newspapers during the war were *Trouw*, *Vrij Nederland*, *Het Parool*, and *De Waarheld*.

As Kuiper struggled beneath the weight of emotions I could only imagine, a face flashed before my eyes: Arty. I hadn't thought about my closest friend in far too long. The harrows of our journeys had stolen him from my mind, but in that moment, all I could see was his awkward smile and the shy tilt of his head, his keen eyes and sharp tongue. I saw his brothers and his mother and father as I strode through their home, their lives playing out before me like a film flickering on the car's glass.

They would have been on a train.

They would've been sent to those places.

To *those* camps.

I hadn't meant to weep. We were talking of the doctor's friends, not those I'd left safe behind their oceanic walls; and yet, my heart lurched as the world around me flew past, and the plight of the people who might help us suddenly came into clear focus. I couldn't feel their loss, but I had imagined it. I felt it in the only way I knew: through the eyes of my own extended family.

That's when a thought settled in my chest like a stone.

"Doctor, do you think they will help us? We're driving to Amsterdam, aren't we?"

He was silent so long, I wondered if he had heard me.

I fumbled for words. "You've been through so much already, and we are not part of your resistance. And, like you said, we're asking people to go on a fool's errand."

"Yes, we are headed to Amsterdam. We take the same road I expect the policemen would've taken your brother on to deliver him to the Nazis. As for helping go into Germany? I do not know. I am confident they will help you escape our borders, but to send men into Germany to save condemned …"

My head snapped toward him, and it felt like all the oxygen had been sucked out of my lungs.

"I am sorry." He caught himself, then continued. "But they are condemned. They are likely on a train of their own, even now. To risk precious lives who might help us here at home … You ask much."

We drove in silence after that, each lost in memories and fears of our own troubled pasts and uncertain futures.

# Chapter Twenty-Two
# Thomas

*"Oh, Roberto. I like ... I don't know how to kiss, or I would kiss you. Where do the noses go? Always I wonder where the noses would go. They're not in the way, are they? I always thought they would be in the way. Look, I can do it myself."*

QUOTE FROM THE FILM *FOR WHOM THE BELL TOLLS*, 1943

The drive to Amsterdam felt eternal. According to Fons, the Nazis tightly controlled traffic into and out of the city, particularly across the bridges from Almere and on the northern end of the city. For that reason, we took a circuitous route, nearly entering the city of Utrecht fifteen miles south of our target, then wound around Uithoorn, Aalsmeer, through Hoofddorp, to enter Amsterdam from the western side, as far from a direct route as possible. The hour-and-a-half trip became a four-hour tour of Holland's heartland.

"You think he'll sleep the whole way there?" I asked as I glanced into the back seat when we were about halfway through the trip.

James stared at the road ahead. "Probably. Whatever the doctor gave him knocked him out."

"I guess it could be worse," I said, earning a sideways glance. "He could be the goofy Fons who was high on morphine. Imagine four hours stuck in a car with that."

James chuckled. "Right you are. Although, he is an amusing fellow when he's high."

I grinned, remembering his silly outbursts. Even the ones in Dutch that none of us could understand had sounded hysterical.

As the outskirts of Amsterdam came into view, with a few multi-story buildings towering in the distance, something in the pit of my stomach clenched. "Is that a giant Nazi flag?"

James followed where I pointed. "Bloody hell."

"Guess it's time for buttholes to pucker."

James nearly spat a laugh. "For what?"

"Time to get into character and on guard."

His cheeks were pinched from his grin. "You Americans …"

I glanced at my watch. "It's nearly eleven o'clock. Where do you think Dr. Kuiper is leading us?"

"I would guess a safe house."

Sure enough, ten minutes later, the doctor's black sedan pulled into a residential area, then stopped on a narrow side street. With his motor running, his door opened and he waved for one of us.

"I'll go. Keep the car running."

James rolled his eyes. "Yes, dear."

I glanced back before closing my door. "Remember to pucker."

Sikes pulled the truck past the doctor's car and stepped out to meet in the middle.

"Quickly, I need to give you instructions," Kuiper said without preamble. "The safe house is four doors down on the right, number four-oh-six. There is an alley two blocks down on the right. The street lights have been out for years and our people ensure they remain dark. Park one vehicle there and walk to the back of the safe house. The other vehicle should park one block west in the parking lot of the abandoned bank building. There are always cars parked there, so it will not raise suspicion."

He paused, eyeing us each, then continued. "Remember, go to the back of the house. There are two doors. Only on the right door, knock one time, pause, then knock two times.""Why don't we just go in together? You can vouch for us," Sikes asked.

"It does not work that way. Please, just do as I ask. We need to break up now. We have stood in this street too long already."

Without waiting for a reply, the doctor folded himself back into his car and slammed the door. Sikes glanced at me. "I'll take the bank. You get the alley. See you in a few."

"Aye, aye, skipper." I gave him a two-fingered salute.

A quarter-hour later, the five of us stood outside the two doors on the back of number four-oh-six. Well, four of us stood. James and I had Fons slumped across our shoulders. We'd had to haul him down the street as though our friend had drunk one too many pints at breakfast, which, looking back on that day, wasn't a very plausible cover. Will gave me a sympathetic shrug of his brows.

*Knock. Knock, knock.*

Sikes rapped his knuckles next to a knocker shaped like a canoe.

A moment later, the door opened and a young girl, no older than fifteen, appeared in the opening. As I looked more closely, the girl's eyes held many more years than her age implied.

"Come in," she said in flawless German.

We stepped inside to find a humble home with neatly painted walls and simple furniture. Colorful rugs covered hardwood floors throughout rooms and hallways alike.

Artwork depicting small boats on peaceful waters adorned the walls, though I noticed a few places where pictures appeared to have been removed. Unfaded paint stood out against the washed-out surrounding wall.

"I will show you to your rooms where you can clean up and rest. Are you hungry?" the girl asked as we climbed the narrow wooden stairs.

"Yes, very," Will said. He was always hungry.

"I will see what can be done."

As she pointed to the first of several empty rooms in a home that was far larger than it appeared from the street, Will asked, "Is the doctor here? Should we be meeting with someone soon?"

"My father works during the day and will not return until well after dark." She turned back toward the open door. "There are three rooms up here and another in the basement."

"Why don't I take this room with Fons, so I can keep an eye on him," James said.

The girl stepped out of the doorway, then pointed to the room across the hall. "That room only has one bed. The bathroom is there, next to that room."

"Woman's prerogative," Sparrow said, elbowing Sikes as she stepped past the big man.

"Aw, honey, really? I hate being split up like this," he said with a wicked gleam in his eye.

Sparrow patted his cheek, more slap than tender pat. "You'll survive, dear. Being apart will make being together again that much more special."

Sikes grunted, his equivalent of a laugh.

"I put the doctor in the room at the end of the hall earlier," the girl said, ignoring the adults' banter.

"Which means my brother and I will go downstairs," Will said, and my pulse quickened. We hadn't been alone together since before the operation in Emden's harbor. I tried not to glance his way, but was sure he snuck a peek as the girl flowed past.

She led us back down the stairs, through a sitting room, then down another even more narrow set of stairs that creaked with each step. Halfway down the steep decline, she reached up and pulled a cord, lighting a naked bulb attached to the ceiling. A lone door stood at the foot of the stairs.

The girl lifted a thin chain from around her neck and unlocked the door with a key that hung from it. We followed her into a wine cellar lined with dust-covered bottles.

"Whoa," Will said. "This is a lot of wine."

Without care for where we were or the girl standing before us, I blurted out, "You should see the cellar at my uncle's ..."

I clamped my mouth shut and tried to narrow my widened eyes.

Will grinned, then leaned down to whisper toward the girl, "Our uncle is more drunk than connoisseur, but Wilhelm is a dreamer."

The girl scrunched her nose at Thomas, then looked at me, shook her head, and stepped across the room, as if to avoid whatever strangeness clung to the pair of us. At the far end, where the light barely reached the corners, several large casks consumed the wall. The girl reached up and pulled the cork from the third cask, and the entire wall swung open.

"Now that's impressive," Will said, as I stared, open-mouthed.

The girl stepped past the barrel-door and flicked a switch on the wall, illuminating a large room with a desk at one end and a long conference table along the other. Multicolored push pins dotted maps of Dutch cities that lined the walls.

"My father meets here."

I glanced around, focusing on the maps. There was so much detail. The pins indicated the location of resistance cells or safe houses, maybe communications relays? There were so many it was hard to make any sense of them. When I looked toward the far end of the room where the desk held court, the girl had stepped up to the wall, flicked a switch, and slid a massive blackboard set on rollers until it smacked into the side wall. She then pressed her hands into the rough stones of the wall and began shoving with all of her weight.

"What's she doing?" Will whispered.

Before I could answer, a seam appeared and the middle third of the wall opened on hinges that must've been mounted on the interior. Warm yellow light flooded out of the room beyond.

The girl looked over her shoulder. "Come on, then."

Will and I exchanged a glance, then followed her through the opening into a small room with a bed, nightstand, and one wooden chair pressed against the far wall. One lonely, unadorned lightbulb swung from the ceiling. While the place was tidy, the walls looked like some animal had gnawed them out of the stone slab that ran beneath the house.

The girl planted her fists on her hips. "The bed is not made for two. Your comfort is less important than your safety." Her tone was as flat as her stare. "There is no restroom down here. You will need to climb the stairs to the main floor to clean up or whatever. I should have lunch ready in an hour or so. Feel free to relax until then."

As she turned to walk away, Will said, "You haven't told us your name."

She glanced back and offered the first smile we'd seen part her lips. "No, I haven't."

A click sounded when the stone closed behind her.

The silence that followed was oppressive. I didn't hear her feet on the floor outside as she strode away. There were no noises from creaky boards above. There was nothing, save Will's breathing from where he stood a few paces away.

"Should we have asked how to use that secret door? We might be stuck down here," he said, running a hand across the nearly invisible seam in the stone. "Did you see how thick that was? It's like we're in a vault."

"Maybe we are," I shrugged. "They probably use this as a safe house for people hiding from the Nazis."

He grunted. "That would be us, remember?"

"Oh, right. I almost forgot, harrowing escape and all."

He turned fully square to me, his eyes searching my face as though examining me fully for the first time since we'd been reunited.

"Are you ... are you okay?" He was tentative, almost shy, as if he wasn't sure where we stood. I couldn't decide whether to laugh or cry ... or let my heart race away with the innocent, unabashed love flowing through his eyes.

My only answer was to step forward and grip his face in both hands, pulling his lips into mine. There wasn't anything gentle in that kiss. It was hunger and passion, pent-up longing, and months of fear, all combined like some explosive experiment waiting for its fuse to be lit.

And I couldn't get enough.

The taste of him filled my mouth. His scent flooded into me, and his arms pulled me tight like a drowning man clinging to a raft.

"God, I missed you so damn much," I said when we came up for air.

Tears streaked his cheeks and his chest heaved. "Will?"

He pressed his forehead into my shoulder.

"I thought I'd lost you, Thomas," he sobbed. "I thought you were gone. I tried to say goodbye. They made me say it. I know they meant well, but I knew you were alive. I could feel it. At least, that's what I told myself."

"I'm right here," I choked out, as I fought to keep myself together.

"Thomas ... I was losing hope. I'm so sorry. I didn't want to. I would never give up on you. You know that. But they said your survival was near impossible ... God, I'm so sorry."

I lifted his chin with my fingers, forcing his eyes to meet mine. "I'm right here, babe. I will *never* leave you again."

Slowly, strength returned to his eyes. "Swear it," he demanded

"I swear it."

"On what?" His lips twisted upward, mischief replacing strength.

"On my family's fortune."

He winced. "Not good enough."

"On everything holy and good."

He cocked his head and quirked his lips. "You're not religious."

I coughed a laugh, as I racked my brain for something meaningful enough to get us past this silly exchange, but the pout of his mouth had turned my brain to mush and my knees to jelly.

"I swear on the Old Timer," I said, invoking the ancient tree that had sheltered our first true embrace.

A brilliant smile crept into his eyes. "Fuck you."

"What?" I said, suddenly alarmed.

"That was the *perfect* swear."

And our lips crashed together again.

# Chapter Twenty-Three

# Will



Quote from the film *The More the Merrier*, 1943

Thomas snatched my cap and tossed it against the far wall, then his fingers dove into my hair, kneading my scalp. I'd lost track of how long we'd stood there kissing. Time didn't matter. The world didn't matter. Only Thomas mattered.

Then I remembered where we were.

"Thomas," I breathed. "Should we be doing this? Down here? In this house?"

He brushed back a rebellious lock of hair that had fallen across my forehead, a smile parting his lips. "We're in a vault behind stone so thick we wouldn't hear bombs falling. There's got to be some kind of lock on that door. Let's bolt it tight."

I started toward the door, but his arm shot out and held me back. "You, sit. Doc said for you to stay off that foot, and I would be a terrible nurse if I let you disobey."

"Nurse?" I teased, lowering myself onto the end of the bed.

"Whatever. You need to stay off your feet, and I like that prescription."

I flopped back, laughing, as he fiddled around where the door met the wall. A moment later, a metallic fingernail scraped across a chalkboard.

"That, my good man, was a bolt sliding into stone. I'm fairly certain Hitler himself couldn't get in here now. And we already established how poorly sound escapes."

I propped up on my elbows. "Whatever shall we do, then?"

He was straddling me before I could sit up, his fingers fumbling with my shirt's buttons.

"I'm going to remind you what you've been missing."

He bent over and kissed me as one button after another flew free. Not having to be told twice, I reached up and returned the favor. A few kisses later, both our shirts had joined my cap on the far side of the room, and Thomas's full weight was pressing me into the center of the bed.

There was no more hesitating, no more wondering or questioning.

We were back together and ready to make up for lost time.

I rubbed my hands down his stomach, feeling the hardness of his muscles, then grabbed the top of his pants and tore his belt free.

"Oh, he's feisty," he teased.

"Get those fucking pants off before I use this belt."

His eyes widened, and I leaned up and took his bottom lip in my teeth.

"Ow!" he squirmed.

"Naked. Now, sailor."

He leapt off the bed, stepped on one leg of his pants, then wriggled out of the other.

"Take mine off," I ordered.

"Dear God, what happened to you while I was gone?" His brows were nearly at his hairline.

"Definitely not this."

He gripped the top of my pants, feeling for my underwear and gripping them with his fingers. In one motion, I went from half-dressed to fully naked and as hard as the stone surrounding us.

His eyes traveled the length of my body, settling on my twitching cock.

"Oh, I've missed him too."

"Shut up, sailor. Underwear. Now."

He glanced down, realizing he was the only one with clothing. A quick tug and shimmy corrected that horrid error.

Then we were in the same position as before, his full weight driving me deep into the lumpy mattress, only this time his skin pressed against mine as his tongue found my earlobe.

I groaned. "You remembered my lobes."

That made him laugh and flop his head on the pillow beside my ear. "Yes, I remembered you like your lobes licked. Did you think ... oh, never mind."

His teeth were the next things I felt, grazing and nipping with the perfect pressure to make me squirm beneath him.

I gripped his back, reveling in the heat, exploring his skin—

"Thomas." He pulled back, concern in his eyes. "What? Are you okay? Am I hurting—"

I traced a line on his back, then another—lines I'd never felt before.

"What are these?" I asked. "Sit up. Let me look." His eyes wouldn't meet mine. "Babe, it's nothing."

"Up and turn, mister. You should know I will have my way today, so stop resisting."

Slowly, he sat up and turned so he faced away from me. So I could see the lines.

Red welts.

"Thomas, what did they do to you?"

His shoulders rose and fell. "It was nothing. Most of the time, they just asked the same questions over and over. It was boring, really."

"Thomas Arthur Jacobs DuPont, don't you fucking lie to me."

This time his chest filled, then he blew out a long breath. "Did Fons—"

'No!" he almost shouted, then calmed. "Sorry, no. Fons was never anything but kind."

When he spoke, his words were quiet and small, as though giving them voice somehow offered them power.

"It was the first day, the first day I was in jail," he said. "The chief wanted to set the tone, I guess, show me what I was in for if I didn't answer his questions."

I waited, but he didn't continue.

"Did you? Answer his questions, I mean?"

A rueful laugh escaped as he turned to face me. "I couldn't. Will, I didn't remember anything. The whole time I was with that family, the ones who found me, I couldn't even remember my name. Well, other than Wilhelm, I remembered that. Who knows why?"

"That must've been awful."

He nodded. "Tell me about it. To not even know who you are? I knew I was somewhere I wasn't supposed to be, but I couldn't even remember being American. German came out like it was my native tongue. I guess that was a good thing. If I'd spoken English ..."

I put a hand on his arm. "What? What is it?"

"I *did* speak English. At least, that's what the chief said. He knew I'd spoken English in my sleep. Someone in that family must've told them. Everything moved so fast, I barely had a moment to think it all through."

My hand rose to press against his cheek. "You're safe now."

He grunted a laugh. "We're in the middle of occupied Holland. Safe isn't exactly the word I would use."

I patted his cheek, a little harder than a caress. "You know what I mean, asshole."

He grinned. "There's the man I fell for."

I couldn't stop the smile exploding across my face. "Yeah, here he is."

Thomas reached up and cupped his hand against my cheek, mirroring my gesture, though with far more gentleness as he pulled me toward him and kissed me deeply. Gone was the wild passion of before. Something far deeper wrapped its cloak about us, enveloping us in its warmth.

Our lips grazed against each other, barely touching, yet filling my chest with light. His tongue slipped past my teeth, teasing my own. Both his hands now held my head, his fingers again woven in my hair, nails digging lightly into my scalp.

I could barely move, barely breathe. In those moments, all the waiting and longing, all the tears and torturous nights, all of it vanished, and the glorious devotion in Thomas's words filled my heart.

He gripped my shoulders and laid me on my side, joining to face me without letting our lips part. Despite the cool air in our cavern bedroom, his sweat slicked my body and eased the friction of our skin.

He rolled me on my back again, this time staying on his side to kiss my neck, his hand feeling its way across my chest, down my stomach. His lips wedged in that soft space above my collarbone he claimed to be his favorite place in the world, and a satisfied grunt tickled my skin.

When he reached my chest, kissing and kissing, his lips wrapped around one nipple, gently teasing, his tongue circling, edging the tip until sensations sparkled across my skin.

"Like that, do you," he growled.

"Uh-huh."

Then he bit down, and I nearly leapt from the bed.

Strong hands held me in place, pressed against my chest and shoulder, as his teeth ground back and forth, sending shock waves of pleasure and pain to every cell in my body. My cock twitched, and I could feel his lips curl against my skin.

When he released my nipple, I breathed a moment's relief.

Too soon.

His hand gripped my balls, pulling them down, and he swallowed my cock until it struck deep in his throat. My body spasmed. He gripped tighter. Then his head rose and fell again … and again. I grabbed his hair, yanked it, shoved his head down, willing myself deeper down his throat, begging him to devour me. My other hand gripped the bedrail, muscles straining, as a waterfall of pressure surged through me.

"Oh no. Not a chance," he said, looking up with my dick an inch from his lips. "Somebody's out of practice."

His shit-eating grin would've been too much if I'd had any control left. I whimpered, desperate for him to take me again.

A finger slipped between my cheeks.

"Oh, Thomas! Shit. I haven't—"

"Shh." His other hand reached up and pressed a finger to my lips. "I don't care."

His finger reached my hole and wiggled slowly, teasing the hairs around it.

"Oh, whoa, wow," I said, artfully.

He pressed against me, not entering, just testing.

My chest swelled with an intake of breath.

"Easy, baby. Let me take care of you."

"Oh, please. Yes," I begged. We were way past me pretending to be in control. Thomas could have me any way he wanted now.

His finger appeared and then vanished into his mouth, coming out coated and dripping.

My cock twitched. He grinned.

The finger vanished and slid past my guard.

"Oh!"

"Relax," he said, the soothing tone of a snake charmer, then slid a bit deeper. "I've got you."

"Yes, you do, Thomas. Dammit, I'm so fucking yours," I said, as his finger slipped in past the knuckle.

"I've dreamed of this so many times. I'm going to fill you up so full."

His fist pressed against my butt as the last of his finger reached its goal.

"Oh, fuck, Thomas."

He pulled back, crooking his finger, tickling inside me in just the right way.

I couldn't fight back the shiver.

His tongue found my nipple again, as his finger slid nearly out, then back in again.

My body couldn't decide whether to twitch or roll or shiver or—

His tongue dropped to the head of my cock and all thought fled.

"Ahh." It swirled around the edge, just under where the skin is tight and sensitive, making me jump and spasm ... and then a second finger joined the first.

"Oh, God, Thomas ..."

He shoved inside, this time harder and rougher, while taking my cock in his mouth.

My body quaked.

His other hand gripped my chest, kneading me like fucking dough that ... but I'd already risen.

And that made me laugh.

Thomas froze.

I looked down to find him staring up at me, one hand on my chest, my cock in his mouth, and two fingers up my ass.

I really tried not to grin. I really, really tried.

"Wha—" the word muffled through cock and tongue.

I laughed out loud.

His fingers slipped out.

"Oh, please no," I said.

He let my cock flop free.

"What's funny?"

He wasn't annoyed, just curious.

"It's dumb. Just keep going."

He sat up, crossed his legs Indian style, then crossed his arms over his chest. "Nope. Speak."

I tossed my head back on the pillow. It had been so damn hot. "It's just ... I mean ... you were ... your hand was kneading my chest."

He cocked his head. "And?"

"Like bread. Like kneading bread ... but I'd already risen." I gave him a sheepish grin.

He didn't laugh. He didn't even move. "That's terrible."

"What?"

"You seriously laughed during hot finger pounding and cock sucking because of a bad bread joke?"

That made me laugh again.

"And there he goes again."

I laughed harder, unable to control it. Before I knew what was happening, Thomas had my legs in the air, thrown over his shoulders, and his fingers were digging into my ribs.

"I'll teach you to laugh at my fingers, dough boy."

Tears streamed down my face, and I could barely breathe. I couldn't remember the last time I'd laughed—

And then his cock shoved inside me, and laughter stuck in my throat.

He pulled back, then slammed into me again so hard my head nearly smacked the headboard.

"Oh, shit!"

He gripped my shoulders, braced himself, and shoved again, spreading my legs wide and pressing them back with his weight. I might've been tight a moment before, but I was now opened wider than I'd ever been in my life.

Stars danced in my eyes and pain surged down my legs.

"Fuck!" I shouted, almost calling a halt, but Thomas didn't hear. He wasn't listening. In my heedless, reckless laughter, he'd somehow found a split second—and a bottle—to slick himself and return for a full frontal assault.

And this sailor was on a mission.

By the fourth time he pounded me into the pillow, pain had almost been replaced by pleasure.

Almost.

Then he gripped my ankles and spread me further.

"Oh—"

I don't know what I was about to say. It didn't matter. Nothing mattered.

Thomas found a way to crawl inside me and shove his entire body up my ass.

And holy mother of pearl, it was the most incredible thing I'd ever felt.

Sweat poured off him. I reached up, pressing a palm to his chest, feeling his muscles taut and flexed. He was exquisite, and he was inside me, filling me. The thought was more than heady, it sent emotions more powerful than any pleasure or pain erupting like tiny volcanoes. Lava raged across my skin. The harder he dove into me, the hotter it became. I didn't warm. I burned.

"I love you so damn much, Will Shaw," he shouted, and all those emotions burst brighter than any explosion. I lost myself in the moment, in this man, in his love and our bodies, the sweat and heat and passion.

That rush from before redoubled, raging in my gut. Thomas grabbed my cock and jerked it hard as he slammed so far inside I thought he might come out my mouth.

"Thomas!" I shouted, my body clenching.

"Don't you fucking come," he raged.

He shoved my legs further back over my head, lifting my ass into the air, then ground into me from an angle that—

"Oh, holy fuck!" I shouted. "Right there, Thomas. God, don't stop. Harder. Fuck me harder."

He did.

My eyes squeezed tight. I grabbed his arms, his rock-hard arms. That sent another shiver.

God, I loved him.

He hit that spot. My body rocked.

He struck again. And again.

And faster.

And deeper.

"Fuck!"

I couldn't hold back any more. Everything in me begged for release, a dam held back by a paper veil, swelling and raging, demanding—

"Ahh!" I shouted as the first wave shot free, coating his chest.

He braced himself and pumped faster.

I shot again.

His body flexed, his arms tightened, his abs clenched.

Then he shouted, a primal, thunderous roar, and I felt liquid warmth flow deep inside.

But he didn't stop. He pushed again and again. Shooting over and over.

Until, sweat soaked and quaking, he doubled over on top of me, his cock still pulsing within, and whispered, "I love you so damn much."

# Chapter Twenty-Four
# **Will**



DUTCH PROVERB, ORIGIN UNKNOWN

There was no bathroom in the basement.

"Is there anything we can clean up with down here?" Thomas asked as he stumbled around the grotto of a bedroom, naked as a streaker in the park. I had to admit, it was a nice thing to watch. "There's no sink, no towels. I don't even see ... oh, wait, here's tissues."

He raised a small box of tissues in triumph, ripped a few free, then tossed the box toward the bed where I still lay sprawled out, a combination of sweaty and sticky, like some disgusting salted caramel left out in the sun.

We'd barely wiped off when the vault-like door rattled. I thought I might have to peel Thomas off the ceiling.

"Quick, get dressed," he hissed, darting about the room to collect our underwear and pants. The door rattled again, but I still couldn't hear anything from the other side. It really was as thick as a bank vault.

A moment later, Thomas pulled the latch, freeing the bolt, and dragged the door open by a leather loop dangling from the edge by a thumb-sized screw.

The girl stood on the other side, her arms crossed, and one brow raised.

"Uh, sorry. We were taking a nap and didn't—"

She held up a palm. "The Nazis hunt more than Jews. I am familiar with *brothers* like you two. My own actual brother was forced onto a train just last year. I believe you may have a shared interest."

Thomas looked back, his mouth open and jaw fixed. I could barely choke out a word.

"It is no matter. This house provides shelter for all. My father would have it no other way."

Thomas turned back to face her. "Uh, I'm sorry, you kind of, I mean, I hadn't ... shit ... oh, I'm sorry. I shouldn't—"

Her lips quirked with her other brow. "Curse? You are truly worried about saying bad words?" She shook her head, and I swear she chuckled. "You Americans. Come upstairs. Lunch is ready."

She turned, but Thomas stepped forward and cleared his throat, causing her to glance back.

Her brows were still arched. "I will not tell your friends. That is, as long as you clean up before lunch. I smell him on you."

She winked, then turned and vanished out the far door to the map room.

Thomas stood in the doorway, one hand on either side, bracing himself, as though he might tumble forward at any moment.

"Well, that was something," I said.

"We've been careless," he muttered.

"What?" I got to my feet and hobbled toward him as he turned back.

"What if she hadn't been so accepting? Or whatever you call it. I'm not sure there's a right word in this world."

"Thomas—"

"No. Will, think about it. She could tell everyone. Are you so sure they would stay with us? Hell, she could turn us in to the Nazis, and then it would be you and me on one of those trains. We can't be so—"

I stepped forward and pressed my fingers to his lips. "Thomas, it's alright. We're safe now. Everyone in this house is a friend and an ally. I'm not suggesting you put on a wig and heels and dance a jig, but I think we can take a moment's breath."

He slumped against the cold stone of the doorway. "It's just ... I was headed toward that fate, Will. I knew it. I was going to die. I can't let that happen to you."

I closed the last of the gap between us and gripped his shoulders. "We're okay, Thomas. *I'm* okay. Just breathe."

He rested his forehead against mine, and a tremble startled me. I wrapped my arms around him and pulled him close. "Hey, you. We're okay," I whispered into his ear, willing my strength into him.

"Uh, guys." Sparrow's voice from across the map room made me jump back. Thomas was pressed firmly against the stone. "It's just me. I came down to check on you two."

She crossed the room to stand across the desk from us, her eyes roaming the table, then the maps, then returning to us. "This is some basement."

Thomas grunted nervously.

"Yeah, that girl shoved us in a vault. Check it out," I said, waving her forward.

She sniffed dramatically as she passed Thomas, then wrinkled her nose and smiled. "Good for you, Will. About time you got laid."

Thomas pushed himself off the stone and fled into the map room. "I'm going to clean up. I'll ... see you up there ... I mean, upstairs ... for lunch. Oh, fuck it."

He shot out of the room faster than the girl had.

Sparrow nearly doubled over. "I don't remember him being quite that shade when we were in the UK."

I laughed, something I'd done precious little of lately. It felt amazing.

"You should be more careful, Will," she said, her tone sobering. "I know, you just got him back, but still … who knows how Sikes or James would react? And Fons. We forget about him. He is a policeman. Or that girl and her father, for that matter."

I blew out a sigh and laced up my shoes. "That girl called us out and she's just fine, from what she said. I'd be more worried about our good doctor than anyone. Fons too."

She nodded, but remained silent as I stood.

"You're right. We'll be more careful from here on out. It was just … God, Sarah … I have him back. He's *really* back."

A maelstrom of emotions I'd thought were in check threatened to shatter the basement's calm. "He was dead and now he's coming home."

She wrapped her arms around me and pulled me close as fresh sobs shook us both. "I really am so happy for you both. You are such good men, but you're better together."

A few heartbeats passed, then I pulled back and stared into her eyes.

"What?" Her brow furrowed.

I barely knew how to form the words. "No one's ever said anything like that to me before."

"Well, it's true."

"I know. I mean, I believe it. I am a better man because of Thomas, and I like to think I help him too." I ran a hand through my hair. "It's just ... the whole world hates us for who we are, but what you just said ... Sarah, thank you."

The last words squeaked out as my voice broke. Her arms were around me so fast, I nearly lost my breath.

"You two are precious to me. Please know that, Will."

I buried my face in her shoulder and let the comfort of a mother's love flood into me. That's what it felt like, at least. My own mother would never ...

I let that thought die quickly.

"Uh, guys, should I leave you two alone?" Thomas snarked from across the desk.

I glanced over Sparrow's shoulder without letting her release me. "Why'd you slink back down here? Good to see your stealth skills haven't gone the way of your sense of humor."

"I'll have you know, I am as witty as I am sneaky." He offered a mocking bow. "Now, come upstairs. Our un-named mistress has lunch prepared and it smells great."

"Her name is Nora," Sparrow said, stepping back and straightening her shirt.

"Nora? She told you her name?" I asked.

"Of course she did. She introduced herself when we first arrived." Sparrow looked from me to Thomas, then snorted. "What now?"

"She made it sound like a secret, like she never told people her name," Thomas explained.

Sparrow cackled at that, patting my butt then stepping out into the map room. "I think she's playing with you two. She's got quite the sharp tongue. You might know that if you hadn't spent the last two hours locked in a cave."

Thomas's face fell. "Two hours?" Sparrow's grin widened as her head slowly bobbed. "Gotta say, I'm impressed."

She patted Thomas's chest on the way by, then smacked his butt, earning a welp and a hop. Her laughter could be heard echoing all the way from the top of the stairs.

Lunch passed without incident. Sikes, James, and Dr. Kuiper showed no hint of discovery. Sparrow and Nora exchanged a few pointed glances—and an occasional grin—but the meal was otherwise uneventful.

"We should take some time to think through our next steps," Sikes said, reclaiming command.

"Would it be alright if we met downstairs, Nora?" Thomas asked, emphasizing her name, as if to get a rise out of the girl.

She did not rise. "That is what it was designed for, meetings and such."

She locked eyes with me when she said "and such," and a tickle of a grin teased one corner of her mouth.

"Thank you," Thomas said, quickly standing.

"Take these with you," Nora said, motioning to a plate half-filled with stroopwafels. The Dutch caramel waffle cookies had James licking his fingers throughout most of the meal. "I will bring tea once the table is cleared."

We filed down into the map room, where Thomas and I quickly settled into chairs around the conference table, while the others examined the maps and push pins.

Sikes whistled. "They are far more organized than I thought. For a mostly non-violent movement, they have a *lot* going on."

"You can tell all that from those pins?" I asked.

Sikes turned and took a seat across from me. "I'm not one hundred percent sure what each represents, but based on placement, the red look like radios, green might be safe houses, and yellow ... I'm guessing those are part of the exit."

"The exit?" Sparrow asked, sitting next to me.

"Yeah, every occupied country has an exit, an escape route used to help those being hunted flee to Allied territory."

"From the last reports I read back in London, the Dutch route hasn't been all that successful," James said.

"It has been a failure."

James and Dr. Kuiper sat as each of us stared at the injured policeman. Fons hadn't spoken a word since we'd joined the group upstairs. I'd assumed whatever drugs the doctor had given him had stolen his personality, but the way his face lined with those words spoke of far deeper pain. His voice was barely a whisper as his head drooped.

"My father tried to help. He truly did." A hand rose to cover part of his face. "The Nazis ... when they first arrived, they were everywhere, soldiers and men in the black of the SS. We were not the first to fall under their heel, but we did fall quickly. They were eager to 'purify' our country. That is how they said it."

Thomas quickly translated his words. "How many—?" he began.

Fons shook his head. "I do not know numbers. No one except the Nazis truly knows, but they brag of removing most Jews from Holland, and I believe it is not false pride speaking."

Fons began murmuring a prayer; the rest of our heads bowed in silence.

"We need to focus on what we can control, on what is ahead of us," Sikes said, shattering the cavern's quiet. "Fons, you said the escape route performed poorly when the Nazis first arrived. What about now?"

The policeman's head lifted as he listened to Thomas's translation, and he replied in a low voice. "They do not care so much anymore. Their eyes are turned east and toward their fatherland. The routes work fairly well now—assuming there is anyone left to shuttle out of this damned place. Most simply shelter in place, praying for the day they might come out of hiding and return home."

"How would it work?" Sikes asked.

"You saw the pins on the map. You would be split into pairs and shuffled from one pin to the next, each pair taking different routes out of the city, then out of Holland and into Belgium. Our friends in Brussels take over from there to get you into France."

"From one occupied country into the next," Thomas muttered.

Fons scoffed. "Do not fool yourself. All of Europe is occupied, no matter what flag the Nazis allow to fly overhead. Any escape requires hundreds or thousands of miles beneath the swastika."

Thomas shifted in his seat. "This is fine, but we aren't trying to escape. We need a way into Germany."

The shift in the group's mood felt as though Sikes had stood and tossed the table into the stone wall.

Thomas looked around, his eyes wide. "What? We discussed this already. We can't leave Heinz and Adam to die."

Sikes stood so fast his chair nearly tipped backward. "We did talk about this and it's insane. You still want to go into the heart of enemy territory where those men, if they're even still alive, are likely surrounded by an entire platoon? Even if you could get into the country without getting caught or shot, how the hell do you plan to retrieve your men, return to Holland, then make the million-mile trek back home? The whole thing is nuts."

Thomas sat back, his eyes steel and his voice calm. "The question is not 'whether' but 'how' we will do it."

Sikes stalked to the far end of the room and pretended to stare at a map.

James, who had also been relatively silent most of the day, leaned forward. "You know I am loath to agree with Sikes on pretty much any topic, but he does have a point. You are not proposing racing across a battlefield to sling a soldier over your shoulder and haul him to safety. You propose raising your arms and walking directly into a line of infantry, all with fully loaded rifles trained on your chest. You will not survive this, and, I am sad to say, neither will your men. It they are alive, they are already dead."

"No!" Sparrow slammed her palm on the table, jerking every head toward her, even that of Sikes from across the room. "We will not leave Heinz to burn in German ovens. This plan is not optional. You two signed up to help us save Wilhelm, and you kept your word. There is no shame in you going home now. But we have a mission to plan."

"This isn't about shame—" Sikes began to object.

"Sikes, shut the fuck up!" Sparrow screamed. I'd never heard her raise her voice like that. From the stunned looks on the faces around the table, no one had. "You two don't even speak German. You *can't* go with us. All we ask is that you help us make a plan with the least shitty odds. Can you do that? Can you *just* do that?"

She slumped back in her chair, her body limp from the surge but her eyes blazing brighter than ever.

Sikes returned her gaze so long I thought he might argue, but the big man simply nodded once and retook his seat. "Of course we can do that. Where do we start?"

# Chapter Twenty-Five
# Thomas

*"My mother drove the bicycle, and Freddie sat on the back and was shooting. Because they were girls, nobody noticed them."*

HANNIE MENGER [1]

"This is useless," I said, tossing myself back in my chair. "Without Nora's father, we have no idea what these people are even capable of."

We'd been in the cellar for more than two hours, studying maps and push pins as though any of us could truly

---

1. Daughter of Hannie Schaft, Dutch resister dubbed "the girl with the red hair" by frustrated Nazis.

make sense of their hidden meaning. All we'd really accomplished was to sketch a plan to get James and Sikes out of Holland. The half-dozen ideas we'd batted about regarding our insertion into Germany were utter rubbish.

James favored driving to the border and crossing on foot, avoiding checkpoints by marching through farmland until we found a place to steal a car. He had no explanation for how we might avoid the watchful eyes of farmers or where we might find a car just waiting to be pinched. Fons ultimately nixed this idea with a description of random German patrols along the full length of the border, each with "shoot on sight" orders for any unwanted guests entering the fatherland.

Sikes returned us to the mission in Emden, suggesting we secure small vessels and paddle around the tip of Germany until we find uninhabited shoreline through which to make our incursion. No one could account for the multiple makeshift ports the Germans had established along their northern coast, or the untold number of soldiers and sailors who might spot a random boat bobbing offshore. Again, Fons put the nail in the coffin with a robust description of the turbulent and frigid North Sea waters this time of year.

For his part, our resident policeman lobbied for a more clandestine approach. "It would be a simple thing to disguise each of you as German farmers. You already have a German-made truck. If the LO is as good as they claim, they should be able to create German documents for each of you. Why not simply drive across as a returning family after selling your goods in Holland?"

Pandemonium erupted as his last words fell upon the table.

"There's no way those papers would fool anyone in the SS. I don't care how good they are," Sikes groused.

James was more polite but equally pointed. "And where is this farm to which they would return? Surely, border guards would ask where home is for these fine folk. Does this cover extend further than a truck and some papers? If they are to pass other checkpoints along the roadways, it would need to. This is simply too thin."

Dr. Kuiper suggested we pretend to be Dutch physicians ordered to travel to Berlin to assist with the war-wounded.

In his typical eloquence, Sikes summed up this last idea with, "We might as well put a bullet in your heads now and save you the trip."

The good doctor lowered his head and stared into his folded hands.

Nora saved us from beating our heads against the stone walls, appearing in the opening of the stairway.

"Dinner is prepared. My father should be home anytime now. Come, while it is hot. Stamppot is not so good when it is cold."

"Stamppot?" Sparrow whispered to Will. He shrugged and shook his head.

During the hours in the cellar, James's hand had rarely been without a stroopwafel oozing its caramel goodness onto his fingers. As we rose to head upstairs, the Brit's eyes darted about, then he snatched up the last of the cookies, greedily devouring it as we rounded the table.

"Stamppot is delicious. Think bangers and mash, but with a twist," he said through stuffed cheeks.

"How does he stay so trim?" Sparrow muttered a tad too loudly.

James laughed and patted his flat stomach. "I could eat the whole of Holland and you would never see it. Consider me blessed."

We arrived in the dining room to a pleasant surprise: the table was set and two massive platters were filled to overflowing in the center, one containing the stamppot and the other cut sausages.

"Whoa," Will said, staring at the sausage pile while sliding his chair back. "Isn't there a war on with rationing and all?"

Nora shrugged. "The Nazis like ration stamps. As long as you present them, you get food. One thing our people are quite skilled at is printing things." She placed her index finger over her lips, then said, "Don't tell them."

Sparrow wrapped an arm around the girl, giving her a half-hug. "I like this one. Can we keep her?"

I wasn't sure if it was Sparrow's question or the horrified look in Nora's eyes, but the entire group devolved into laughter, lighting the poor girl's cheeks red and sending her scooting into the kitchen.

"I believe you scared the poor rabbit," James said with a smirk.

We left plans for escape or incursion into enemy territory in the basement, giving dinner an almost festive atmosphere. Even Sikes managed a smile or two, though his dour countenance remained throughout most of the meal.

Dr. Kuiper was about to drop his napkin on his plate when the front door rattled and a man of indeterminate middle age stepped in. He hung his hat on a wall peg, then turned and took in his guests.

"Papa!" Nora shot to her feet and raced into the entranceway, reminding me of how a small child might greet a returning parent. The man wrapped his arms around the girl and pressed his cheek into the top of her head.

"Take nothing for granted in the midst of a war, isn't that what we're told?" Sparrow's voice was more sigh than words.

The man looked over his daughter's head and spoke so we could all hear. "Would you introduce me to our guests, my dear Nora?"

She led him by the hand to the table, motioning with an open palm to each of us.

"You remembered all our names?" Will asked.

Nora blushed at the praise.

"She is brilliant, is she not?" The man beamed, then kissed his daughter's head, again like a father might a much younger girl. It was, perhaps, the most touching gesture I'd seen since returning from captivity.

As Nora left his side, the man offered a tilt of his head. "Gentlemen and lady, welcome to our home. Please call me Adriaan."

With a practiced formality that somehow felt casual, Adriaan circled the table to shake each of our hands, a firm grip snapped up and down once.

Greetings complete, he looked to Nora and said, "I will take my dinner downstairs. There is much we must discuss and not a moment to waste."

"Yes, Papa," she said, all coldness in her features fully melted under her father's gaze.

"If you would follow me down, please," Adriaan said, stepping toward the stairs with a sly grin. "Feel free to bring your glasses. Planning can be such thirsty business, and not all the casks below are doorways."

The clouds around Sikes parted as he nearly elbowed Sparrow out of the way. "Ale? Whiskey? Don't keep a boy in suspense, Adriaan."

Our host's laughter was the peeling of merry bells at the holidays. "Come find out. It would be a crime to let an American die of thirst in my home."

"Are they always this happy?" Will whispered.

I shrugged my brows. "It's creeping me out a little, but I kind of like it too."

As he chuckled, Sparrow butted in. "Boys, soak it up. This is what making lemonade out of lemons looks like. We could all use a little more of it in our lives these days."

Sikes, never to be outdone, said, "Add vodka to that lemonade and I'm on board."

James groaned and called from halfway down the stairs, "Stop encouraging the cad. We are not rid of him quite yet."

Before letting us settle back into our chairs, Adriaan had each of us pass our glass to be filled at the spout of a barrel. Golden liquid flowed freely and nearly reached the brim before he handed it back.

"That's my kind of pour. You need Americans around these parts? I could stay a little longer if you're tending bar." Sikes lifted his glass and slurped to keep any from spilling over the edge.

Adriaan's amusement echoed off the stone, somehow brightening the dim cavern. "You would be welcome, my friend."

"See, we're friends. You kids need to treat me right now," he said toward us.

Sparrow stepped up and stabbed a finger into his meaty chest. "Act right and we will, big boy."

"At least you got the size—"

A chorus of "Oh" and "No," paired with a healthy round of laughter, drowned out whatever off-color words followed.

The moment we'd settled into our seats, Adriaan stood at the head and ended all laughter. "The SD man who was supposed to take Wilhelm into custody arrived in Amsterdam earlier today, forcing us to accelerate the plan. You must leave for Germany tonight."

# Chapter Twenty-Six
# Thomas



Anonymous survivor of a Nazi concentration camp

"SD? I thought he was SS," Sparrow whispered to Will.

Adriaan's sudden, raptor-like gaze snapped to her. "The *Sicherheitsdienst* is the security service within the seven-headed hydra that truly rules Germany. The SS are insidious, but it is the men of the SD who handle interrogations and high-level prisoners."

"Wait"—Sikes nearly dropped his half-empty glass on the table—"what did you say about leaving tonight?"

Adriaan sat. "Much of this day was spent planning, then rearranging that plan. As arranged, the Allies sent fighters to intercept the SD man's transport. Unfortunately, the Nazis brought an escort of their own. A dogfight ensued, and, while the transport received enough damage to make her inoperable for the moment, she was able to land. Our man inside *de bezetter*[1] reported a red-faced officer arriving late in the morning. He remained at the headquarters for approximately one hour then stormed out of the building with a low-level man chasing behind. It is our understanding he intends to drive back to Germany tomorrow. He was offered a return flight but refused to risk facing Allied fighters again."

"Why does that matter? Why do we need to rush because one Nazi is rattled and running home?" James asked.

"Because the orders for that scared little rat is to return with Wilhelm to Germany, collect your men who are currently held in a prison in Oldenburg, then question the three of them for information regarding the attack on the port." He paused to let that sink in, then raised his glass.

---

1. The Dutch people referred to the occupying Nazi government as "de bezetter," which translates to "the occupier" in English.

"And … because you will assume *his* identity as part of our plan."

"We're what?" I nearly spat across the table.

Adriaan folded his hands before him and spoke with deliberate calm. "You asked for a way into Germany, one that would allow you access to rescue your men, one that gave the maximum amount of cover. There are very few roles in German society today that are questioned less than the officers of the SD. I wish we had time to sharpen your accents, but that cannot be helped."

"Roll this truck back a minute," Sikes said. "Are you seriously suggesting they pose as not just any SD officer but this actual officer? By name?"

Adriaan nodded. "Yes. We have reliable information that he is the one who has been tasked with collecting the prisoners related to the Emden attack. The Germans have even given his mission a name: *Rüsselkäfer.*"

"Weevil?" Will asked.

"Your German vocabulary is quite good." Adriaan's eyes widened as he nodded. "When transfer papers are presented, protocol will require a phone call to SD headquarters before they are handed over. Nazis are nothing if not lovers of rules and procedures; and, given the priority the Reich has placed on these particular men, the chance a warden would shirk conventions is nil. No other name will work."

"Forgive me for saying so, but I am now quite happy we are not joining you on holiday this year," James said with an ironic quirk that held no amusement.

"What is this?" Adriaan's brows knitted. "What do you mean that you are not going?"

Sikes leaned on his elbows. "It's just those two. We're going back to England."

"Three," Sparrow said, giving Sikes a sharp stare. "The three of us."

Sikes glared, but kept quiet.

Adriaan thought a moment, then said, "I suppose that does make things better. Fewer people will attract fewer eyes; though a woman traveling with you would be most unusual."

"Make me a nurse," Sparrow said without hesitation. "The mighty colonel was injured and insisted on medical accompaniment."

"Hmm." Adriaan steepled his fingers. "There is sense in that, I suppose, especially since Tobias *is* injured."

"It explains my limp," Will said. "Who is this man we are to impersonate? What do we know about him?"

"Standartenführer Horst Ewers," Adriaan answered. "Our men are well placed inside the SS, but not so much in the SD. We know little more than his name. We could not even produce a photo."

"A colonel? Shit, people will know him. He'll be recognized," Sikes said.

"It is a risk, but you must not underestimate the chaos that is taking place in Germany at the moment. The eastern front is a disaster, the Americans are entering the war in force, German cities are being bombed with regularity, and Hitler is raging in every direction." Adriaan sat back in his chair. "The Nazis are scrambling to shore up their homeland defenses, which means men are being moved quickly. Besides, if we struggled to find a photo of this man, then he may not be well known. SD officers often guard their identity, unlike their counterparts in the SS."

Adriaan rose and refilled his glass. When he returned, he leaned over the back of his chair. "The real trick will be getting you there before the real standartenführer arrives. Imagine what would happen if you arrived after—"

"Can we not imagine that, please," Sparrow said.

"We'll need to be far away before he discovers what's happened," I added. "The moment the Germans realize, all hell will break loose."

"Yes, that too," Adriaan nodded.

"And you think we can just slip through the cracks," Will muttered.

Adriaan thought a moment, then said quietly, "I think you must. We debated many plans. This is one we believe ... well, it was the least terrible."

"You inspire such confidence." Sikes pushed up from the table, snatched up his empty glass, and strode toward the far end with the barrels.

"I have not been confident in a very long time," Adriaan said quietly as he stared into the table.

No one spoke. No heads turned. No gazes shifted. I could feel the silence that followed echoing off the stone walls.

The rush of liquid into a glass shattered the shell of quiet.

"How do we get there?" I finally asked.

Adriaan's head snapped up, as though he'd woken from a dream. "In a car, of course."

# Chapter Twenty-Seven

# Egret

*"I shall never forget how I was roused one night by the groans of a fellow prisoner, who threw himself about in his sleep, obviously having a horrible nightmare. Since I had always been especially sorry for people who suffered from fearful dreams or deliria, I wanted to wake the poor man. Suddenly I drew back the hand which was ready to shake him, frightened at the thing I was about to do. At that moment I became intensely conscious of the fact that no dream, no matter how horrible, could be as bad as the reality of the camp which surrounded us, and to which I was about to recall him."*

Viktor E. Frankl, *Man's Search for Meaning*

Darkness. My companion.

I was surrounded by lifeless bodies, men still alive yet no longer living. The smell of them choked my senses, but the sight …

Eight of us inhabited a cell made for two. Our captors cared little for comfort—at least, not *our* comfort. When we'd first entered our cage, twelve stood beside us. None had room to lie down. Sitting required coordination and resulted in legs sprawling atop others. Thankfully, the guards removed those who'd lost hope before the rest of us could sicken.

Death was renamed escape.

The days and nights merged into an endless blank reel of boredom. It was impossible to know, with any certainty, how long we'd been there. I guessed weeks. Adam thought longer.

Once each day, we received a tin cup of water, every two or three days, a cup of broth.

Adam grew pale and gaunt, as if to blend in with those around us. I supposed I'd done the same, though I could not see myself. The lack of a mirror was a small blessing.

On most days, two of the men huddled in the far corner, their hands clasped tightly together, a gesture worthy of derision and welts and blood, should it be seen. Their eyes had grown dull, duller than when we'd first arrived, though shades of darkness mattered little in that place. On occasion, the pair's heads would lift from the gloom, and their eyes would meet. For fleeting moments, a semblance of life would spark in their gaze.

I felt it in my chest. However small it had become, whatever it was they truly held between them, it swelled in my chest each time I saw it.

I couldn't comprehend what I witnessed. I couldn't say it gave me hope. That word did not translate in the language of our despair; and yet, it did remind me of something beautiful, a smattering of color in the monochromatic world that was now our fate.

It almost made me smile. Almost.

"At least they don't beat us anymore," Adam whispered. Speaking louder was *verboten*, a word we'd come to loathe.

I looked around our cell at the bruises and scars on the others. A few wounds wept still.

Adam and I bore none, save the still unhealed wounds from our original mission and a handful of cuts and boot prints left by the first to capture us.

"Why?" I asked. My voice tasted bitter on my tongue and sounded even more so.

His head turned. "Why what?"

"Why don't they beat us?" I motioned with my eyes. "Look around. We're the only ones."

He scanned our cellmates, as if truly seeing them for the first time.

"I ... I don't know."

"They haven't really questioned us either," I said. "Think about it. Other than that first day after they dragged us away from the dock, they've barely looked in our direction. Does that make sense to you?"

Adam's head lolled back toward me. "Nothing makes sense in here."

"And our guards have changed."

He scrunched his brow. "Huh?"

"There isn't a single guard from those first days. In fact, I think this is a different group than just a few days ago." I motioned outside, where three guards diced at a rickety table. "Why would they change? I could see one or two, but *all* of them?"

"I don't know," he said, letting his head fall back against the bars. "I don't really care."

I couldn't raise my arm without disturbing others, so I gripped his forearm and squeezed. "Adam, look at me. Don't you fucking give up."

"Okay, Charlie. I'll try," he said, without conviction, then lowered his head.

I knew we—the other birds and I—shouldn't have shared our real names with the submarine crew, but it felt right at the time, and in this moment, I was glad for it. If I was going to die here, I didn't want to be some fake profile of a person. I wanted to be myself. Charlie Booher. Not a soldier, but a human.

I squeezed his arm again, willing strength into him, strength I barely felt myself.

Outside the cage, a guard pocketed the dice, and the trio vanished. A click sounded and the small light above our cell extinguished.

My friend darkness returned.

# Chapter Twenty-Eight
# Will

*"She was just a girl. What could she possibly have done?"*

Quote from an unnamed Dutch royal [1]

"This has to be the most ridiculous, insane plan I've ever heard," I said.

---

1. Regarding rumors a young Audrey Hepburn participated in the Dutch resistance. She was, in fact, closely aligned with Dr. Hendrik Visser 't Hooft, a local resistance leader.

We'd been driving for nearly an hour, meticulously following the circuitous route marked on the map Adriaan had provided. Like our entry into Amsterdam, our exit sent us many miles out of the way to avoid known roadblocks and checkpoints. When added together, we would travel two hundred twenty miles in nearly five hours, all under the cover of darkness.

We'd been in the car for thirty minutes and my ass already hurt.

Thomas had been unusually quiet as we'd said our goodbyes to James, Sikes, Fons, Nora, and Adriaan. He'd been even more so in the car. He and Sparrow sat in the back, while the unfurled map and I consumed the front.

Sparrow's hands appeared on the back of the passenger's seat a heartbeat before her face. "You don't like road trips?"

I gave her a sideways glare. "Not when they involve pit stops to change into my Nazi interrogator uniform and pretending Thomas is our prisoner. I can't even count the number of things that could go wrong." "I can't really argue, but I couldn't think of a better plan either," she said, propping her chin on the seat back. "I guess we could just go home, hope Heinz and Adam make it out okay."

"Seriously?" I scoffed, dithering between amusement and annoyance.

"Of course not. I wouldn't leave them to that fate any more than you would." Her hand found my shoulder.

When I peeked at her, her lips formed a tight line. "Try to stay positive. It's the only way we'll get through this."

I glanced back at Thomas through the rearview mirror. He was staring out the window.

"What are you so quiet about?" I asked.

His gaze shifted to meet mine in the mirror. "Just thinking."

"Great, now he's thinking," I said, trying to make a joke without coming across sharp. I whispered loudly to Sparrow, "His thinking is usually when I know to run."

She offered a shallow smile, but her mouth returned to neutral far too quickly.

Thomas's eyes remained fixed in the mirror when I glanced back again.

"Sorry. Guess I'm a little punchy," I said.

Thomas nodded, then resumed his window gazing.

"How much longer before we stop?" Sparrow asked, awkwardly reaching over to reposition the map.

"I'd guess another hour and a half, maybe a little more. That should put us on the west side of Hardenberg. Adriaan said to stop on a side road before the fields give way. I'm assuming we'll be able to tell where that point is in the light of the moon?"

She glanced out the window. "It is pretty full."

"What time was the colonel supposed to leave tomorrow?"

"Adriaan wasn't sure, but thought he would leave early," she said into the window. "He said to assume an eight o'clock departure, which would give us around an eight-hour head start."

"Okay, that's eight hours once we get there to locate the warden, retrieve our men, and get as far away as possible."

Sparrow looked toward me. "If things go according to plan, we really only have to wait for one phone call. The guards shouldn't take too long bringing prisoners from a cell, especially since this isn't a proper prison."

"This sounds too easy. It makes me want to throw up," I said. After a moment's thought, I asked, "What happens when the colonel shows up at the border presenting papers with the same name I'm about to use?"

"Shit, we should've used a different identity to enter the country," Thomas said, turning his attention fully toward our conversation. "How long is the drive from the border to Oldenburg?"

Sparrow grabbed the map and held it up to the moonlight in the window. "It looks like seventy or eighty miles, depending on which route we take. The one Adriaan suggested is more like ninety."

"So, time to get from the border to the prison with five hours to spare?" I asked.

"Something like that. We need to get away quickly enough to beat the colonel to the checkpoint. Once he raises the alarm, it'll be nearly impossible to get back into Holland by road," Thomas said.

"Let's hope the good colonel likes to sleep in. That would give us a little more time," I said.

"I wouldn't count on that," Sparrow said. "Sounds like this guy has a real stick up his ass."

I nearly spat a laugh.

"What?" she asked with a smirk.

"Sorry, you just caught me off guard."

"Can't a lady swear these days? It is 1943 and we're in the middle of a goddamn war. If I can't say an occasional fuck or shit now, when will I ever?"

I shook my head and tried not to laugh again.

"And why would a lady want to curse like a sailor?" Thomas waded deeper into the conversation.

Sparrow sat back. "Because girls are every bit as bad ass as boys, you just don't notice until you need us."

Thomas grunted, and a quick check in the mirror revealed a broad smile.

"As I recall, I have been the one to include you in everything, my dear," I said, proud of whatever that made me. "I always notice you."

Thomas's grin widened. "And I was just the one to get you into this mess, getting captured and all."

"First of all, Tobias, you have never noticed me, especially when your living, breathing Hollywood hunk is nearby." Sparrow reached up and patted Thomas's cheek like a reproving mother. "And yes, dear, you really should work on *not* getting captured. It threw my whole social calendar into a tizzy."

Thomas chuckled. "We can't have that now, can we? The Germans take over Europe but mess up Anny's calendar, and it's tizzies all around. What has the world come to?"

"One does love one's social schedule to remain blemish free," she singsonged in a terrible British accent.

I glanced back at Thomas through the mirror again. "We still have four hours in this car together. Can you gag her or something?"

He laughed and raised his palms. "Don't put me in the middle of your spat. I was calmly watching the countryside when you sucked me into this mess."

A quiet contentment settled after that, each of us lost in our own private thoughts. My mind wandered to our days at Harvard, carefree and curious, hopeful for what the future might bring. I couldn't help but picture Arty's goofy grin staring back at me. My roommate had been a staple in my life in those days. At first, when my parents had died, he'd kept me afloat. I'm not sure I could've made it through without him.

As our university years rolled by, he became my most steadfast companion, the friend others dreamed of having, the one who would have your back no matter the odds.

The thought of spindly Arty squaring up to some bully nearly made me laugh out loud, though I knew he would do it if he thought someone he cared for was in danger. He was a spark of light and joy in this dark world. People like him were the reason we fought, the reason we hoped for better days when old men's wars no longer bled the world of her young.

I could see us sitting around the table, enjoying a meal. Janie, the sassy aristocrat who'd pierced the veil of our brotherhood, throwing her head back and laughing with full-throated enthusiasm, drawing every eye in the room. She could've drawn those eyes without laughing. Janie was a force of nature, a presence, a disturbance in the atmosphere one could not ignore. She was as much a sister to me as Arty was my brother. My chosen family.

My heart longed for the simple pleasure of those days, for a life where the most harrowing decision involved the flavors of milkshakes rather than the path into enemy territory. Most of all, I longed for the sense of belonging that came with our mismatched found family. The handful of days I'd spent with Arty's family, celebrating a holiday I knew little about, felt like a favorite shirt, worn and soft, snug in just the right way, a comfort on a crisp day. That visit had been the first time since I'd lost my parents that I'd felt that sense of belonging and comfort.

And then I'd met Thomas. And my world shifted.

I'd never loved a man. I'd never even been attracted to one; at least, not that I understood as such. When we'd met, a chance encounter in the middle of campus, something stirred in my soul I'd not known existed before that moment. The first time his fingers grazed my cheek, the flame in my soul blazed and singed every part of me, marking me as his for all time. There was no resisting his touch, no escape from his gaze. His laugh thrilled my ears. His smile warmed my heart. His very presence tickled the tiny hairs on my skin and sent my heart racing.

He never had to ask me to be his. I always was. I always would be.

The urge to look at him, to feel his gaze burrowing into my deepest thoughts, was nearly overwhelming. Had I not been driving ...

"Is this where we're supposed to stop and change?" Sparrow's voice clipped short my reminiscence.

"Oh, really? Already?" I tried to recover. "Check the map."

I caught her examining me, but didn't turn to give her a better view. The rattle of the map told me she'd given up her wordless interrogation.

"Yeah, this is it. There should be a side road any minute now. Adriaan put a note here that says it won't have a sign or a name. It's just a dirt road used by farmers who own the land nearby."

"Sounds like the perfect place for a dressing room," Thomas said, a grin in his voice.

We'd barely seen other cars so far on our journey, once we'd left Amsterdam and her surroundings. We probably could've changed in the middle of the main road and remained unseen. Still, I was relieved when the side road, indeed a poorly maintained dirt path, appeared ahead on our right.

"The note says to turn in and go for a quarter-mile before stopping," Sparrow instructed.

A plume of dust kicked up as we made the turn, following us until we stopped and taking forever to dissipate. If there had been anyone watching for cars, we'd just announced our presence.

"Sorry, babe," I said, leaning forward and kissing Thomas on the cheek as I clamped the second cuff on his wrist. "If you weren't so much trouble, we wouldn't have to lock you up like this."

His lips twisted. "If I wasn't so much trouble, you wouldn't love me like you do."

I shrugged through a chuckle. "Probably true—the trouble part. The jury's still out on the loving you that much."

"Hey!"

"Boys," Sparrow cut in. We both turned. "Can you tease each other after we go into Nazi territory, avoid getting killed, save our friends, and return home … again, without getting killed?"

"When you say it like that, sure. It sounds so exciting," Thomas smirked.

"God, I hate you both." Sparrow threw her arms in the air, wheeled, and folded herself into the passenger seat.

Thomas's grin was wide, his eyes bright, when I turned back. "You know I love you more than breathing, right?"

I searched his eyes. "Where'd that come from?" He raised his bound hands and tried to trace fingers across my face. "I guess I had time to think—not that I needed it to know how much I love you. Will, you're everything to me. I don't want a day to go by without telling you that. Okay?"

I grabbed his head in both hands and pulled him into a rough, deep kiss. The car, the farms, the world, faded away. There was only Thomas and me, and that kiss.

Until Sparrow's window screamed as she rolled it down.

"Guys, seriously? I know this is a dirt shit path, but a farmer could drive up on a horse or plow at any moment."

Our lips parted as I choked out a laugh. "A plow? How would a farmer ride a plow?" She stuck her arm out the window and raised her middle finger, then vanished back inside the car and rolled up the glass.

"You've been such a bad influence on her while I was in prison," Thomas said, his smirk returning.

"What can I say? I live to teach."

I helped Thomas fold himself into the back seat, then resumed my spot as driver. "Where would ma'am and sir like to go today? A park? Perhaps a lovely luncheon spot?"

Sparrow shook her head, but a smile crept across her lips. "How about German for lunch? Wilhelm, does that sound alright with you? This nice secret policeman has offered to chauffer us for the day. Isn't that kind of the Reich?"

"Terribly kind. Did you see the bracelets the young man gave me? A gift before our lunch. What will they think of next?"

I leaned over and pretended to bang my forehead against the steering wheel. "Can we just go now?"

"Carry on, good man." Sparrow made a haughty gesture with one hand, then turned away as if I were too far below her station to sit squarely beside.

"This is going to be a long ride," I muttered as I turned the car around.

# Chapter Twenty-Nine

# Egret

*"The world must know what happened, and never forget."*

Dwight D. Eisenhower

We hadn't seen a guard in a day, maybe two. I was beginning to lose count of everything. My stomach had quit growling, which I assumed was its way of surrendering to hunger. Sitting for so long had made most of my muscles sore; though, in an odd way, I was thankful for that. At least I could still feel something.

Adam was losing his fight. His eyes would open, but I doubted they ever saw much. I'd stopped urging him to fight a few days back. It wasn't helping and he didn't seem to appreciate the encouragement. In the still of the night, I wondered if he was right.

One of the others, one of the men whose hands rarely parted, stared at me across the cell.

"What?" I asked quietly, my voice worn sandpaper against my throat.

"I am Holger."

We'd lived in our iron box for that long, and it was the first time he'd spoken to me, the first time anyone had offered a name. If a jailer's boot had kicked my head, I couldn't have been more surprised.

"Uh, I'm Heinz." Clawing fingers pulled and tore at my chest. It was my conscience's way of pointing out how this doomed man had reached out his hand and I'd given him only falseness. "Charlie. Call me Charlie."

His lips twitched but didn't curl.

"This is Joachim." He motioned, ever so slightly, with his head. A wince told me the effort had cost him.

I studied the pair. Starvation had stolen years. It was impossible to tell their age, though I suspected neither had seen a thirtieth birthday.

"Are you two ..." He looked to Adam.

I shook my head. "No."

I couldn't read his expression that followed. Confusion? Disappointment? Curiosity? If his mind begged a question, he chose not to ask it.

"How long have you two …" I wasn't sure how to ask the question.

"Almost seven years. We met at university before all this madness."

With each word, his voice grew strength. It was a bit like watching a child rise and stand that first time, then repeat the effort without wobbling.

"We were so young. It seems a lifetime ago." His eyes drifted further away. "I remember the first time I saw Joachim. He sat alone, eating at a table in the corner of the dining room, nearly shrouded in shadow. His eyes squinted as he strained to read a book. There were plenty of empty seats with more light, and the silliness of him straining intrigued me."

When he lost himself in time, I asked, "What happened?"

"He told me to go away." He coughed, a reflex of the body unused to laughing. "He wanted to read in peace, but I insisted he would damage his eyes doing so in such darkness. I sat beside him and threatened to tell him folktales until he moved."

"Folktales?"

He shrugged. "It was the best I could think of in the moment. He was quite handsome."

His head turned and his gaze held Joachim. I remained silent, giving him his moment.

Without turning, he continued. "He surrendered, and, in the years that followed, we were never far apart."

The feeling I'd somehow intruded on life's most private moment was nearly overwhelming, and I found myself staring pointedly at my shoes.

"Joachim is a jeweler. He makes the most beautiful things. I would show you, but the Nazis took everything."

"And you?"

"A teacher, in a primary school. I have always loved children. We ... we would have wanted children of our own if ..." Reality skewered the last of his statement. "We had to hide, of course. Even before all of this, we could not be ourselves to others. Still, we were happy. Joachim always made me happy."

He spoke in past tense, as though happiness was impossible at any time but in the past, a whiff of smoke one tried to grasp as it drifted away on a distant breeze.

He stared a moment longer. "Your accent. I cannot place it. Where are you from?"

The sudden jolt through my body nearly drew me to my feet.

Was he *questioning* me? Was this emaciated skeleton of a man part of some sick Nazi plot to extract information? It seemed unfathomable, even for those bastards.

I quickly replayed the endless days and nights as I'd watched this pair comfort and hold each other. There was no way anyone could fake that love, that compassion. There was no way the Nazis could possess such a thing. I was being ridiculous. This man—this kind, loving man—was nothing like our captors.

Had I been lost so long in the dark I'd forgotten how to see goodness?

"West of here, but I have lived in many places, including America. Travel does something to the accent, does it not?"

He eyed me, though I couldn't tell if his vacant expression was surprise, disbelief, or perpetual hunger.

"America," he said wistfully, allowing his head to press back against a bar. His gaze drifted toward the ceiling. "What I would give to be home right now..."

"I can't argue with that," was all I could think to say.

After a moment's reflection, Holger looked back to me. "In America, would we"—he nodded at Joachim—"would we be able to live ... without fear?"

My heart clinched. This huddled mass was desperate to dream. He dared not hope. And yet, his question begged for it. How was I supposed to tell him they would be as unwelcome in the Land of the Free as they were here? They might enjoy a larger cell, but a prison would still be their fate. How could I rob him of his vision of a better life, his desire to simply live and love and be free?

"Yes, you would be welcomed and loved," I lied.

His lips twitched again, this time forming the slightest smile, the first I'd seen in months.

Yet the claw about my heart refused to release.

# Chapter Thirty

# Will



*"In the dance of shadows and light, hope was our steady partner, leading us through the wartime waltz with grace and resilience."*

UNKNOWN DUTCH CIVILIAN

As the checkpoint at the German–Dutch border faded into the distance, I felt each of us inhale our first deep breaths.

"Well, that was fun," I said, trying to slice through the tension that still hung thicker and more acrid than burned butter.

Sparrow reached over and swatted the back of my head. "Eyes on the road."

"Hey!"

She shrugged and turned away.

"Printheth Thparrow doth not enjoy thy joketh," Thomas drawled, adding a thick lisp.

I grinned at him through the rearview. "Methinks the lady doth protest too much."

Sparrow's daggers stabbed in my direction once more. "If you're going to quote *Hamlet*, at least get the wording right."

"What's wrong with my wording?"

"The text reads, and I quote"—she cleared her throat dramatically—"the lady doth protest too much, methinks."

I rolled my eyes. "I misplaced 'methinks' and you call that a literary crime?"

"A quote is a quote, good sir, and a rascal thou art." She folded her arms in defiant triumph.

Thomas laughed from the back seat. "Who would've thought we would be joking on our way through the German countryside?"

And the jovial mood died.

"At least that first checkpoint went well," Sparrow said, her gaze returning out the window. "Those guards took one look at your uniform and almost shit themselves."

"They looked pretty bored when we drove up," Thomas said.

"Traffic has been light, almost non-existent. They may not get more than a handful of cars passing through each day. That would put any patrol to sleep." She thought a moment, then added, "What's more surprising is how lax they were with a car at night. I would've thought any vehicle traveling at two in the morning would draw greater scrutiny."

"Like you said, they were bored. They're guarding a border crossing between Germany and a German-suppressed country, and it's not like the Dutch have mounted any serious violent resistance. And what Dutch citizen in their right mind would want to cross *into* Germany right now?"

"Yeah, I guess you're right," she said. "Still seemed weird."

"And then, along comes Colonel Will Shaw and his big baton." Thomas patted my shoulder. Sparrow groaned.

"I think it's my gun, not baton, dear prisoner."

"Oh, right. Although I'm fairly certain theirs were bigger."I shot him a glare.

"Their guns, babe. Your baton is clearly the biggest around."

"Guys! Lady present. A little respect, please," Sparrow snapped, though I was fairly certain a smile threaded her words.

"Methinks—""If you say one more word—""The lady—"Sparrow rounded and flashed Thomas a vulgar gesture.

He laughed again. "Some lady. With fingers like that—"

"Babe, it's not polite to talk about how a lady uses her fingers," Will teased.

Sparrow punched my shoulder, causing the car to swerve.

"Easy," I said.

"I give up on you two." She recrossed her arms and stared at the road ahead, ignoring our boyish snickering.

We saw more cars along the German roads, mostly military vehicles racing about. No one paid any mind to a random black sedan of German make, one of thousands servicing the Reich. Adriaan said he'd "liberated" it from the motor pool in Amsterdam, replacing it with a car once owned by a Jewish family no longer in Holland. When I asked why he hadn't simply given us the family's car to drive, he said, "In Germany, the staff car will draw less attention. Plus, I can use this to point the finger at one of the higher-ranking officers."

"I don't follow," I said.

"The Germans are meticulous. They track everything. Someone will notice and report the swap. An investigation will follow. I will leave false clues, sending them in every direction. Our Nazi friends will spend days, perhaps weeks, chasing their tails. That is time they are not tormenting our people or chasing after you."

Adriaan was clever.

Nearly an hour and a half after we crossed the border, around four in the morning, we reached a side road with a large white sign with the Nazi eagle and swastika and black lettering that read simply, *EINGANG VERBOTEN. ENTRANCE FORBIDDEN.*

"Who puts a prison in an airport?" Sparrow asked.

Thomas leaned forward so his head was nearly even with ours in the front seat. "I asked Adriaan about that. He said this is more of a waystation, a temporary holding facility until prisoners are sorted and moved to a final location."

"Final location." The words tasted sour in my mouth. "I hate everything about this place."

"Okay," Thomas said, his voice shifting to that of a navy commander. "Eyes sharp. From here on out, we are our covers. I won't be able to help at all since I'm supposed to be the despondent prisoner. Anny, unfortunately, you can only speak when spoken to, being a woman and a Dutch nurse. That means everything rests on you, Tobias—or, should I say, Standartenführer Ewers."

I nodded, trying to project a confidence I didn't feel.

"Remember, you're an SD colonel. You've spent a lifetime ordering people around and you expect to receive immediate obedience. You don't need to overplay being an ass though. A quiet voice and stern glare are often more frightening to subordinates than a lot of shouting. If someone pushes back, pull out your notebook and ask for their name for your records. That usually works with American military. I would guess the same is true here."

I was almost to the gate when my stomach fell. "How do we account for you being in a car with a nurse unguarded? When I go inside to present my papers, you'll be in here with a Dutch nurse. The Nazis would never leave a prisoner like that. Hell, neither would we."

Thomas, usually quick with a plan, remained silent.

"How could we miss that?" Sparrow asked.

"Slump over," I said.

"What?" Thomas asked.

"Slump over like I've knocked you out somehow. She's a nurse. We'd have drugs. I'll make it work."

We were out of time.

The wheels squealed as we slowed before a lowered traffic arm adorned with tiny versions of the Nazi symbols we'd seen on the sign. A glass-paneled guard shack attached to a much larger building stood to one side of the arm. Before we'd fully halted, four guards poured out of the shack, each with rifles at the ready. One stood in front of the car, two on the driver's side, and one took up a position on the passenger's side.

I rolled down my window and handed my papers to the soldier before he could ask.

He glanced at my uniform, then my rank insignia, and I could almost hear his spine stiffen. "Hello, Colonel. My men will inspect the vehicle while I make a call. Please wait here."

"Sergeant," I said, in an almost soothing tone. "Is all this necessary? I am in a hurry to retrieve two prisoners and get back to Berlin. This is of the highest priority to senior leadership."

The soldier glanced across at Sparrow, then peered into the back seat where Thomas lay. "Who is that man?"

"An *American* prisoner," I said, with deliberate pause on the nationality. "One you *never* saw. Do you understand, Sergeant?"

The guard stared into my eyes, then his head snapped up as he shouted, "Make it quick." He looked back down toward me. "Only a moment, sir."

"Thank you, Sergeant," I said, trying to sound grateful but annoyed. "I will be sure not to remember *your* name as well."

The sergeant's eyes widened slightly, then he darted back to his shack.

The other men scurried about, glaring inside at Thomas and Sparrow, then running mirrors attached to long poles under the car. They even asked for the keys so they could search the trunk.

A moment later, the team's leader returned and handed my papers back. "Drive straight through. Take the third turn to your right. Your building is the last one on the left."

"Very good," I said, folding and stuffing my papers into my coat.

"Heil Hitler." The soldier's heels clicked together like the firing of a rifle. His salute might have been carved in stone.

"Yes, Heil Hitler," I said, raising a half-hearted palm. "If only the guards at the border were as efficient as your team. Well done, Sergeant."

The man looked stunned at the compliment but offered a stiff nod and waved us through as the gate arm lifted.

The moment my window was closed, Thomas whispered, his voice muffled, "Good job, but don't give them more info than they ask for. Now they know we crossed the border."

"Shit," I said. "Good point."

My pulse was racing and the collar on the Nazi coat itched fiercely against my skin. The pints of sweat pouring out of my body probably didn't help on that score. I took a few deep breaths and some semblance of calm returned.

The two-runway airfield looked more like a military base attached to a rural airport. The runways, such as they were, did not boast of large bombers or fierce fighters. In fact, the only planes visible were two twin-engine birds that looked more civilian than military.

Soldiers milled about, a few walking with purpose, but most showing no sign of urgency.

"Doesn't look like this place received the love from the Allies Emden has," Thomas said.

"Yeah," Sparrow agreed. "I don't see any damage. It doesn't look like a high-priority target."

"Probably right," I said, turning to look out the opposite window as we passed a building marked *Headquarter s.*The third turn was a dead end into an L-shaped building that forced us to turn right. We rounded the corner and pulled into a parking space at the last building before a fence that separated the complex from the runway. Above a lone door was a plaque bearing the twin lightning bolts of the SS. One lone guard stood to the right of the door, his rifle slung over his shoulder and a weary look in his eyes.

"Here we go," I said as my door groaned open.

# Chapter Thirty-One
# Will

*"You are the heroes. You are the heroes every
day."*


HERMINE SANTRUSCHITZ GIES [1]


The soldier guarding the door snapped to attention
as I approached. His hand flew into the air and he
barked a crisp, "Heil Hitler."

"Heil Hitler." I returned his salute. "Is the warden in?"

The guard's eyes darted from his forward-facing blank-
ness to where I stood a stride away.

---

1. Better known as Miep Gies, helped hide Anne Frank
   and her family from the Nazis and saved her diaries.

"It is not a tough question, soldier. Is the warden in?" I repeated in a quiet tone a teacher might use with a student who'd clearly not read the assignment.

"Yes, sir, Colonel, sir." His eyes snapped back to the indistinct distance before him.

"Good." I waited.

His eyes shifted to me, then he jolted into action, reaching behind to open the door so quickly his rifle nearly fell from his shoulder.

I cocked a brow, then shook my head, again the disappointed teacher.

The interior of the building felt smaller than the main floor of Adriaan's home back in Amsterdam. One clerk sat behind a metal desk, nearly obscured by a stack of papers several inches high. The pecking of keys stilled the moment I stepped through the door.

"Sir!" The man fumbled to his feet, then snapped his heels together in a firecracker salute. I glanced to where his coat lay haphazardly tossed across the seat of a chair, then eyed the rumpled shirt whose yellowed pits had likely not seen laundering since the war began. The man noticed my examination and shuffled uncomfortably, failing to maintain his rigid position of attention.

"Where is the warden?" I asked quietly.

The lines around his eyes relaxed a touch. "In his office, sir."

I waited. He remained still.

"Inform him SS-Standartenführer Ewers is here to take possession of two prisoners." When he didn't move immediately, I pursed my lips like I'd seen other Nazi officers do. "Now."

The man scurried from behind his desk and vanished through one of two doors on the far wall. A moment later, he returned with a rotund, balding man in an equally disheveled uniform.

"Standartenführer, welcome, sir. I did not expect you—"

I held up a palm, then reached into my coat pocket, retrieving the transfer orders the LO had falsified for us. "Captain, the prisoners. Now, if you please. I must be back in Berlin today to begin their questioning and I am already weary of the road. Please do not steal more time from me today."

The captain's eyes flashed and he ran his stubby fingers over his scalp. "Of course, Standartenführer. I will need to call to verify your orders, you understand?"

"Fine. Be quick about it."

The captain needed no further encouragement, leaving me alone with his clerk. I glanced around for another chair, but there were no others.

"Let me get that for you, sir," the clerk said, hurrying around his desk to snatch up his coat. "There. Please, have a seat. Can I get you anything?"

"A glass of water, please." I wasn't thirsty, but I figured as long as the man was attending a task, he wasn't examining me.

The captain took longer than I'd hoped, particularly based on the way the color drained from his face upon my arrival. I set the empty glass on the clerk's desk and squared with the captain when he entered.

He held out the orders for me to take back. "Berlin confirms your orders, sir, but—"

"But?" I raised a brow.

He looked down, then back into my eyes. "Berlin is terminating this holding station. When our prisoners are transferred, we are to be reassigned and this building turned over to the Luftwaffe. This is one of the few airfields the enemy has not harassed and command wishes to use that to our advantage."

He nodded as if he'd explained everything perfectly.

"Captain, I fail to understand how this impacts my prisoners or mission."

He shuffled again. "Standartenführer, sir, I have been ordered to transfer *all* of my prisoners into your custody."

My throat seized. "All of them? All eight?"

He nodded quickly. "Yes, sir."

"This is ridiculous," I said, straining to come up with some argument, any argument, to resist, but this was an order from SD headquarters. That's who the captain would've called. A colonel would never defy such a command, would he?

"I have one of my guards preparing the prisoners now. Some may need … assistance. I will see to it."

I fought the bile that rose. "Captain, I have one car. There is a prisoner in the back seat and my nurse in the front with me. Where should I put eight prisoners?"

The captain smiled, as though he was about to solve all the world's problems. "We have a bus, sir. It is large enough to accommodate you all. There are metal bars to secure the prisoners too. Command wishes you to return the bus to the motor pool in Berlin as part of our decommissioning."

"And what am I to do with the additional six prisoners?" I didn't have to feign annoyance any longer.

"I was only told to hand them over to you, sir. Oh, and I am to have Staff Sergeant Ambrose"—he gestured to the clerk—"accompany you as a driver. I will have his belongings sent in the next few days. Unless …"

"Unless what, Captain?"

"You could simply call and ask." He motioned to the telephone on the clerk's desk. I didn't think he was suspicious, simply trying to mollify the increasingly angry senior officer standing in his foyer while removing himself from the center of the cookie.

I spat a laugh. "Captain, what fool questions orders?"

My gaze then fell to Ambrose, whose pallor was decidedly more ashen than it had been upon my arrival. "Well,

Staff Sergeant, have the prisoners loaded and bring the bus around. We have hours of driving ahead of us."

"Yes, sir," Ambrose said, his voice resigned, before stepping out the second door on the far wall.

The captain made to flee back toward his office, but I yanked his leash with a question. "Captain, what of the other prisoners? What do I have on my hands now? More Jews?"His face screwed up in utter distaste. "Worse, sir. Deviants."

I didn't have to pretend disgust. The captain smiled in satisfaction at our clear agreement on the matter, never suspecting our shared displeasure was for far different reasons.

"I will wait outside. Thank you for your assistance, Captain."

I didn't look back or slow my stride. How were we supposed to make any of this work? Six additional prisoners? And a Nazi driver? He'd know the minute we turned west instead of east that something was wrong.

A million questions swirled. I barely heard the door guard salute.

The moment the car door closed behind me, I let out a breath I hadn't realized I'd been holding.

"So?" Sparrow asked.

"Orders are confirmed, but they're making us take six more prisoners ... and a bus ... and a driver."

"What?" Thomas hissed from his prone position in the back.

"Yeah, a young kid. They're closing down this unit, disbanding it. We're helping them by moving their last prisoners." I wanted to bang my head on the steering wheel for real this time. "How the hell are we supposed to pull this off?"

"I'll have to go in the bus, chained up with the others," Thomas said in the staccato tone I recognized every time we had to plan something. "Will, you drive the bus. Let the kid drive the car."

"That doesn't make sense," Sparrow said. "An SD colonel wouldn't drive a prisoner bus."

"She's right," I said.

"Fine. Will drives the car. Sparrow's with him because she's his nurse. I'm chained with the other prisoners, and the kid drives the bus. That doesn't answer how we get rid of the soldier or what we do with the extra six people," Thomas said.

Sparrow turned in her seat to face me. "We'll need some excuse to stop—a restroom break or something. You and I will have to take the driver out while the others are chained up."

"What time is it?" Thomas asked.

"A little past five, I think. Why?" I asked.

"An uptight colonel might want breakfast," he said. "Insist he takes you two to the officers' mess before we leave. Find an opportunity to take him out before we even leave the base."

"You seriously want me to kill a Nazi on the base? Say we don't get caught, what would we do with the body?" I said, a little too loudly.

"Quiet," Sparrow urged. "We'll figure that out. We can't let him leave with us. If we can get his uniform, Wilhelm can become our driver."

A moment later, Thomas said, "That could work."

"Assuming we find the right time and place to stab the kid," I said, exasperated but without a better option.

"Planning session over," Sparrow said, her finger pointing to the black-painted bus pulling around from behind the building. It huffed to a stop before our parking space and we watched Ambrose stand and climb down.

"Go," Thomas said. "Time to move."

"Fuck me," was all I could think to say as I opened my door.

# Chapter Thirty-Two
# Will



*"We were not heroes by choice but by circumstance, facing the unknown with a courage born of necessity."*

Unknown resistance fighter

Ambrose thought I'd lost my mind when I told him I wanted breakfast before leaving the base. By the tightness of his lips and the pinch of his eyes, he clearly had to fight back the urge to argue. Thankfully, fear of the vaunted SS and SD outweighed this simple soldier's common sense, and his eyes lowered in resignation.

"We should move the prisoner in your car to the bus, cuff him like the others," he said, looking past me toward the car.

I nodded. "Good idea, Sergeant. We administered a high dose of sedatives to the man, but one can never be too careful with spies."

"Spies?" Ambrose's eyes flared wide. He blinked a few times, then said, "Uh, sir, I can take care of that for you. No need for you to handle prisoners."

I laughed as though he'd said the funniest thing possible. "It's alright, Sergeant. Handling prisoners is what we do, and these three Americans are of special interest to the Reich. Remain here a moment."

His brow furrowed, but again he didn't resist. "Yes, sir."

"Wait here," I instructed, then strode to the car, opening the door for Sparrow to exit before turning my attention to Thomas in the back seat.

"I have to move you to the bus with the others," I whispered quickly. "Act drugged."

Thomas proved to be a frustratingly brilliant actor, turning his body into an amorphous mass of limbs and muscle. I tried to haul him out, but his weight nearly dragged me down.

"Not *that* drugged," I hissed.

I stood him up and gripped his arm roughly, shoving him before me as he staggered aimlessly wherever he was pointed. Ambrose watched from the bus's door with interest.

"We may have given him enough for the entire trip," I said as I passed the sergeant.

"Better to keep the bastards quiet, sir."

As we stepped up onto the bus, Thomas and I froze. Egret sat in the third row. His eyes flashed with recognition, but he kept his expression still. Adam sat one row behind. Neither he nor any of the others who passed as humans looked up.

Something caught in my throat as I scanned the prisoners. Cheeks were not meant to be sunken. Bones in the arms and legs should be less prominent than muscle. Eyes were meant to hold brightness and life.

The resignation of death sat before me.

"Go on," I said in English. "Sit your ass down."

I shoved Thomas roughly toward the back of the bus where one long seat, meant to accommodate three, only held two. The way the pair huddled, hands clasped with fingers entwined, drew me up short.

Thomas sat, but still my eyes were fixed.

I forgot to breathe.

One head turned up, then the man's eyes followed my gaze, and we both stared at their hands. In a minor act of defiance that gave me hope these souls might still be saved, the man looked back up and glared.

Each thud of my heart was a hammer strike in my chest. I wanted to reach up and tear it out, to never again feel whatever agony swelled within.

My eyes whipped to Thomas, desperate for the sun of his gaze to warm my skin, but his head remained bowed.

I wheeled and fled the bus.

"The officers' mess is that building over there," Ambrose said as I stepped onto firm ground. He pointed across several small parking lots to a building that sat just past the massive hangar where the clanging of mallets on metal never ceased, even at this early hour of the morning.

"Good. I need coffee," I said, stepping away from the bus as though being near it might set my body aflame.

"I'm afraid you may have to settle for tea," Ambrose said, scurrying to follow. "The ration ended months ago. Still, we have not received any."

I paused as we reached the car where Sparrow waited. "Come, Anny, the sergeant says we must settle for tea. Let us get this breakfast over with so we may return to civilization in Berlin."

Sparrow's eyes said I might've overplayed my part a touch, but Ambrose took it all in stride.

There were six tables, each accommodating four chairs. Only two were occupied by bleary-eyed officers eating quietly near the corner. Sparrow and I sat as far from them as the layout allowed. Ambrose walked around the building to another entrance that led to the enlisted men's dining hall.

Tepid tea and stale scones were the order of the day. I immediately missed the hospitality of our Dutch friends. After a second cup, Sparrow and I rose to find Ambrose leaning against the wall beside the officers' entrance.

"Ready to go, Colonel?" he said, straightening.

"Almost," I said, glancing at Sparrow. "My nurse has a professional curiosity we would like to settle."

The sergeant glanced at her, then back to me. "Sir?"

"She would like to see where these men have been held and how they were transferred to the bus."

Ambrose's brow furrowed again. "You want to see the holding cell?"

"Now," I added with a bit of force. "If you please."

"Uh, okay. I mean, yes, sir. Right away, Colonel. Follow me."

As Ambrose stepped away, his back staring at us as we followed, Sparrow shot me a "what the hell are you up to?" glance.

I wanted to say, "I have no idea. I'm winging it here," but all I could do was dart my eyes meaningfully toward Ambrose, then back to her.

We stepped into an empty office, the sergeant's desk chair uninhabited and silence permeating every corner of the building.

We stepped through the door that was not the captain's office.

No hallway greeted us, only a room containing an empty cage of iron bars three fingers thick. The door stood open.

There were no cots or chairs, no sinks or toilets, only the cage and the fecal remains of far too many who'd been stuffed into it.

I covered my nose and mouth and willed myself not to look away. Sparrow did the same but averted her gaze.

"Where is the captain?" I asked, threading my voice with annoyance.

"If he is not in his office, he may be gathering his personal items. His orders were to pack and report to Bremen for assignment."

"Bremen," I muttered to myself, recalling reports and reels of relentless Allied bombing of the city a year earlier, and of likely more devastating ones to come. "Poor man."

Ambrose glanced up. "We will all be poor men once the Americans land."

I nearly staggered back as his comment slapped me across the face. "Sergeant?"

He cocked his head, a weary, resigned look entering his eyes. "Sir, the eastern front is lost. Africa is falling. Command is activating operations for homeland defense. We should have never brought this war ..."

My mind whirled. I couldn't believe what this man—no, this *boy*—was saying. I stared into his eyes, a youthful gaze that had barely seen eighteen winters.

I wanted to scream.

What was *I* supposed to say? How should I respond? How would a colonel in the SD, a man charged with guarding the beating heart of the Reich, react?

I stepped forward and slapped the sergeant across the cheek so hard his head snapped back and a red mark formed. Ambrose stumbled, grasping his face, his eyes turning up in widened shock.

"You are a soldier of the Reich. Act like it or you will end up in one of these cells," I growled.

"Yes, sir," Ambrose mumbled, still cowed.

"Where are the guards?" I demanded.

"Relieved, sir. There is no one left to guard."

Sparrow shot forward and swung a baton I hadn't noticed her grab while we stood in the foyer. It struck the sergeant's head, knocking him to his knees. He gripped the bars for support as she struck again, this time in the softness behind his neck that stole his consciousness and sent his limp form to the ground.

"Quickly, grab those cuffs and something to gag him with," she said.

"We should kill him and hide his body."

"Please, no more killing than we have to. He's just a boy." She paused, staring up at me. "Besides, where would we hide him? Neither of us knows this place. It's more likely we'd be spotted."

I looked down and saw the sleeping face of a child, smooth and unmarred by time, and I knew she was right. It didn't matter that this boy would shoot us if given the chance. It didn't matter that he would hate me for who I loved. We could not become him. We could not become his hatred. Not if we hoped to return home with some semblance of ourselves intact. This war had already stolen so much. We could not give it the last of our humanity, even if it put our lives at greater risk.

I nodded once, then dragged Ambrose into the cell. Once inside, I cuffed one wrist, wound the chain through a bar, then cuffed the other. Sparrow stuffed his mouth with a wadded cloth, then tied another around his head to secure the gag. I searched one of his pockets, then the other, relieved to find the keys to the prisoners' cuffs and the bus.

"Let's go," I said, closing the cell door behind me.

The sky was just beginning to shed night's shroud as we stepped out of the building. Only a couple of soldiers and mechanics could be seen ambling lazily from one building to another. No planes flew. The runway was still.

"The car?" Sparrow asked.

"We should stick together." I thought a moment and handed her a set of keys. "No, you drive the car. I'll take the bus."

"Where are we going?" she asked.

"Plan B rally point," I said, invoking the only back-up built into Adriaan's plan.

She gripped my arm, squeezing gently, then strode purposefully toward the car. When I stepped onto the bus, Egret's head snapped up. Adam's didn't, nor did any of the others, save for Thomas in the rear. When I reached Egret's row and my extended hand revealed keys to their constraints, a few curious gazes found their way upward.

"Wait until we're well past the guard shack at the gate, then unlock everyone. Have them leave the cuffs on their wrists in case we get stopped," I said in English, widening already curious eyes. "It's fucking good to see you, Egret."

The man I knew, albeit bedraggled and weary, smiled, and I thought the sun might've risen inside that bus. His voice rasped but my heart soared at the sound. "You too, Emu. Still a stupid name."

I shook my head and smiled. Despite it all, his humor remained. Hope lived still.

"Aliases only from here. And keep everyone quiet. We have a long drive ahead."

The steering wheel turned slowly, like straining against a wheel while fighting angry waves in a small boat. The brakes screamed as we rolled to a stop just inside the mechanical arm.

"Papers," a disinterested guard demanded with an outstretched palm. No others joined him. There was no inspection. We were assumed to be safe, as we were already inside the compound.

I reached inside my coat and handed the man my identification and the amended transfer orders given to me by the warden.

"The woman in the car behind us is my nurse," I said in an attempt to head off any conversation he might have with Sparrow.

"Where's your driver? Orders say Ambrose is supposed to be with you." The guard continued staring at the paper while waiting for my answer.

"No idea. He did not show up this morning, and I have no use for a soldier who cannot be punctual. Berlin waits for no man."

The guard eyed me a moment, then his gaze fell to my collar. I held my breath as he took the papers back to his shack, only allowing myself air once he returned and waved us through.

The arm lifted. The engine roared. We passed beneath, and Sparrow followed unhindered.

We'd made it a quarter-mile when I heard the sound.

The unmistakable wail of an alarm.

# Chapter Thirty-Three
# Thomas



UNKNOWN SURVIVOR

Egret had just freed my wrists when a distant cry pierced the quiet morning.

"Dammit!" I said, looking up as Egret braced himself. The bus lurched as Will tried to add distance between us and the base. "We're never going to get away in this thing."

Egret's mouth opened, but one of the men sitting beside me, the ones who'd been holding each other, spoke. "There is a lot."

"What?" I asked, switching to German.

The man's voice was a gravelly whisper, nearly drowned out by the sound of our flight. "We lived in Oldenburg before ..."

"A lot? What about a lot?"

"There is a lot where the Germans park vehicles. There are many cars and buses," he said.

"What would—" Egret began.

I understood. "Get his hands free." Without taking my eyes off the man, I asked, "Can you stand? Can you come to the front?"

He glanced at the man clinging to him, then looked back up. "Yes. You may need to help me."

"Come on," I said as his cuffs snapped open. We staggered, banging into seats and prisoners alike. None complained. Egret held the man aloft from behind, while I let his weight lean against me as I led us forward.

Will heard the commotion and glanced back through a mirror. Terror filled his eyes.

"Tobias," I said. "This man knows where we can hide until the search settles."

I stepped down into the stairwell to allow the man to squat beside Will. His balance faltered and he fell forward, slamming into the bus's metal frame.

"Here, let me help you," I said, pulling him upright.

"They make cars and buses close to here. There is a lot for storage."

"Just tell me where to turn," Will said.

The man looked around, gaining his bearings.

A horn honked desperately behind.

Outside, the dull gray of the airport and surrounding buildings was quickly replaced by the greens and browns of farms that spread in every direction.

"We're out in the open. We need to get off this road now," I said.

Will shot me a glance, then returned his attention to the road. The man sitting beside me looked between us, a curiosity in his gaze, then he turned to face the oncoming roadway. "This road will dead-end onto Metjendorfer Street. Turn right. You will come to Heidkamper very quickly. Turn left. The lot is only a quarter-mile or so down that road, on the right."

"Got it," Will said. "Hold on."

The bus roared as Will slammed the pedal to the floor. The man lost his balance again, spilling into me in the stairwell. I wrapped my arms around his skeletal body and carefully set him upright on the floor beside the driver's seat.

"Thank you," he said, as his eyes examined me. There was no fear in his eyes, certainly not like there was raging through every part of me. He was oddly calm. "I am Holger."

The casual introduction collided with our frenetic escape, and I stared back, as if seeing a new animal at a zoo.

"Wilhelm. He's Tobias."

Holger looked up at Will, then back toward me. His lips twitched, ever so slightly, then his brittle fingers reached up and closed around my forearm. "We are the same, you and I, your Tobias and my Joachim."

If the Nazis had dropped a bomb on our bus, I could not have been more stunned.

Here we were, a world away from home, a lifetime from the simple pleasures of our freedom, using cover identities to hide code names beneath disguises, and this emaciated man saw through it all and embraced the men we truly were.

I opened my mouth to speak, yet words fled. I swayed when the bus swerved, but this time it was Holger holding me upright, gifting me what little strength he had to offer.

His eyes never left mine. His hand remained locked on my arm.

"There's the dead end," Will announced, excitement mixed with panic in his voice.

I knew I should look, should watch where we turned. Holger's head should rise above the bus's dash to ensure we followed the proper path, but we were frozen, locked in a journey between us I couldn't understand.

The bus slowed enough to turn, but felt like gravity would rend us from the road when Will actually took the sharp curve.

"Hold on!" he shouted to everyone aboard.

When the bus leveled out, I realized neither Holger nor I had released the other's gaze.

His grip squeezed, almost a gentle caress, and his eyes softened into understanding.

"Yes," I said. My voice sounded in my ears as one beneath water listening to another standing above; distant, vague, incomprehensible.

Holger's hand released my arm and rose to graze my cheek in the purest gesture my heart could fathom.

"You two need a moment alone?" Will snarled as he slowed and banked the bus leftward, making the second turn onto Heidkamper. His note of jealousy in the most absurd and desperate of circumstances made me bark out a laugh. I glanced down to find Holger smiling for the first time since I'd been loaded onto the bus. For a man so drained of life, I realized in that moment how wonderfully he lived each moment afforded him.

The bus slowed again.

"Is this it?" Will asked, pointing to a massive lot with hundreds of vehicles.

"Yes," Holger wheezed.

"There's nothing around for miles but farms. If they check here, we're dead," Will said.

"I'm open to better ideas, but this thing can't go much faster than you drove it. They'd catch us if we kept running, especially if they sent planes up to look for us."

Will turned into the lot and headed toward a section filled with identical buses. I stood and looked through the length of the bus out the rear window, relieved to see Sparrow still close behind. Then I saw the plume of dust chasing both the bus and car, and my heart seized again.

"Let me out. You can go park in the middle of those buses. I'll send Sparrow to the other side with the cars, then we'll come join you. There's no reason to be separated."

Will turned toward me as the bus ground to a halt. "No, not again. Never again."

As I reached for the handle to open the door, Holger's hand gripped my wrist. His words nearly flooded my eyes. "Thank you, Wilhelm. Thank you for saving us."

# Chapter Thirty-Four

# Thomas



Sparrow and I drove the car to the opposite corner of the lot farthest from the entrance. There were several other black sedans of similar make and style, and larger vehicles obscured the view from the road. We got out and snuck from one car to the next, crouched over, pausing at each stop to ensure we remained well hidden.

"God, this is taking forever," Sparrow whispered.

I peeked through the windows of the car we hid behind to confirm we were still alone.

"Ten more rows, I think. This must be part of their Bremen fleet storage. There's far too many vehicles here for Oldenburg," I said, letting the strategic implications roll through my mind.

We scurried to our next hiding spot.

"How are they?" she asked.

I cocked a brow.

"The prisoners," she said. Then her eyes dipped and she added in a barely audible whisper, "How is Egret?"

I gripped her shoulder. "Egret will be fine. Adam looks really rough. The others ... they're alive."

Another check ahead, then I whispered, "Silence until we get into the bus. We're getting closer to the edge." She nodded, though her eyes begged for more than my simple words had offered.

The moment we stepped onto the bus, she shoved past me and barreled down the aisle, nearly knocking Egret off his feet. Weary eyes turned to watch her arms wrap tightly about him and her lips press into his. Tears flowed almost immediately.

"Get down," I said, somewhere between a whisper and a shout.

The pair ducked without releasing each other, falling to their knees, then crumpling into a pile on the hard metal floor. They didn't care. They didn't look up or let go.

We were transfixed. I doubted the prisoners had seen genuine happiness in months, perhaps longer. The only love they'd likely witnessed came from Holger and Joachim.

I was fairly certain Will and I shared one mind. We'd known of the couple's physical connection. We were thousands of miles from home and people had needs. What I hadn't expected was the deep emotional connection so clearly on display. Sparrow hadn't just enjoyed the rugged man's company, she'd fallen for him. And, by the streaks on Egret's face, he'd done the same with her.

I don't know how long they sat there like that, embracing, kissing, weeping. It was only when Will's hand clasped mine that I startled out of my daydream. My eyes shot down and a jolt of terror seized me. We weren't exactly in public, but we were in front of several strangers. We could never ...

Then I caught Joachim's smile, the first I'd seen from the man, even when he was huddling with Holger. His eyes grew bright again, and his cheeks filled with a life I'd thought might be lost to him. I followed his gaze to our clasped hands, then met his eyes once more.

I'll never know what unspoken words bound us together in that moment, but we would forever be brothers, Joachim and I.

"We need to get everyone out of their seats and onto the floor," Will whispered, tugging urgently at my hand. "If a patrol checks this place, they can't see heads poking up."

"Right," I said, suddenly alarmed at my lapse in awareness.

"Everyone," I called. "We need to hide here for a few hours to let the patrols exhaust themselves. I'm sorry to ask this, but please either lie flat on the seat or sit on the floor."

Holger coughed, the result of an unexpected chuckle gone wrong. When I looked down, he said through wheezes, "We have been in a cage, sitting in our own piss and shit. I think the floor of a bus will be just fine."

In moments, Sparrow and Egret had joined Will and me near the front of the bus. The others gathered close, huddling shoulder to shoulder in the aisleway and on the floor between seats. Adam stared lifelessly from where he sat alone near the back of the bus.

"Heinz, are you well enough to fight?" I asked, suddenly aware we had no plan should the Nazis show up.

"No, probably not. I haven't eaten a proper meal in … I can't remember when. You could probably blow on me and I would fall over." Egret's gaze narrowed as he considered something, then he shifted widened eyes to our clasped hands and pointed. "You two?"

*Oh, shit.*

Egret had never known about Will and me.

Sparrow had pierced our veil early on, but the men of our contingent remained clueless. Will and I had talked about how to handle exactly this situation, ultimately agreeing that avoiding it altogether was our best course.

There would be no more avoiding of this issue.

No other words were needed. Everyone on that bus knew exactly what he meant. Every man there had faced a similar accusation. We knew the hesitation in the way he asked his question. We recognized the point of his finger.

They understood the terror that flooded both of our faces. Empathy flowed through the gazes of every former prisoner as I grappled with how to respond.

In the end, Will's bravery overtook my own. "Yes," he said simply, then looked at Sparrow, then back toward Egret. "You two?"

She covered her mouth to stifle a girlish giggle that threatened to light every corner of the bus with sunlight. Egret's smile did just that. "Yeah, if she'll have me."

Somehow, magically, thankfully, that was the last time we ever spoke of the matter.

Sparrow and Egret, Will and I—we simply were.

And it was beautiful.

I sucked in a breath, not even realizing how badly I'd needed to steady myself, then looked to Egret.

"Okay, you're responsible for keeping these men out of the way. Anny, Wilhelm, and I will handle whatever we have to." I took a mental inventory. "We have three pistols and two knives, not enough to hold off more than a few men, but it'll have to do."

"We just can't be found. It's as simple as that," Sparrow said.

I nodded. "Right. Let's keep quiet for a while. We should be able to hear cars on this dirt and gravel, but I'd rather not take any chances of someone sneaking up on us."

The entire group fell into an uneasy silence. Some closed their eyes, willing sleep. Others, afraid of what dreams might come, stared into nothing.

Joachim and Holger held each other.

Sparrow rested her head on Egret's chest, her arms wrapped tightly about him. He never stopped stroking her hair.

Will's fingers entwined with mine and he occasionally squeezed, drawing my eyes to his. I wasn't sure if he was reminding me of his love or reassuring himself I was still there. Either way, we were together, and I would die before letting anyone tear us apart again.

Hours passed. The sun yawned and stretched across the sky.

No Nazis came. In fact, no one came.

I'd expected workers to retrieve vehicles, mechanics to remove others to be serviced, some form of ordinary activity, but none of that occurred.

I motioned for everyone to remain low and rose to my knees. The buses on either side obscured the view, but I could make out the road in the distance through the rear. The road remained silent and untraveled. Looking out the front, I could see beyond the lot, across distant fields that sprawled forever. It was late autumn, nearly winter. The ground was packed and hard, the fields barren and silent.

"Anything?" Sparrow whispered.

I shook my head. "Stay here. I'm going to step out and make sure."

Will's eyes flared and his grip tightened before releasing my hand.

"I'll be right back."

I didn't have to go far, just around the line of buses, to clear the field of view. A few birds rummaged through garbage strewn about. The wind whistled through the rows of vehicles. Puffy white clouds eased across a brilliant sky.

And everything was, as I suspected, quiet and undisturbed.

As I looked toward the far corner where our sedan was parked, I remembered the few supplies Adriaan and Nora had packed for us. The poor men we'd brought along were desperate, starving, dehydrated. What little remained would barely whet their palates, but it was more than the Germans had fed them. It would have to do for now.

I snaked my way through the vehicle maze, careful to keep my head down, retrieved two backpacks from the trunk, then returned to the bus.

"Anything?" Will asked urgently as I stepped up onto the bus.

I shook my head. "No. But I brought something for the others to eat. There's a canteen with some water too."

Every eye on the bus, even Adam's, snapped toward the front, hope mingled with doubt pouring through their gazes. Even now, after we'd freed them from their cage, trepidation wafted off them like some tangible ache they couldn't escape.

I watched as they passed the canteen back. No one drank greedily. Each sipped and passed it to the next, ensuring everyone received relief. When the meager pack of food made its way about, warm expressions turned to surprise and delight. Never before had I seen a simple cookie invoke tears of joy. First bites were chewed slowly, so slowly, inducing groans that warmed my spirit. Again, no one had to monitor the stores. These men shared a bond and cared for one another so gently.

A man seated on the other side of Joachim smiled as caramel stuck to his fingers. Like an Olympian raising a medal, his finger lifted into the air before he brought it to his mouth to lick it clean. It was like watching children try candy for the first time, and I couldn't stop grinning.

"I was a baker," the Olympic caramel eater said, his voice an echo of a whisper. "Before all this, I made things like this."

Sparrow lifted her head and turned to the man. "What's your name?"

His smile widened. "Dieter."

A name is such a simple thing, yet it holds such substantial weight and power. These men had not owned their names since their captivity. Use of them was forbidden, punishable by whatever barbaric means the guards could conjure.

To be asked his name was a luxury. To be able to answer, beyond treasure.

Before I realized what was happening, others scooted close.

"I am Hans." He was a bookseller specializing in ancient volumes. His shop was celebrated throughout Germany as one of the finest.

"Reynard," the oldest said eagerly. He'd been a school teacher. His eyes were kind and sure.

"My name is Karl," the last man said. His hair was black, thick, and plastered to his head from lack of washing. His eyes were green with flecks of gold. There was such depth and sadness in them. "I was a musician. I miss my music so."

I looked toward the back where Adam sat, hoping the shift in the group might lift him from his daze. He remained unmoved, his eyes little more than glass, seeing less than a mirror whose only craft was reflection.

A moment passed, then Dieter whispered a memory, recounting some of the many items he'd make each morning. As his gaze drifted into the past, a smile curled his lips and remained until his telling was done.

Then Karl spoke, then Hans, and Reynard.

We listened until the sky was painted with the sun's evening kiss.

It startled me when Dieter turned toward Will and asked, "Who are you? Who were you ... before?"

Will's eyes found mine and held, as if asking ...

"My name is Tobias," he began. "I worked with ancient artifacts; I preserved history."

Hans lit up. "Antiquities? My books might be called that as well."

Dieter ended the stream before it could flow. "And you?" he asked me.

"Wilhelm. I ... I was a translator. I love languages."

Egret and Sparrow followed, recounting their cover stories to perfection.

Only one person refused his tale.

I made my way carefully past the men and sat beside Adam. He didn't even look up as I approached.

"Adam, how do you feel?" It was such a stupid question. I knew that the moment it left my lips, but I had to ask.

He didn't answer.

"Adam, look at me." He remained unmoved.

I reached up and gripped his chin, forcing his head to turn.

I nearly shuddered at his gaze. It was the bottom of a forgotten vase, dark and cold—and empty.

I lowered my voice so the others could not hear. "It's me, Adam. Thomas. You remember me, right?" His nod was barely perceptible. Had my fingers not clung to his chin, I might never have known it occurred.

"Good," I said. "We're going to get everyone to a safe house, get you cleaned up and fed."

Something in his eyes shifted at that. "Home?" he croaked.

"Yes, Adam," I nearly choked. "I'm taking you home."

# Chapter Thirty-Five
# **Will**

*"Hope is the power of being cheerful in circum-
stances that we know to be desperate."*

G.K Chesterton [1]

As dusk deepened, everyone rose and stretched, grateful to be off the numbing metal bus floor. We'd spent the afternoon as comfortably as our confines and fear of discovery would allow. I think our stink on the floorboard inflicted more damage on Sparrow, Thomas, and me, as the others were now used to far worse.

---

1. English writer, 1874–1936.

"Where do we go now?" I asked as Thomas made his way back to the front.

"The Plan B safe house," he said matter-of-factly.

The LO had devised a simple plan: get in, get out, get home. There hadn't been time for anything more elaborate. Thankfully, they did also include a back-up in case things went haywire, which tended to happen when infiltrating the enemy's homeland. Our back-up plan was a safe house south of a small village called Papenburg, a few miles from the Dutch–German border.

"Safe house? In Germany?" Holger asked from his seat across from Thomas.

Thomas nodded. "We haven't learned of much formal resistance in Germany, but there are a few who still own a conscience. We should be able to hold up safely if we can make it to Papenburg."

"The borders are going to be sealed up tight," Egret said.

"Yeah." Sparrow nodded. "I would love to have seen when the real colonel arrived and discovered all his prisoners missing. I bet he wanted to burn the country down."

"We won't be able to cross for a while," Thomas said, more thought than statement. It chilled further discussion.

"Alright," he said after a few moments of silence. "It's nearly dark. Tobias, do you have the map? We need to plan our route."

"Right here," I said, pointing beside the driver's seat to the neatly folded map.

---

Headlights were terrifying, especially when they came in pairs or threes. Each time cars passed headed in the opposite direction, my breath stilled and my heart leapt into my throat.

Yet none stopped. No cars wheeled about in pursuit.

Almost an hour after leaving the lot, we pulled onto a long drive leading to a sprawling farmhouse in the middle of fields of swaying tallgrass.

"Is every safe house on a farm?" I asked absently.

Thomas grunted. "Seems like it. It's better than risking a town or city where we have to worry about prying eyes around every corner."

"True," I said.

"Stop the bus," Thomas said when we were about fifty yards from the house. "Stay here. I'll go greet our host. They might not take kindly to a bus rolling up unannounced. Have your gun at the ready, just in case."

He squeezed my shoulder, then stepped out into the night. Thomas continued to impress me. He might let his guard down a little too easily—like we all did—but his mind was as keen as ever. As he shrank into the distance, I realized for the thousandth time that I not only loved this man, I respected him.

A moment later, the light flashed on and off in the distance, a signal I assumed meant we could approach. As we rolled up to the house, Thomas, an older man, and a bent woman stood on a deep porch that wrapped around the home. The man raised a hand in greeting, then pointed to where he wanted me to park.

The old woman stepped back and her eyes widened as I stepped off the bus still wearing the uniform of an SD colonel.

"It is a disguise. I'm not a Nazi," I explained quickly.

The woman's shoulders relaxed, but her gaze remained fixed as I stepped onto the porch.

I nearly fell over when Thomas stepped forward, grabbed my hand, and turned back to the old woman. "This is Tobias. He's my partner."

"Why didn't you say that to start with, Wilhelm? He's rather handsome, even in that black thing." She scowled at him, then her tension evaporated and a broad smile stretched across her weathered face. "Come, let's get you some proper clothes. I think we've all seen enough of those uniforms to last a lifetime. You can call me Oma." [2]

---

2. German word for grandma, granny, or grandmother.

She stepped forward and wrapped her bony arm in mine but froze before turning.

"Dear God," she muttered, crossing herself with her free hand as Holger and Joachim stepped off the bus. Her husband was off the porch and across the yard faster than I thought the gray-topped man could move. As the others stepped down, the old man grabbed hands and arms or offered his own, helping them to steady their balance.

"When was the last time these boys ate? Or bathed?" she asked to no one in particular.

"The Germans fed them broth every few days. They pretty much lived in what you see. The smell is terrible," I whispered, suddenly conscious of them hearing us talk about them.

"This is madness. This whole damned war is ..." She shook her head. "Their stomachs won't take much now, but I'll get them fit again. You, my cute little Nazi, come with me. You can change and help me in the kitchen."

Thomas winked when I looked up with pleading eyes. "He is a cute little Nazi, isn't he?"

Without missing a beat, she raised a finger toward Thomas. "And you, Mister, you will help these poor souls bathe and change. My husband will round them up some clothes while you handle the baths. Don't leave them in there alone. When they get to this point, sometimes they just duck under and don't come back up. Trust me on this."

Thomas blinked, stunned by both her orders and the idea she'd seen wasted former prisoners drown themselves in her bath.

Oma crossed herself once more and dragged me inside.

I chopped root vegetables while Oma prepared a bland soup with a small amount of beef.

"I'll make something a bit heartier for the rest of us, but those boys won't tolerate much more for their first proper meal." She thought a moment, then her eyes brightened. "Bread. They can probably handle bread. I have a few loaves I made just this morning. Perfect."

I wasn't sure if she was talking to me or herself. Either way, she seemed pleased with her arrangements, and even more so that someone was helping her in the kitchen. Once the soup was prepared and simmering, she led me through the house to a room at the far end of a long hallway.

"We had seven children," she said, touching the door to the room like it was precious. "This was our oldest's room."

"Where is he now?"

"We lost him in the war." Her eyes fell. "We lost them all." My heart ached for this woman. My hand found her arm, and she leaned into me, nestling her face in my chest.

The only thing I could do was wrap my arms around her and give her what comfort I could. When she pulled back, she hadn't shed a tear and her eyes were again steel.

"We have all lost much," she whispered, smoothing the spot on my coat where her cheek had pressed. "Come, let's get you changed."

She had a keen eye. Her eldest had been close to my size. When I returned to the kitchen in brown breeches and a light blue shirt, she whistled. "Now there's a right handsome fella."

I blushed and grinned, which only encouraged her.

"Keep flushin' like that and you'll make this old woman's heart race," she chuckled as she stirred the soup. "Why don't you go help Wilhelm finish up? This soup just needs to simmer."

"Yes, ma'am."

She cackled. "Ma'am, like I'm some lady. I love it."

Most of the men had been bathed and were adjusting the clothing formerly worn by Oma's other sons. Nothing fit. They had so little muscle on their bones that belts had to be cinched tight just to keep pants up. Still, they were clean and somewhat refreshed. Joachim almost looked relaxed as he smiled up at Holger.

"Don't you look nice?" I said.

Holger grinned but struggled to get his fingers to complete his task.

"Here, let me," I said, reaching up and fastening the button, then smoothing his shirt as Oma had done to mine. "There, look at him, Joachim. Isn't he handsome?"

Joachim's smile widened, an effort that looked painful but there was joy returning to his eyes.

"Oma is making soup. Why don't you go in the kitchen and keep her company while I help Wilhelm?"

Holger gripped my arm and pulled me into a tight embrace, then stepped back.

"What was that for?" I asked.

He squeezed my arm. "Everything. That is what you have given us."

I nearly ran to the bathroom, not trusting myself to keep from drowning in a waterfall of emotions. I'd only made it one step inside when the last of my control fled.

Adam was sitting in a tub of brackish water. He stared blankly into the faucet. Thomas was kneeling over him, sponging his back gently, speaking words I could not hear, soft and low. When Thomas glanced over his shoulder, so hollow were his eyes that I had to grip the sink to stay upright.

I shut the door and dropped to my knees, wrapping my arm around him. "Babe, I'm here."

He stared into my eyes, fighting his own tears.

Adam never spoke. His gaze never shifted.

"You go change. Oma will find you clothes. I'll finish here," I said, helping Thomas stand. He nodded weakly but didn't move to leave. I gripped his face with both hands and pressed my forehead into his. "We'll make this right. It'll be alright," I whispered over and over.

At last, when his strength had returned, he pressed a soft kiss to my lips and closed the door behind him.

I turned to my task, returning to my knees and draining the dirty water from the tub.

"Let's get your hair clean, then get you into some warm clothes, alright?"

Adam didn't respond.

I watched a moment. He was an empty shell. He'd been so full of life.

Anger welled within me and I gripped his chin, forcing him to look at me.

"Adam, you listen to me. We sail all that way to save the world only to lose you? We care about you, Adam Roth. You're our brother and I'm not letting you go. You hear me? You stay with me."

Maybe it was the play of the bathroom light on the draining water.

Maybe it was what I hoped to see.

I swear, Adam's eyes narrowed and his head shifted.

# Chapter Thirty-Six

# Thomas

*"The only limit to our realization of tomorrow
will be our doubts of today."*

FRANKLIN D. ROOSEVELT

Autumn surrendered to winter.

Oma's soup grew into meaty stew, then full meals. The men regained their strength. Even Adam began to look human again, though the vacancy in his eyes remained. How does one impart the will to care again? Is it even possible? Oma's constant clucking and persistent tending healed nearly every wound. I began to think the woman could work any miracle, trusting in her kindness to salve the deeper wounds that could not be seen.

Some things were beyond mortal strength.

The old man we'd come to call Opa[1] and I sat alone on the porch, huddled beneath heavy blankets to stave off winter's chill. He sat out there most mornings to watch the sun rise, claiming the cold helped him think. As I watched my breath float away, I wondered if it didn't do the opposite, at least to me.

"The Allied bombings are increasing," Opa said, shattering our silent contemplation. "They assaulted Frankfurt a few days ago. The talk is of terrible damage and uncontrollable fires."

I nodded. "It won't be long before troops arrive from America. If they're bombing the interior like that, it's to prepare for something."

Opa peered over his spectacles and sipped his tea. "The men in town say they have pulled many of their patrols from the border to protect the south and east." His words were deliberate, his gaze meaningful.

"You think it's time?" I asked.

He set his cup on a saucer and laced his fingers across his belly. "If there is something coming, best you be gone before it arrives. You might not be able to leave once it starts."

---

1. German term for grandpa, the informal of grandfather.

There was no way anyone could make contact via radio with Allies in Holland, not from German soil. The Nazis had become ever more efficient in ferreting out transmitters, and the use of them in their own territory was unthinkable. No one in Holland, Britain, or America knew we still lived. No one could assist with our escape.

"What do you suggest?" I asked, recognizing the gaze of a man who had more to tell.

His lips twitched and he leaned forward, as if to impart some conspiratorial code. "There is a cavern near the village of Neuheede, an abandoned salt mine."

"A salt mine?" Images of stalactites, pitch-black caves, and tons of collapsing earth burying us alive flashed to mind.

Opa nodded. "The salt mine only goes so far, but the caves continue for several miles."

I waited, disliking this plan more by the moment.

"The caves open on the Holland side of the border. The mouth is set in a pile of obscure boulders outside the farming village of Bourtange. If we can get you into the mine, there is an underground canal that will ferry you beneath the border. You will have to find transport to Amsterdam, but I expect the Nazis will be most distracted at the moment."

"You've put thought into this?" I asked.

His grin was my only answer.

"When?"

"Best not wait too long," he said. "Two, three days at most."

I thought a moment. "The others?"

He grabbed his cup and took a warming sip. "They have recovered much but they cannot make that trip. They should stay here, with us, at least through winter."

The last thing I wanted to do was separate. Joachim and Holger had become fast friends, brothers to Will and me. We would both be loath to say goodbye, but Opa was right and I knew it.

"Alright. Two days? If the weather is good?"

He nodded. "Two days."

The next day was unseasonably warm. Opa sat on the porch, cradling his mug of tea as the sun's fingers gripped the horizon. It was the first day in weeks he wasn't buried beneath a mountain of blankets for his morning ritual.

"Morning," he said, raising his mug in salute.

The old man's smile warmed my heart as well as any blanket could my skin.

"Good morning," I said. "Oma's already hard at work in the kitchen."

He grunted through a sip. "She has always been an early riser. We are alike in that way."

"From what I can tell, you are a match pair in almost every way."

His eyes glittered at that. "I suppose we are."

"There was another surprise waiting for me in the kitchen just now."

"Oh?"

I settled into the seat beside him and stared into the yellowing sky. "Dieter was kneading dough beside her."

Opa nearly spilled his tea. "Oh, that is good. That is very good."

"It really is. And yesterday, Karl was picking at an old guitar he found somewhere." My grin matched his. "If you had told me all those weeks ago that Dieter would return to a kitchen so soon, I would've thought you were touched. You two are miracle workers."

"Oma would say I'm plenty touched, though perhaps not for that reason." He chuckled. "There's nothing like a full belly and a warm, safe place to rest one's head to restore the spirit. I'd say you and Tobias share in the credit there too. Seeing the pair of you dote on each other might melt the ice in Hitler's veins."

I groaned at the invocation of the Führer's name. "I'm not sure anything could do *that*."

"If there's any justice in the world, Allied bombs will soon enough."

I raised my mug. "Hear, hear."

The moment stretched in pleasant silence. I could've spent years at the old man's side. A part of me wanted to forget the war and all the world's troubles and simply hide in that home filled with laughter and love. Alas, such things were not meant to be.

"You have not told the others of our plan? Not even Tobias?" he asked, shattering visions of Will growing old in the kitchen with Oma.

"No, not yet," I said. "They deserve another day."

He eyed me, though I didn't turn from the sunrise. The warmth of his smile was as clear on my skin as that of the newborn sun.

"You are a fine man, Wilhelm, a very fine man. You remind me so much of our Alric."

His voice trailed off, as if speaking the name aloud stole some part of him.

"He was your oldest?"

Opa nodded, though his eyes were far away.

"Oma mentioned him to Will but didn't share his name."A flock of birds, late for their winter respite, took flight at the far end of the field.

"Did she tell you how he died?"

"No, only that he was lost to the war."

He shifted in his seat and set his mug on the wooden table between us.

"He was a stubborn boy. Before the war began, when Hitler was little more than a noisy man with a microphone, he talked of fighting back, of doing something to stop what he called evil rising." He shook his head slowly. "He was too smart by half."

He lifted his mug and sipped, pressing it to his lips for an eternal moment before returning it to the table. "When the Nazis began rounding up the Jews, it was too much for Alric. He had many Jewish friends at university and could not watch them suffer under Hitler's boot. He helped a few of them and their families flee into Holland. Others were too late."

He turned and met my gaze again. "He died, almost a year ago, attacking a train headed for one of the camps. I do not know what they would have done if they had succeeded. Where would he take hundreds? It seemed so foolish."

"He died trying to save people," I said quietly. "He died a hero."

The wrinkles about his eyes tightened as he considered those words, then he nodded and his gaze fell to his hands.

"You pay me too much honor comparing me to him."

Then Opa did the last thing I expected. He reached across and gripped my arm, iron fingers digging into the flesh. His eyes searched mine, brilliant beams slicing through the darkness. I could feel them piercing every part of me.

"You honor him by the life you lead, Wilhelm. Do not take that away from an old man. I am proud of the boy he was, but I am growing so proud of the man I see before me."

Something slammed into my throat as I tried to speak.

His eyes welled, and I felt my own threatening to give way. His gaze held firm.

I struggled to speak. "Thank you, Opa," was all I could think to say.

Another moment passed and he released me, returning his attention to the horizon. "It is a beautiful day, is it not?"

I couldn't stop staring at the old man. "Yes, I believe it will be."

# Chapter Thirty-Seven
## Thomas

*"To love and be loved is to feel the sun from both sides."*

DAVID VISCOTT [1]

T hat night, as the others sat together listening to Karl play lighthearted tunes, Will and I took a walk through Opa's fields. There were no roads nearby. Anyone bored enough to spy on the old couple would have to cross an open plain or trek the lonely drive.

---

1. American psychiatrist, author, and media personality, 1938–1996.

The night was clear, though the moon was a sliver of itself. A million fireflies struggled against the sky's dark web above.

Another hour would reveal our breaths. The nip in the air was life itself.

We'd been freed from our cages, but being cooped up in a house for weeks on end was an entirely different prison. It felt good to be outside, to stretch and move.

Will remained quiet far too long after I outlined the plan for our departure the next day. I was about to ask his thoughts when he finally spoke.

"I don't love it, but when was the last time we had a plan with decent odds?"

I couldn't argue with that. Just once, I'd like the odds stacked in our favor as we began a mission.

"And I'm not sure Adam should come with us," he continued. "I don't want to leave him behind, but he's in no shape to run. Maybe this place is better for him, at least for now."

I sucked in a breath. The same debate had raged in my head all day. "Should we just ask him? Let him choose?"

Will thought a moment. "I'm not sure he's in a mind to be able to make that kind of decision."

"But?" I could hear the word in his tone.

"But ... who are we to decide for him? He deserves to choose his own fate."

I hated that answer, but he was right. Adam hadn't been himself since well before we'd found him, that much was clear. Egret said he started fading a week or so into their captivity. Throughout our training in Scotland and our mission at sea, he'd seemed so strong, so invincible. It felt as though we'd already lost him.

"We need to tell the others tonight," I said.

"Yeah," was his only reply.

I was dreading that conversation. We'd only known the former prisoners a few weeks, but they already felt like family. There's a strange bond that forms when you're responsible for the fate of another person. When their life is literally in your hands, it's stronger still. I'd miss Holger and Joachim most of all. We were so alike, the four of us. In another life, another time, definitely another place, we might've been the closest of friends.

My heart sank at the thought of leaving them behind.

"The mines make a weird sort of sense," I said, desperate to escape the melancholy that threatened and defend Opa's idea. "We'll be about as out of sight as possible."

"Hidden beneath a bazillion tons of rock and dirt? Right." Will shuddered. "You know, I really hate confined spaces." I stopped walking and turned. "You never told me that."

He shrugged. "You never invited me spelunking before."

I chuckled. "Such a big word. You trying to turn me on?"

"If that turned you on, just wait till I tell you about my arachnophobia."

"Dear God, confined spaces *and* heights? What else have you been hiding?"

"Spiders, you idiot. Acrophobia is heights." He shoved my shoulder playfully. "I don't love those either, by the way."

"You're scared of pretty much everything, but you're really smart and that's fucking hot. Say that last one again. Take it slow for me."

He laughed, pressed both hands to my chest, and shoved. My foot caught on the ridge of one of the field's rows and I toppled backward onto my butt.

He was on me before I could protest.

"Show me how turned on you are," he breathed, his mouth wet and hot against my own.

It had been more than a month since we'd been alone together, enjoying the naked pleasure of youthful love. Our kisses were passionate and our hands searched greedily. He pulsed above me, driving my own arousal to dance beside his. I wanted to fill myself with his scent, to devour him. I wanted every part of him and—

"Why do we have to be in a stupid field?" he groaned as we ground against each other. "I want you so bad."

"Me too, babe, but ..."

"But what?"

"There's a turnip in my back."

His head jerked upright. "A what?"

I shifted, wincing, then reached back and lifted the offending object. "Okay, maybe it's a rock."

He laughed and stood. "You are such an idiot."

"Hey! Where are you going?"

"Nothing kills the mood like a turnip." He extended a hand to help me up. "Let's head back before it gets any colder."

# Chapter Thirty-Eight

# Thomas

*"The middle of the road is where the white line
is, and that's the worst place to drive."*

ROBERT FROST [1]

Adam insisted on returning with us. It wasn't a surprise, but the disappointment in Will's eyes mirrored my own. He was a broken man and we feared leaving the warmth of the farmhouse spelled disaster for his recovery. Alas, he was also a grown man with a mind of his own, and we respected his decision.

Our goodbyes were beyond bittersweet.

---

1. American poet and author, 1874–1963.

Will, Holger, and Joachim clung together, the three whispering private thoughts before facing the group. When Oma wrapped her ancient arms around Will, I thought the ground might shake, she cried so hard. I was sure some of her tears were shed for her lost boys as much as for us. A mother's grief is never complete.

What I hadn't expected, and perhaps I was naive, was how hard facing Opa would be.

"The Nazi patrols at the border remain only four-man teams," he said, repeating the intelligence from his network of gray-haired tea and coffee aficionados who whispered often about such things. "Perhaps the increased activity by the Allies has your pursuers chasing other prey?"

"We can certainly hope so," I said. My eyes drifted past the old man to where our friends stood surrounding Will, Sparrow, and Egret. "We will take care of them. God willing, they will be strong again soon, in body and in mind."

"God willing," he repeated.

When I started to turn away, he gripped my shoulder.

"Opa?"

"You could ... you could stay." He struggled to meet my gaze.

I grabbed him then, pulling him tight against me and holding him with all my strength. "You have no idea how much I would like that. But there are others to save."

"You are so alike." He pulled back, his hands still gripping my arms, his eyes swelling. "Be safe, Wilhelm."

"Thank you, Opa."I realized something in that moment that gave me pause.

"Wilhelm?" he asked, his brow furrowed.

"We never learned your names."

He smiled. "No, you did not, as I suspect we have not learned yours."

I wanted to object, to argue, to beg for that last closeness to bind us together, but words failed to form. He stole them from me.

"It is as it should be."

I nodded, wishing to never leave his gaze, then turned to gather the others. Opa had acquired a car, from where he did not say, which was now laden with baked goods and camping supplies the couple thought we might need on our journey home.

"There are a few extra batteries for your torches. I wish we had more, but they are so scarce these days," Oma said, pointing to the pack that held her precious cargo.

"Three guns and two knives," I said to myself.

"Hope we don't have to use any of them," Sparrow chirped. I hadn't realized anyone had heard me.

"Right," I said with a nod and tight grin.

We piled into the car, Will and me in the front, Sparrow sandwiched between Egret and Adam in the back. If we hadn't all known our destination and the dangers the journey might entail, the whole thing would've felt like a merry holiday with our closest friends.

Adam's hollow stare was a persistent reminder of the truth of the matter.

"We're only about ten minutes from the mine's entrance. Opa suggested we park a half-mile away and walk the rest. He thinks the place has been abandoned long enough for no one to notice, but didn't want us to take unnecessary chances."

"Wouldn't be the first time the Nazis left eyes in place a lot longer than we expected," Egret said.

"Right," I replied. Our instructors at Camp X had told plenty of stories where operatives were killed or captured because the enemy had given the appearance of relaxed vigilance, only to be deeply hidden and waiting for their moment to pounce.

"How you holding up back there, Adam?" I hoped the action of a mission might jar something loose in his mind.

"Fine," was all I received. His eyes never even left the window.

A few moments later, he surprised me by speaking up. "There's a car behind us."I glanced in the mirror to find a dot in the distance. "You can see that?"

"It's been back there since we picked up this road. We only took one turn, but it turned with us and it's stayed that same distance the whole way."

*Not dead after all*, I thought, wishing the thing that spurred him to life could be something other than armed pursuit.

"Keep an eye on them. Maybe it's nothing," I said, not believing my own words. Adam always had good instincts. If his hackles were raised, there was something amiss.

We reached a dirt road not far from the mine, the waypoint Opa had suggested would make a good parking spot. As our car rolled to a stop, I watched in the rearview as our tail slowed at the turn but continued past.

"Looks like they're gone," Will said.

I opened my door. "Let's move. Grab the packs. We're exposed until we get into those trees."

Egret, Will, and I slung packs over our backs, while Sparrow checked a gun then handed it to Will. I tossed the keys under the driver's seat and we set off across the open field, headed toward a forested area that began at the far end.

Halfway across, the sound of a car door slamming turned my head.

I spotted the telltale smear of Nazi black as a blond man stepped from a car parked behind our sedan. A second man rounded the car, then pointed in our direction.

"Dammit, run!" I barked.

The field was rough and rocky, far too uneven for a car. I glanced back to see the black dots giving chase on foot.

"They're coming. We've got to move!" I shouted.

As we made it to the tree line, Adam doubled over, heaving. "I can't run anymore. My lungs are burning."

"Here, Tobias, get his other side." We launched him into a fireman's carry. "Anny, Heinz, run ahead. Secure the cave entrance. We'll follow as fast as we can."

We hobbled forward as quickly as possible, watching Sparrow and Egret weave in and out of trees, eventually vanishing from view.

The sound of twigs snapping in the distance spurred us on. They were getting closer.

The trees gave way to open grass. Massive boulders like small hills, five times the height of a man, lay strewn about. A dozen yards ahead, the ground opened in a massive maw. Sparrow and Egret stood just outside, giving us the all-clear signal, urging us on.

"They're right behind us!" I shouted.

A gun fired.

"Shit! You've got to run now, Adam!" We set him down and shoved him forward, running after him.

Another shot fired, echoing off the stone. Will pointed his gun behind and fired aimlessly into the trees.

"Save your ammo," I shouted.

His shot had bought us only a moment.

"They're behind you!" Sparrow screamed, raising her gun.

They fired again.

Adam's body hurled forward into the grass.

"Adam!" I shouted, stumbling to grab him.

"Leave me," he said, slapping my arm away, then wrenched the gun from Will's hand. "I'll hold them off. Go!"He struggled to his knees, then raised the gun, aiming at the men chasing us.

There was no time to think. No time to fight.

We ran.

Another shot fired, then another. We couldn't tell whose was whose.

Then more rang out.

Then nothing.

The four of us entered the cavern's jaws and an eerie silence enveloped us.

Sparrow and Egret had torches ready, but their light was a dim reflection in the absolute darkness of the cavern.

Still, we ran.

"Which way?" Egret whispered, his voice booming in the cave.

"Straight. Every time it forks, go left," I said, repeating Opa's instructions.

One tunnel bled into another, then another. We were too far ahead to see lights behind us, but the slap of boots against stone echoed in the salty cave.

Out of breath, Egret slowed, then stopped, holding up a finger, begging for a moment's breath.

Will and I shared a frightened glare.

"Give us the guns," I whispered. "You go. Tobias and I will take care of them."

"Wilhelm, no—" Sparrow's eyes were wide.

"We won't lose them. Go!"

Reluctantly, Sparrow and Egret handed over the last of our guns, then turned to hobble forward. When their light vanished into the distance, I flicked ours off, casting us in the inkiest blackness.

Will and I pressed ourselves against the cavern's side, hunched behind a turn to guard the approach. His breathing was thunder in my ears, though I doubted any sane man could've heard it.

A beam of gold sliced through the gloom, moving like a desperate eye, searching in every direction.

A second beam appeared. Booted steps grew louder. The ragged huffing of men.

Will fired. The deafening shot bounded off the cavern walls, nearly driving all sense from my head.

The beams faltered, then focused, then surged forward.

I fired at one beam. Then Will did too.

Still, they came.

Then one stilled, and a shot rang out.

Will screamed. My heart seized.

And the second beam brightened my face.

"Do not move!" said a voice in angry German.

I flicked my torch on, lighting every corner of the dark cave.

"Drop it!" the voice barked.

My torch rattled to the floor and I caught sight of the man behind the gun.

"Standartenführer Ewers?" I was stunned. The colonel had indeed pursued us across the fatherland.

"You wounded the Reich at Emden, then you embarrassed me in my own homeland. You will trouble us no more." The clicking of a revolver cocking into place chilled my blood. The barrel pointed unerringly between my eyes.

I watched him squeeze the trigger, and a shot rang out.

I fell to the stone, covering my ears.

My ears.

I was alive.

Slowly, my head rose, as a second beam shone on my face, blinding my vision.

The wielder lowered it, and the stars in my eyes subsided.

Will lay on the ground nearby, blood pooling about him. I fell to his side, all alias protocols turning to dust in my mind.

"Will! Look at me, Will. Oh, God, no!" The light brightened about Will's prone form. His eyes fluttered open. "My leg. I'm okay."

I searched frantically, feeling gently, desperate for it to be true.

Then I remembered the man with the gun and turned.

"Sergeant Ambrose?"

The man stood with his weapon lowered, a torch in his other hand.

I looked for the gun I'd just held. I'd dropped it. When Will fell …

Then I saw the colonel swimming in a pool of blackness.

"You killed him?" I could barely process the scene.

I remembered the gun I'd dropped, then lunged toward it and spun.

Ambrose bent down and set his revolver on the ground.

My jaw flexed. What was he playing at?

"I won't harm you. Either of you. Let me help."

I hovered protectively over Will. "Why would you help us? Why did you—?"

Ambrose nodded. "You saved my brother."

I looked to Will. Confusion muddled his eyes as much as mine.

"Who?"

The flash of a gun lit the cavern behind us and deadened my ears.

Ambrose's black coat grew darker, spreading outward from a perfect hole in his chest. His eyes widened, then he fell forward.

Will lifted his arm and fired into the darkness beyond. Another cry echoed down the cavern, followed by a thump then silence.

It was only then my mind caught up to the reality of the situation. Adam. Ambrose.

Will.

I grew dizzy. My breath came in rapid gulps, my vision blurred, and I tumbled backward into the cave's wall, unable to think or feel or ...

# Chapter Thirty-Nine
## Thomas

*"Do I not destroy my enemies when I make them my friends?"*

ABRAHAM LINCOLN

When I came to, Will was staring into the cave's ceiling. He'd managed to wrap a rough bandage on his own leg. Ambrose lay a few feet away, a blood-soaked bandage resting on his chest, another discarded beside. My flashlight sat upturned, casting an eerie glow across the pimpled roof.

I crawled over and gripped the back of Will's neck. "Are you—?"

"I'm okay," he said. "It went clean through my leg."

He was alive. I'd thought I'd lost him again. My life had ended a second time.

I breathed, pressing my forehead to his. "I swear you're trying to kill me, Will Shaw."

He looked up.

"If you ever take a bullet for me again, I'll shoot you myself. I thought—"

His lips pressed into mine, and time stopped.

The war vanished.

The world vanished.

It was only Will and me.

And we were okay. We were going to be alright.

The tang of his tears reached my lips.

"Cry baby," I teased.

He shoved me back. "Idiot."

His smile lit the cave like a thousand suns.

Then I remembered where we were. The cave. The chase.

The man who'd saved us.

"Ambrose?" I asked, glancing down at the young, frightfully pale face.

Will shook his head. "He's still alive, but barely. I did what I could. There's just so much blood."

I followed his gaze to the well of life spilled beneath him. "Why?" I asked.

"Why does anyone die in this fucking war?"

"No. That's not what I meant," I said. "He *saved* us. Why?"

Will shook his head again, unwilling to look away as Ambrose's breathing grew thinner and slower. He scooted carefully to sit beside him, then reached under and cradled his head. "I don't know. He—"

Words leaked out, barely a whisper.

Will leaned down. "What? I'm here. We're with you. What did you say?"

Ambrose's eyes fluttered open, struggling to focus. "Brother," he hissed.

"Brother? You have a brother?" Will asked.

For a brief instant, the German's eyes cleared and a smile formed on his bloody lips. "You saved ... my brother. Thank you."

Will looked up. I shook my head, baffled.

"What are you talking about?" Will asked. "What brother?"

A low hiss slipped free of his lips. His chest stilled. Unseeing eyes remained fixed on Will. The last word he spoke was, "Holger."

# Chapter Forty

# Will

*"There is nothing like returning to a place that remains unchanged to find the ways in which you yourself have altered."*

Nelson Mandela

It felt wrong, leaving Ambrose to lie in a tomb of salt.

More wrong still, to leave Adam lying on a bed of open grass.

But there was nothing to be done for either of them.

The smooth, rounded cavern gave way to the jagged teeth of untouched caves as we descended below the earth. In places, stones ground so closely together we feared we might not make it through. My leg had stopped bleeding, but the stabbing pain never ebbed, and the ankle I'd twisted some time ago decided to complain with every step. The best part of the trek was how Thomas had to hold me close to keep me upright. If we had to trudge through the belly of the earth, at least I did it in his arms.

"Is that running water?" My voice boomed in my ears.

"Opa said there'd be a canal down here."

A dozen paces later, Thomas's torch light shimmered off a shallow river flowing down the center of the passageway.

"If only we had a boat." The idea of wading for a mile or more in chilly water made my leg throb harder.

"It's barely ankle deep. I don't think a boat would help, babe," he said. "Let's stop for a minute. Your leg could probably use a break."

"Yeah, but not too long. Anny and Heinz are probably wondering whether we made it."

The water never rose to our knees, but it did span the cavern in places, forcing us to slog through as its icy fingers pricked at our skin. By the time the cavern began to ascend once more, we were exhausted, soaked, and fighting against chattering teeth.

"Up there," Thomas said, his voice rising above a whisper for the first time since we'd left Ambrose at the cavern's entrance. He switched off his flashlight and a weak stream of sunlight slipped between the rocks to guide our steps.

"I've never been so glad to see the sun," I said.

Thomas squeezed me against him. "Almost there, babe."

Egret's face was the first thing I saw as Thomas shoved my butt higher.

"Take my hand," he said, extending his meaty paw.

Sparrow threw herself beside me the moment she saw me emerge with a bloody bandage wrapped around my leg.

"Guess I got shot." I smiled weakly, gritting against the pain.

"Will!" she cried. Egret cleared his throat, and her face flushed. "I mean, Tobias. Shit."

"Language, please," Egret teased.

"Fuck off." She raised her middle finger, then focused on my leg. "Let me look at that. What a terrible bandage."

"Sorry, nurse. It was all we had in the bowels of the earth."

"Right." She offered an apologetic glance, then went about unwrapping my binding and replacing it with a fresh one from her pack. How she managed to keep the darn thing while fleeing through a complex network of caves was a mystery I made a mental note to unravel later.

Thomas flopped down beside me the moment he emerged. "That's enough spelunking for a lifetime."

I turned my head, careful not to move my leg. "At least you learned a new word."

His grin somehow eased the pain.

"Okay, boss, I've already scouted the area. We're alone up here. Nothing around for miles," Egret said. It was the first time I'd seen the Egret of old, the confident, almost swaggering brute of a man, who would run headlong into situations, heedless of everything, sometimes without checking to see if there was a solid wall or steep cliff ahead.

"

The village is about two miles that way."We followed where he pointed to a smear on the horizon that resembled a few buildings huddled together around a narrow road.

"Any luck finding a vehicle?" Thomas asked.

Egret shook his head. "I didn't want to approach until you got here."

"Alright," Thomas said. "Tobias is in no shape to walk. Anny, you stay with him and do what you can with his leg. Heinz, let's go steal a car."

"Sounds like a Friday night back home," Egret responded.

Sparrow's eyes widened. "Who *were* you back then? The town thief?"

"I prefer the term liberator, especially in present circumstances." He winked and turned away to follow Thomas.

Sparrow stared after him.

"You really love him, don't you?" I asked when the others were too far away to hear.

"Yeah. I guess I do." Her lips curled and her eyes drifted. "Only God knows why."

It was midnight when we rolled to a stop in front of the Amsterdam safe house. Nora, apparently ignoring the beauty sleep requirement for fifteen-year-old girls, greeted us at the door. "We are all full. You will need to come back another night.

"Thomas's features fell so quickly, the girl couldn't hold back a rumbling laugh. "Come in. It is good to see you returned in one piece." She watched me limp forward, then added, "Mostly one piece."

I shrugged and let the girl wrap my neck with her arms and peck my cheek. Her touch was no longer formal. We'd become something more through our mutual survival. I was beginning to see how war was funny like that.

Our good doctor was no longer in residence, Nora explained, having returned home with Fons, so another would have to be called in to ensure my leg and foot healed properly. To our surprise, Lieutenant James and Major Sikes were still there. Not surprisingly, James was tipsy and Sikes was utterly drunk.

"Fucking Germans bottled up the bay," Sikes said as we stepped into the basement map room. "We've been trying to find a way into France, but they're pouring troops and tanks in there too. Must be a shitstorm coming."

"I haven't minded one bit." James licked his fingers free of caramel. "This is a lovely country, a deliciously lovely place."

Nora didn't ask if we were tired. She didn't try to shoo James and Sikes from their seats. She simply motioned to the empty chairs and went about setting glasses before us, then scurried upstairs to prepare a midnight snack.

"What the hell happened to you?" Sikes said, glancing down at my leg as I sat next to him. "You're supposed to dodge the bullets, not run into them."

I was too glad to see the burly man to be annoyed. "Guess I missed that memo."

Despite our protests, Nora roused Adriaan.

"There have been far too few reasons to celebrate of late. I am happy to sacrifice a little sleep to welcome friends home again," he said, raising his glass.

Hours passed as we traded tales of all that had happened in the time we'd been apart. It had only been months, but in war, days were lifetimes. Months were an eternity.

By our third round of whiskey, which Nora said was all they had left after months of hosting Sikes and James, Sparrow had moved from her chair to sit in Egret's lap. One of his arms wrapped around her, while the other hand traced lazy circles across her upturned palm.

Thomas and I remained seated across the table from one another, our gazes the only thing we dared let touch. Egret knowing about us was enough of a breach. We dared not widen that circle further.

Still, we were safe and among friends again.

For a moment, we knew peace.

As the stories and laughter slowed, Adriaan excused himself, dragging James and Sikes upstairs behind him. Nora insisted Thomas and I take the basement bedroom again, claiming Thomas's snoring could wake the dead. Sparrow nearly snorted tea at that.

Egret took Sparrow's hand and led her upstairs. They would no longer sleep in separate rooms.

I knew we needed to form a plan, to find a way to return to London so we could rejoin the effort to defeat the Axis, but my aching leg and weary mind demanded rest first. Thomas and I fell asleep in each other's arms almost as soon as our heads hit the pillows.

# Chapter Forty-One
# Thomas

The darkness of our vault-turned-bedroom was absolute, as was the silence. No sunlight streamed in through cracks in the non-existent windows. The chirping of birds didn't pry my mind awake with pleasant thoughts of a hopeful morning.

I blinked, desperate to inject a bit of moisture into eyes that felt of sandpaper. My hand was invisible as it lifted, then rubbed, willing tears to flow. In an odd way, the void of that space was both at once comforting, disconcerting, and utterly disorienting. In the fog of waking, I struggled to remember if I lay in a bed in a Dutch prison, the home of farmers, or somewhere else. All three places had haunted my dreams, the people from each location, even more so.

Then Will stirred.

He didn't wake, simply released a heavy sigh and rolled onto his side to face me.

My eyes couldn't see his face, but my mind knew every angle, every curve, every line. Without thinking, I reached out and traced the outline of his hair, gently lifting it off the forehead I felt beneath.

How could such a simple act in utter darkness warm my soul?

Will was the clearest image my mind could ever conjure, yet our love remained a mystery. How had I, as flawed and broken as any man, earned this unfathomable treasure? How had Will come to love me so much that he would travel across the globe, risk war and ruin, on the slimmest hope of bringing me home? How could such love even be real?

My chest swelled as memories invaded the moment's solitude.

It hadn't been so long ago that we walked the cobbled stones of Harvard, ignorant of the other's presence, oblivious to the life that would unfurl before us like a tapestry of the richest silks and finest spun gold.

Our meeting had been by chance.

Or some divine hand.

Who knew how the heavens or gods or whoever spun the strands of fate guided such things?

Who cared?

My fingers brushed the skin of his cheek, and the thrill of his warmth trickled into me. I felt the muscles of my mouth tighten and my cheeks rise.

This man.

My God.

"Good morning."

His gentle whisper was barely a breath.

Then his hand crept from under the covers to caress the back of mine, still pressed against his cheek.

"Good morning to you, too."

He pulled the covers tight around his shoulders and nuzzled closer so the heat of our bodies embraced. I took my hand from his cheek, wrapped it around his shoulder, and pulled him into me. His head burrowed into the softness between my chin and collarbone. I felt his chilly nose press into my skin.

"This is my favorite place in the whole world," he breathed.

My heart nearly burst at that.

I squeezed him, holding him to me, desperate for him to be closer. My arms trembled, and I felt the tremor of emotion welling just beneath the surface.

"Babe? What is it?"

I kissed his forehead, not trusting my voice.

The first tears fell.

He pulled back, and his hands gripped my face, his thumbs wiping the moisture.

"Thomas, what's wrong? I'm here, babe. I'm right here."

I pressed my forehead against his and released the last of my control. Every moment of fear and longing, of sadness and pain, of hopelessness and regret, everything I'd felt since we'd been separated came flooding out. I sobbed, my chest heaving, my face wrecked with tears, as I had not done since I'd been a babe in my mother's arms.

Will wrapped himself around me, held me close, and whispered soothing words I didn't hear.

I don't know how long we lay like that, how long he held me, how long I poured myself out before him.

I didn't care.

Will held me, and that was all that mattered.

The world be damned.

We'd come so close . . . so close to losing each other, to losing everything.

I was in his arms, and nothing would ever steal that from us again.

When, at last, the tears had dried, Will's hands gently lifted my head from his shoulder, and I felt his breath drift across my skin a moment before the softness of his lips met the roughness of mine. Our lips lingered, touching, an embrace so perfect and pure, and I knew, in that sublime moment, the true depth of our love.

He pulled back, only a little, then kissed me again. And again.

His hands found my head again, his fingers gently twining in my hair, stroking and kneading, a blind man recalling a memory from the past.

My tears returned, but neither of us cared. Their tang seasoned our passion as his tongue teased past my teeth.

My hands traced circles on his back, feeling the lines of his bones and muscles beneath, remembering the perfect canvas I once knew better than my own, savoring the knowledge it was mine, and mine alone.

Will moaned, and I felt him stiffen against my stomach.

The same sensation, one I hadn't felt since we'd been parted, grew against him, as well.

When our lips parted, I thought the world might have fled. Then they grazed my neck, and I knew life once more.

He kissed my skin, grazed teeth against the tenderness, gradually lower and lower.

His fingers gripped my nipples, gently at first, then firmer. When his mouth closed around them, and his teeth clamped down, I thought stars might've bloomed in the blackness.

I reached down to run my hand across the back of his head, but he grabbed my wrist and slammed it back onto the bed. I couldn't see his eyes but knew, without doubt, the hungry, fiery gaze that blazed within them.

Then he kissed my stomach, and I shivered.

His fingers teased the divots of my hips.

His cheek brushed my hardened cock, and I felt wetness leak onto him.

On any other day, the stubble of his face would've sparked pain. But on that morning, in that bed, I reveled in the agony his whiskers inflicted.

I was alive.

With Will.

His lips closed around the head of my cock, and I felt him swirl the drops before a swallow. The tip of his tongue dragged against the underside of my head, the most sensitive place on my body, and I cried out.

"Fuck!"

His hands reached up and gripped my chest, squeezing, claiming me.

Then he took all of me.

His head rose and fell, my cock scraping the back of his throat with each bob.

His lips locked around my shaft.

His tongue swirled.

One hand left my chest and gripped my base, pulling my balls taut, hardening my cock to its limit.

I arched my back.

"Will!"

Still, he drove me into him.

Still he squeezed and stroked and pulled.

My abs clenched.

My chest tightened.

And he released me.

Before I knew what was happening, his body hovered above mine, and he spat into his palm.

I could barely think.

My breaths came in gasps.

And then I was inside him.

"Oh, God, Will."

His lips covered mine.

His tongue pressed against my own.

His hands gripped my head.

And slower than anyone had ever moved, he rose.

Then somehow slower, he fell, easing me deep within his body, forcing every inch of me inside him as deep as I could press.

He held us there so long I thought he might not move again, then he began to rise.

More kisses.

More caresses.

He nearly slipped out before pressing down once more.

My whole body shook.

All I could think was how badly I wanted to be inside him, to be one with him, to fill him. I gripped his sides and began to pull, but he refused to go faster.

"Slow," he hissed. "As slow as you can."

It was like holding back a hurricane with a tissue.

But I tried.

God, I tried.

Each time he rose, my whole body wanted to rise with him. Each time he fell, I thought my life might pour out.

I reached up and gripped him, his cock covered in pre-cum. The thought sent a jolt through me I feared beyond control.

Still, he rose.

Still, he fell.

I stroked him.

He groaned.

His back arched as he fell, and I somehow drove deeper.

I felt him clinch.

My pleasure swelled.

His nails bit into my shoulders.

He rose faster.

My chest heaved.

He slammed down.

And the last of my walls fell away.

"Will!"

"Fuck!"

I felt his warmth on my chest the moment my own burst free.

Again and again, no longer heeding his own deliberate pace, he slammed his body down, driving me in, forcing everything out of me . . . into him.

When, at last, he stilled, he refused to free me, angling himself so we held each other, still joined, still one.

We fell asleep as one.

And for the first time since we'd been parted, the dreams did not return.

# Epilogue

## Thomas

By the time we stepped into the Bedfordshire safe house again, it was 1944. I should've known better but getting from the Netherlands back to England had been far more of an adventure than I'd expected.

It took weeks for the Dutch to plan our flight to safety, then another few weeks to make the trek across Belgium, then into France. I had expected German patrols to be vigilant once we reached French soil, but the Nazis appeared too distracted with defensive preparations to care about a small band posing as poor farmers, complete with run-down trucks and dirty, torn clothing. Adriaan had truly outdone himself with the planning of our escape.

We were ultimately retrieved from an abandoned French town by fishing boats formerly owned by local fishermen in one of the villages that dotted the coast of Britain.

I'd never been so glad to see the stodgy old buildings of England's capital.

London was abuzz with activity. The RAF and American Air Force were more closely partnered than at any time during the war. We couldn't see the full scope of their plans, but it was clear this would be a pivotal year in the war.

Sparrow and Egret were sent back into Europe a few months later, each headed in a different direction with different objectives. With her language skills, I suspected Sparrow might land in France. Egret was a wildcard.

Their parting was one of the most heartbreaking scenes I'd ever witnessed. In the time we'd spent holed up in Amsterdam, then traveling across Europe, the love between them had grown deeper than either Will or I had realized. I tried to argue with command, to allow them to act together, as a team, but the needs of the war were greater than any individual—or couple.

We would miss them terribly.

At the personal request of Jamison Hurt, a man whose true affiliation we still could not guess, Will and I were assigned to assist the British intelligence services in their planning of special operations.

I asked Hurt how he had the power to pull such strings, but he simply shrugged and said, "I am the King's man."

Neither of us expected to remain in London more than a few months. Our skills were unique. Surely, the OSS would need us somewhere, digging into secrets or wreaking havoc on the enemy. It's what we were trained to do.

We spent the next year and a half wondering when our good luck, being assigned together in the heart of Britain, would run out.

But that call never came.

After a month in the Bedfordshire safe house, Hurt appeared with keys to a flat closer to London, insisting the Crown needed the space in the safe house for others. We suspected the heart buried deep within the snooty spy had finally warmed to us—at least, that's what we hoped. In an odd way, we liked the strange man.

There was nothing idyllic about our time in London.

We planned operations designed to kill and destroy. We spent every waking hour—and those were long hours—consumed with the horrors of war, the consequences of battle, the devastation inflicted by hateful, evil men.

Every day, the people of the city wondered if Nazi planes would return.

Every day, we feared for our troops and the fate of Europe, of mankind.

And yet, we were together.

Will slept in my arms each night, his head nuzzled between my chin and collarbone, in that perfect place that brought each of us peace. I woke to his smile, to brush back that unruly lock I hoped he would never cut.

In the midst of so much sadness, we found great peace and joy.

When, at last, Europe celebrated the end of hostilities, Will and I were among the one million souls who flooded the streets of London, cheering, singing, drinking, and waving as the world turned the page on a terrible chapter. A week later, Hurt arrived at Bedfordshire with a second sealed missive, this time bearing the King's seal.

"Any hints?" Will teased as the snarky Brit held the note with two hands toward me.

"I would never presume to speak for the Crown," he said formally. Then he cupped his mouth and whispered, "But I think it's from *America*, not Buckingham."

Will and I shared a quick glance, then he tore the envelope open.

*Emu and Condor,*

*You have exceeded even my expectations, which is rather difficult to do.*

*On behalf of the President and a grateful nation, thank you for your service and sacrifice.*

*Few will ever know of your deeds, yet all will enjoy the freedom that follows.*

*Unfortunately, our eye must ever be vigilant. While one foe is defeated, others rise, and our job is never truly complete. Despite what some may think, we need you both, together. You make quite the team.*

*In two weeks' time, a plane will return you to the United States.*

*Until then, Godspeed.*

*Manakin*

**The adventures of Will and Thomas will continue**

. . .

# Also By Casey Morales

# About the Author

Casey Morales is an LGBT storyteller and the author of multiple bestselling MM romance novels. Born in the Southern United States, Casey is an avid tennis player, aspiring chef, dog lover, and ravenous consumer of gummy bears.

www.ingramcontent.com/pod-product-compliance
Lightning Source LLC
Chambersburg PA
CBHW051258130726
47987CB00004B/1576